Woman for Sale

Shirley Eldridge

A catalogue record for this book is available from the National Library of Australia

ISBN-13: 978-1-922727-70-1

Linellen Press
265 Boomerang Road
Oldbury, Western Australia
www.linellenpress.com.au

This story was inspired by real events.

To *Rose*, motivated by her desire to help others, thank you for allowing your story to be told.

The outcome in this story would never have been possible without assistance and direction from two religious groups. (Special thanks to Sister A.T.) as well as A.C.R.A.T.H.

Contents

Contents..v

Chapter 1 1

Chapter 2 9

Chapter 3 18

Chapter 4 27

Chapter 5 34

Chapter 6 48

Chapter 7 58

Chapter 8 67

Chapter 9 71

Chapter 10 84

Chapter 11 92

Chapter 12 101

Chapter 13 107

Chapter 14 116

Chapter 15 128

Chapter 16 137

Chapter 17 147

Chapter 18 155

Chapter 19 158

Chapter 20 168

Chapter 21 178

Chapter 22 191

Chapter 23 201

Chapter 24 217

Chapter 25 232

Chapter 26 241

Chapter 27 247

Appendix: 253

About the Author..257

Chapter 1

On the rough dirt pathway outside a rusty iron dwelling, two barefoot girls drew circles with their sticks, while inside, their frazzled mother fed their three-month-old brother cradled on her lap. The mother stared expressionless at the corroded formwork that divided their home from their neighbour's. Behind the framework hung an old sheet, giving her a small degree of privacy.

Eventually, she adjusted her tee-shirt, crouched and placed the baby on a mattress on the floor then walked outside into the steamy Filipino air. At least the blue plastic tarpaulin overhead provided protection from the sun, but the air hung as still and foul as the inside of a second-hand coffin.

Rose plonked herself into the stained plastic chair and turned to her neighbour with barely the energy to smile.

'Has Ramil been in touch yet?' her neighbour, Darna, asked.

Rose shook her head.

The woman frowned. 'It's been five days now. How can a husband just disappear?' She pushed a damp strand of hair from her forehead. 'We reckon he's found a job on a ship.'

Rose sighed. She thought the same thing. One extra mouth to feed with just the casual work he picked up here and there proved too much for Ramil to cope with. Their relationship had become strained with four of them now living in such a confined space, never mind the addition of a crying baby. Ramil had been spending his days and his evenings down on the waterfront.

She wiggled the plastic thong on her foot and swallowed her

pride. 'I don't suppose you could spare some rice?'

'Oh, Rose, you know I would if I could. Let me look after the baby while you go and see if you can borrow from someone else?'

Rose hadn't eaten for a couple of days. She'd made sure the girls had something though, but now there was nothing. Nothing at all. Maybe if she walked, she could find a mango tree? *No*, she shook her head, *in this squatters' area there are no fruit-bearing trees that haven't already been raided.* There was, though, endless corrugated iron, scrap iron formwork, rough concrete, plastic sheets and tarpaulins. Water had to be fetched from the illegal tap someone had plumbed in at the end of their street. But she would have to borrow a neighbour's trolley to haul the water barrel. And then there was fuel for the lamps – it wouldn't last forever.

Levering herself out of the chair, the move draining her energy, she said to Jasmin and Iris, her girls, 'I'll be back soon. Be good.' Then she wandered down the crudely formed alleyway bordered on both sides by shoddily built houses, many no better than her own, looking for help.

Pulling up the bottom of her tee-shirt, Rose tried to dry her face, but the shirt was already soaked with sweat so it made no difference. For almost an hour, she wandered along the broken concrete pathways asking anyone who'd listen to her plea for help. She walked until her feet hurt, and her head hurt, her heart aching at the thought of not being able to feed her children when night fell. In time, her steps failed her, and the swirling in her head forced her to collapse on a stool outside a sari sari store. A skinny, toothless woman came out from behind a rough-hewn but laden counter and knelt in front of her, holding up a water bottle.

'Here. Drink.' She lifted the water to Rose's mouth, then proceeded to fan Rose's face with a woven palm fan.

Rose finally sat up straight and took a deep breath. 'You are so kind, *tita*. I am needing some food for my children. Please, please can you help me?'

The wizened old woman rose with an ease that defied her appearance, and, without saying a word, disappeared into the store. She returned with a small bowl of rice, insisting Rose eat. Then she passed her a plastic bag of rice with two potatoes on top. 'Off you go now my child,' she said, helping Rose to her feet.

Much later, Rose staggered into her neighbour's place. Darna held the baby while he sucked on the knuckle of her little finger. Rose stretched out her arms and Darna handed him back.

'I'm glad to see you have something. Here, drink,' she urged, passing a bottle to Rose who gulped noisily, the baby now pressed to her shoulder. She passed the bottle back, nodding in gratitude. Then she took her precious food and baby home.

Jasmin sat cross-legged on an old rug on the floor, writing a fancy heading for her written homework in a lined pad provided by the local school.

'I know that's important to you, Jazz, and I'm glad you work hard, but will you take Aaron?'

Jasmin arose with ease, lifted a grumbling Aaron into her arms and waltzed outside with him.

Where in goodness name did that girl get her energy from? she thought gratefully. Desperately she wanted to sit, but there was food to prepare, urgently, for every morning when she watched the girls go off to school for the 6 am to 12 noon shift, she knew that, lately, their stomachs had been almost empty. She filled a saucepan with water from one of the buckets before placing it over the flame from the gas bottle burner, which she knew would soon be out of gas too.

Once she had doled out the meagre meal, she called the girls in, and watched them silently scoff down the rice. *They're already growing out of those secondhand tee-shirts*, she thought, *and that's without the help of much nourishment.* Till now, Ramil had picked up enough work to feed and basically clothe the family. But no more.

Glancing over at their green checked uniforms hanging on wire hangers airing out for tomorrow, she thought, *at least now they'll have energy for tomorrow.* Their long black hair was tied back and she was glad their pretty, delicate faces still reflected an enthusiasm that had deserted her long ago, yet she found the energy for a gentle return smile when Iris grinned at her, sporting a missing tooth.

After eating a small portion of the food, feeding Aaron and putting him down, Rose sat and watched the girls quietly doing their homework on the floor, the quiet giving her more time to think clearly.

There was no doubt Ramil had abandoned his family, even though he'd taken none of his clothing, which now hung listlessly in front of her on the iron formwork wall.

Tensions had been escalating for months between them. She enjoyed the peace that surrounded her now without his yelling and temper explosions, but inside that pseudo-peace fear was growing. She'd never had to carry the burden of two children and a baby alone. She felt weighted down, crushed and crumpled with the responsibility. Who could she turn to? Not her mum and dad – they lived on an island and had nothing to offer. So where was the money to come from? The only handout given in the Philippines was a basic education, which Rose had, and through the fog of her current insecurity, she knew she had to get a job.

But where? How?

Big money can bemade from jobs overseas. Everyone knows that. And labour is the Philippines' biggest export. If I were adequately fed, I could work hard and long hours like others before me.

She wandered outside. 'Darna, I'm thinking about working

overseas.'

'You crazy, Rose?'

'How else do I get out of this predicament?'

'Who you got to look after the kids?'

The kids. She couldn't bear to think too much about being separated from them. But her mind took her there anyway as she pictured her eldest, Jazz, about to hit double figures. Jazz was passionate about art and music. *Who will encourage her?* Then her thoughts shifted to Iris, just two years younger. She already had a decent command of the English language. *Smart girls. Tiny for their ages. And as for baby Aaron … No, no. I mustn't think this way. To help them, I must get work. Focus on that.*

She looked Darna in the eyes. 'Yeah. There's my sister, Annlyn …' Rose's gaze strayed across the pathway, so engrossed in the vision in her head of Annlyn with her children that she didn't even register seeing the two little children in a plastic tub across from them being bathed by their mother. She answered Darna once she'd sorted her thoughts. '… but Annlyn is pretty desperate too. Her husband doesn't get much work and they have two other mouths to feed. Do you think that could work?'

'Where is your sister?'

'Not too far away. The other side of Pan-Philippine Highway. Squatters too, but they're much better off. They've even got electricity. And a TV.' Rose pictured the crude but spacious dwelling and could image another three children along with Annlyn's two managing to live in it.

Darna nodded slowly and supportively.

'What if I can get a job on a cruise ship and send money home and support all of them? My family *and* Annlyn's. This is what families do to survive, Darna.'

Her heart skipped at the prospect of her plan working; she wasn't sure whether it was a sign of fear or excitement. 'You know they employ Filipinos.' She waved her hands. 'You've seen them working on the cruise ships on TV.'

She visualised the richness, the opulence she'd been overwhelmed with on the television screen – all totally beyond her scope of understanding. When she tried to place herself in that environment she failed. 'But I'm prepared to do anything you know, like scrub floors, wash dishes – whatever it takes.'

'Do you know anyone down on the docks?' Darna asked skeptically.

Rose shrugged. *That's irrelevant.* 'Well, my English is passable. I doubt they need much Tagalog though.'

She looked towards the sky where the sun had set, and sniffed the air. So many smells: sweat, dirt, cooking odours, rotting foods, her own tired feet. Determinedly she declared, 'I'm going to see Annlyn tomorrow, and work out something.' And with that, she dragged herself out of the chair and padded the few steps to home. Too exhausted to even wash her feet, she curled up on the mattress with her two sleeping girls and cuddled Aaron. With a dose of sheer exhaustion, blended with raw fear mixed with a morsel of hope, she fell into a deep sleep, despite the noises of the functioning families around her.

The following day, once the girls left for their early school start, Rose washed, soaping herself up then using a dipper to lift the water from the barrel to rinse off. She noted the big drum needed to be filled from the common tap soon. Tying baby Aaron to her chest in a sling, she said good-bye to Darna and trekked the difficult distance to her sister's home.

No breeze blew in the narrow alleyways, and perspiration soon dripped down her face, neck, and between her breasts. Nevertheless, she nodded and forced a smile as she was greeted by acquaintances and strangers along the way, and moved aside to allow the tricycle riders passage. Usually, she'd take a trike ride to her sister's, but she had no pesos at all. The riders, in turn dodged children and stray dogs, sometimes even chickens. Rose reached the highway, crossed the eight lanes at the traffic lights, and, after wandering through a littered wilderness, entered another squatters' area.

Annlyn's home was similar to Rose's, but was older and larger, causing Rose's envy, and it sported electricity, albeit via an illegal connection cable. Her husband, like Ramil, went off every day looking for casual work. Annlyn's two children were also at school.

Ramil this time had shot through without topping her phone up and Rose had no money left on her phone, so she arrived unexpected.

Rose and Annlyn hugged tightly, squashing the three-month-old baby between them, his squeal soon breaking their hold. Over a mug of instant coffee, with a fan drying her out, Rose explained her predicament and her proposal.

'Sounds like a good idea, Rose.'

Rose stared at her sister, astounded at the easy reception she'd received.

'I think we can work something out. Your job will have to pay well, but I hear some jobs do.'

'I could send back enough money for my three and your two as well.' Rose glanced over at the table, which was covered in bits of wire, beads, glue and clasps. 'Do you sell much?'

Annlyn's lips pursed and she shook her head. 'No one seems to have much money for this stuff, but I get enough to keep doing it. More coffee?'

Coffee at the moment was a luxury for Rose so she nodded, feeling ecstatic and grateful that her sister showed enthusiasm for her proposal. She watched as Annlyn pulled out her phone.

'Let me find the nearest employment agency and let's act on this, Rose.'

'You got Wi-Fi?'

'Yeah. Tapped into someone who hasn't got security.' Annlyn

wrote down the address of the nearest agency to Rose's home.

'I'll take whatever I'm offered. I promise.'

'Make sure it pays well, that's all.'

After drinking more coffee topped up with milk and fortified with sugar, Rose found the energy to trundle home carrying, not just Aaron, but a bag containing decent shoes and a skirt and top borrowed from Annlyn for the interview, along with a few precious pesos.

Chapter 2

The following day after Rose saw the girls off to school, Darna again cared for little Aaron while Rose put on her sister's clothes, brushed her thick black hair till is shone, tied it back, and, in the borrowed shoes, headed off.

She found the pop-up agency located behind a small shop front, its two staff members sitting behind desks furnished with laptops and bordered by stacks of papers and files. One of the women arose from interviewing and handed Rose a form attached to a clip board to fill out while she sat in a plastic chair and waited her turn. With the form written in English, Rose guessed this was her first test. It had been a long time since she'd worked, and her heart thumped loudly in her ears. She hoped they didn't ask for her level of education as she finished school at fourteen. While English had been compulsory, she'd acquired most of hers from American television shows. She sat patiently with her application, all completed except the date because she didn't know what day it was.

She glanced at the other candidates, feeling intimidated by the younger, more confident women who entered after her. Her legs trembled when her turn came to be interviewed.

'Stand there and turn around,' the older woman, dressed smartly in a green sleeveless top and skirt, requested in an accent unfamiliar to Rose. 'Yes,' she continued, 'you can sit now. You're slim and attractive. You'd look perfect in a uniform.' She smiled softly at Rose, before reading through the application.

Rose watched as she scribbled in the date: Fifteenth of

October 2014. Rose had totally lost track of time.

Looking up, the interviewer said, 'Why do you want to work overseas? I see you have a family.'

Rose explained her circumstances.

'You have family, but they can't support you? You need to support them?'

After the woman made notes about Rose's family, she put Rose at ease. 'This is very common. Please relax. I just need to understand. Now, to place you well, I need to ask your religion.'

'Catholic, ma'am.'

The woman nodded and scribbled a few more words on the application form, then leaned back, smiling. 'I think we might have just the thing for you, Rose. Not too far away either. Not like the Middle East where a lot of young women go.'

Rose's sigh released the tightness in her shoulders. *Could getting a job really be this easy?*

Leaning forward, still holding Rose's application, the interviewer put her forearms on the desk, and said brightly, 'We can offer a waitressing job in a hotel restaurant in Bangkok.'

Rose sat silently. *Ah, so that's where she's from.* Not expecting an offer straight away, it was a lot to take in. While she knew where Bangkok was, she knew very little about Thailand. She clasped her hands together, unsure if she was pleased or scared.

'You'll be expected to work during the day and in the evenings. They can be long hours. But there are breaks. Your uniforms, accommodation and meals will be provided. You'll receive a regular wage but ...' Here, the woman paused and smiled for effect, '... the best thing about this work is the tips.'

'Oh.' Rose didn't know what else to say. She'd never been to a hotel restaurant. She'd seen them on television, and was aware how swish they were and knew the tips could be generous. Yes, suddenly things were looking up.

The woman again broke into Rose's thoughts. 'This job won't

wait, dear. The next person I interview might snatch it up. But if you accept now, I'll move on to organising passport, work visa, plane ticket and the like.'

'Um … oh, well, um…,' Rose stammered, overwhelmed by the suddenness of decision making.

The interviewer raised her eyebrows and nodded to Rose in encouragement.

'Yes, yes. I accept,' she said, her heart pounding so hard she could feel the blood rushing to her head.

More details were forthcoming over the next hour, during which Rose signed more forms.

'I'll be in touch as soon as paperwork is finalised. That should be in a week or two. Time to go and get everything in order.'

Rose staggered out of the agency, her thoughts muddled. So many questions she forgot to ask. But I don't have a choice, she rationalised. I promised to take the first job offered. I am not really abandoning my baby and my precious girls. Lots of women have to do this. If they can, I can. Thank goodness I have Annlyn to rely on.

Nonetheless, her shoulders drooped, and she felt a pain in her chest as she walked home.

Over the next few weeks, Rose began to sell her and Ramil's possessions, item by item, in order to continue feeding her family. Every time a piece of costume jewellery brought back a memory, she shut it down. This was no time for an emotional display. *No. Deep breath and move on.* She kept, though, her plain silver bracelet, a gift from her grandparents. Annlyn wore an identical one. All other trinkets collected over her lifetime went. When the last items sold, she would give the pesos to Annlyn to help feed the children till she sent the first of her wages home. She was now ready to fill two red, blue and white plastic zipper bags, loaned to her by Annlyn, with the children's clothes and possessions – her meagre belongings for travel would fit easily into one zipper bag.

Leaving her little family took all the strength Rose could muster, strength she didn't know she had. On Sunday, she held her children close at mass at the Church of the Holy Rosary and prayed like she'd never prayed before. Her hold on Aaron, even though he was swaddled to her, was so tight he squealed. She enclosed one arm around Jasmin and the other around Iris to pull them closer but they too squirmed with discomfort, so she eased off. *Dear God*, she thought, *how do women do this? But I have to … I have to.* It became a chant, repeating over and over as she stroked the mass of black hair on Aaron's head, then stroked his dear little round face. After mass, she used Annlyn's phone to call her parents. Her phone still had no money on it to make a call, although she could still receive calls.

'We will help where we can,' her mother assured her, but that was all.

Tears welled again in Rose's eyes; she swiped them away.

'What is it, Mum? What is going on?' Jasmin threw her arms around her mother's waist, interrupting Rose's conversation with her mother. Till now, Rose had not spoken of the upcoming events with her daughters. She'd been avoiding it and hiding her planning from them. The pain and heartache she expected and predicted would erupt for all of them frightened her and she wasn't sure she could hold herself together when it did explode.

Rose said, her voice breaking, 'Mum, I've got to go. My girls need me.' A sob escaped her when she terminated the call.

Passing the phone back to Annlyn, and still trying to hold herself together, she farewelled Annlyn and said to her girls, 'Come with me.'

She sat them both down in the back pew of the now empty Church and gazed at the two beautiful fragile faces framed by neat jet-black hair. Both watched her with wide, open eyes, sensing something was wrong. One at a time Rose held their face in her hands and stared into those dark pretty eyes. They were so slender from lack of nourishment a puff of wind would knock them over.

'You've watched me selling things?'

The girls nodded. Aaron, however, grabbed a handful of her hair and tried to eat it. She ignored his gesture. At least he was quiet. She took a deep breath. 'Your father isn't coming back, so I'm going away to work. Your lovely Aunty Annlyn will take care of you and your brother.' *There, it is said.*

Jasmin and Iris fell to their knees in front of her and wailed, their heads on her knees. She stroked their hair. Aaron fussed and wriggled and kicked her thighs, responding to the collective sadness around him.

Finally, little Iris said, amongst her sobs, 'Will she feed us?' She automatically put her tiny hand on Aaron to try to calm him.

'Oh, yes, my darlings. I will make sure she has enough money to buy you plenty of food.' *How precious*, she thought with gratitude. *The thing most missing in their lives is not their absent father, nor my imminent departure, but food. Totally understandable, given recent times. But that is just Iris's concern*, she realised when Jasmin lifted her head and looked into her eyes.

'When will you come home?'

This was a moment she hadn't prepared for. She had no idea how to answer that.

Before she could respond, Jasmin added, 'Dad didn't come back. How do we know for sure you'll come back?' She threw her head back against her mother, looking for a bit of her mum's body not already claimed to cling to.

'Oh, my beautiful girls.' Rose rubbed their shoulders. 'I could never, *never* leave you. *Never!* I'm just over in Bangkok. You'll have to look it up at school on the map. We can talk on one of the apps on Aunty Annlyn's phone. You can send me pictures.

I can send you pictures. We won't be cut off.'

The girls' crying subsided to spasmodic hiccupping and Rose wiped their tears and sighed. When their emotions were more under control, she responded to more of their concerns, till finally they were done talking and headed home.

Rose functioned on automatic pilot through each of the following days, doing the usual chores of collecting water from huge buckets on a trolley, disposing of rubbish and body waste, washing, cleaning, cooking, and ironing at the shared illegal electricity outlets at the end of the lane. She took her phone there regularly to recharge it, ready for the all-important call to travel. With all these daily chores, she accommodated little Aaron, toting him around tied to her chest like a second skin, and feeding him meagerly from her breast.

She would not allow standards to drop, and the two girls attended school with clean and crisp uniforms. If they were hung, she told them, straight after a wash, they held their shape and didn't crumple. Rose taught them how to polish their shoes, wash their socks and underwear daily, and showed them how to fold their clothes. Their reaction, to her surprise, was again accepting.

Darna came rushing to her open doorway one morning, looking serious. 'Come. Come and read the notice board.' She tugged at Rose's arm.

'What is it?' Unable to tell whether Darna was anxious or excited, Rose grabbed up Aaron and hurried down to the communal area where a crowd had gathered. A deep hum of concern pervaded the air. Darna pushed Rose through so she could read the notice for herself.

The large government poster featured the country's colourful coat of arms at the top. The centre of the coat of arms featured an eight-rayed sun, each ray representing one of the eight provinces. Rose ignored its familiarity and read silently, feeling ill at the proclamation that the vast residential area in Barangay Bagong Tondo in Manila had been declared illegal. The government planned to tear it down for redevelopment. They were giving the families only a month to vacate. This included Annlyn's area.

Rose's knees wobbled. She already felt sticky and clammy from rushing to see the notice, but now she also felt faint and dizzy and thought she'd collapse. The woman beside Rose, seeing her reaction to the first half of the notice, patted her arm and said comfortingly, 'Keep reading.'

As Rose read the smaller print in the bottom section, hope began to rise, like a headache lifting after a dose of aspirin. Yes, families could apply for resettlement in the government's new project areas. The forms were available at a local government office or online. Rose, holding a now whimpering Aaron closer, pushed her way out to find Darna.

Darna, grinning widely, gave Rose a friendly punch on her arm. 'See, your kids are going to be fine. We'll all apply.'

'But we'll have rent to pay as well. We've never paid rent. I must work even harder. And we have to see if the two families will qualify for housing together.' It was so much information to absorb.

Very soon, she and Annlyn met up to fill in the application. Rose pointed at the conditions nominated. 'Look, look … with five kids, you qualify for three bedrooms.' They high-fived each other.

Finally, the call to travel came. She needed to appear at the agency, ready to go in four days.

When Jasmin and Iris arrived home from school, they were bewildered by their mother's behaviour as she grabbed them and hugged them one at a time, spinning then around.

'What is it?' Jasmin said, peeling off her damp socks after escaping the crushing hold.

'It's time, my beautiful girls. Look at you. You're going to be fine with Aunty Annlyn.'

Rose spent time with each of them, trying to give off positive vibes even though she felt anxious, maybe even a little scared, yet excited when she thought of the opportunities that would arise for them from the money she'd be sending home.

'Sure, we'll be fine with Aunty Annlyn, Mum.'

Good. I have said it so often they are beginning to believe it. But Rose could tell they didn't understand the dimensions of their future. The last thing she needed now was to revisit the explosion of emotions. It was hard enough to suppress her own.

On the day prior to her departure, she sold the last of the household goods and, with a significant payment, allowed another family to move into her now-vacated humble home. She was devoid of feelings for it. She waited at Darna's for the girls to arrive home from school then messaged her local trike rider, who transported them all to Annlyn's where Rose and the children spent the night on the floor entangled in each other's limbs, Rose unable and unwilling to let them go. No one slept.

The next morning, utterly exhausted, Rose, her eyes red and nose runny, tried to say goodbye to her children. Jasmin and Iris didn't look any better than her. Reality had smashed into them all like a gale force wind, depleting them of any strength they thought they might have had. The girls refused to let their mother go. Rose didn't care. Doubts ricocheted around her head like a never-ending echo. *What am I doing?*

Through a teary haze, she saw Aaron already settled in Annlyn's arms. No words were spoken, but primeval sounds from her and her girls filled the air.

Rose could find nothing at all to say to fit the enormity of her departure. When they were interrupted by Rose's trike rider reappearing to take her and her lone zipper bag to the agency, Annlyn, grim-faced, with her spare arm, dragged Jasmin and Iris from their mother. Rose held each tiny head and kissed it in turn, her tears dribbling on them. She gave her sister and Aaron a quick hug, then turned and left before she changed her mind.

Chapter 3

Inside the agency, four other young women waited. An over-weight, weather-beaten Chinese gentleman with stained crooked teeth introduced himself as Mr Wang. His creased clothes strained against his frame.

'I escort all way to new work,' he said in a heavy accent. 'Now, who this?' He opened the passports in his hand one by one and called their names; handed them out with other documentation, explaining them to each girl. When Rose accepted hers, her nose crinkled at his stale breath.

They were then loaded onto a mini bus where they nervously introduced themselves, and talked about where they were from. They were all fairly local, Rose discovered, and they would all be working together as waitresses. She instantly realised she was the oldest in the group.

Rose didn't really feel like talking; her heart was racing. The others soon fell silent too and she suspected they also suffered from doubts as she did. Mr Wang sat up front by the driver.

Time passed.

Finally Rose said, 'Who has flown before?'

All heads shook.

The flight departed Ninoy Aquino Manila Airport for Hanoi. Rose had never been in an airport terminal before, and huddled close to the girls she had just met. If she became separated from the group, how would she ever find her way back home? When Mr Wang moved, she moved to stay on his heels. This place reminded her of the sights and sounds of her neighbourhood, magnified a thousand times. While announcements constantly blared, people scurried – people with different facial features, who dressed differently, who spoke in languages she didn't know. Electronic boards flashed airline names and times and statuses.

Relief fell upon her after they passed through the formal sections of the terminal and reached the departure lounge. Not much talking went on during the wait, each girl in awe of their surroundings. After walking along a long tunnel, they reached the aircraft door. Rose's anxiety level reached maximum again. She put her hand on her heart to stop its pounding, all the while keeping her eyes on Mr Wang's back.

Her jaw clenched on take-off and her knuckles turned white as she clung to the armrests, stayed locked on till the plane levelled out. Maria sat on one side of her, Marisol on the other. They too clutched the armrests. Mr Wang sat in the seat across the aisle, with Angel and Princess beside him, the girls wearing an earbud each, and listening to music on their shared phone.

The snacks served on the flight represented more food served in one sitting than Rose had seen in many weeks; she savoured every mouthful, trying not to think of her children, or feel guilty because she was the one eating. Her gaze swept around the other girls. They were petite and slender, as though they too had suffered from lack of nourishment over time.

On arrival in Hanoi, after clearing Customs, Rose again felt panic rising. Mr Wang gathered them together to collect their bags from the carousel, and Rose almost cried when she found her clothes spilling out of a long tear along the side of her red, white and blue plastic zipper bag. Devastated, she showed it to Mr Wang.

'We buy proper bag. You pay back later,' he said offhandedly, and ushered them all to another mini bus. 'We go long trip where you will live,' he said before climbing in beside the driver.

The white mini bus lacked side windows, but, was at least air-conditioned. For the first time, they all sighed with relief and relaxed.

'I wonder what colour our uniform will be?' young Angel bounced excitedly. Her name was apt: she was a picture of childish innocence with the prettiest of smiles, Rose noted. They then talked animatedly about colour preferences. 'Black with a little white apron with a bib,' Angel wished, '… with a butterfly embroidered on the corner of the bib.'

Rose didn't participate much in the conversation. She was more a listener than a talker. She noted Angel and Princess were inseparable. 'How do you two know each other?' she eventually asked.

They laughed and threw their arms around one other.

'She's my big sister,' Angel said. 'Two whole years bigger.'

Princess simply smiled.

'What brings you to waitressing work?'

'Oh, we'll send money home to our mother. That's our job now,' Princess said. 'There are five other children at home.'

Maria burst in, 'How old are you?'

'Eighteen,' Angel said.

'You shouldn't have to do this if you don't want to.'

'No, no, we do want to. It'll be fun being together.'

Maria shook her head. Rose heard her mutter, 'Silly children.'

'What about you then, Maria?' Rose asked.

'What about me?'

'What brings you here?'

'That's my business.' At that, the atmosphere fell flat and silence fell between them.

Eventually Rose turned to Marisol, who appeared almost skeletal. Her collar bones protruded so much Rose wondered if she might be anorexic. She was the tallest in the group, with fine features and a long neck. Rose was so in awe – she could have strutted the catwalks of the fashion houses in the big cities with that boyish body.

'You?'

Marisol tucked a strand of her shiny shoulder-length hair behind her ear and looked down at her nails. Without lifting her head again, she said softly, 'I'm looking after family too.'

No one thought to ask Rose about her circumstances, but Rose knew none of the others was married or had children. She was also the oldest by a number of years. These young women made her feel more of a mother than ever, and somewhat responsible.

True to his word, Mr Wang ordered the driver to stop at a row of stalls off a main highway where he purchased a cheap bright orange suitcase for Rose. 'You pay first money.'

She nodded, and transferred her meagre belongings into the case, including the outfit Annlyn had loaned her and then gifted her. *Thank goodness uniforms will be provided.*

Angel and Princess giggled their way through the journey.

Hours later, they were given a comfort stop and issued with pre-packaged food and bottled water. No one complained. *I'll bet they are as hungry as I am*, Rose thought. *Mr Wang though, shouldn't be.* His belly protruded like a third trimester pregnancy from his ill-fitting lightweight suit.

The roads here were just as busy as at home, with the same constant honking and vehicles swerving. The outside air was also no easier to breathe. The girls chatted about the food they were eating, which was unfamiliar to them.

'Enough talk,' Mr Wang suddenly snapped. 'Get going.' He crushed his cigarette out on the ground with his heel then pointed to the sliding door of the bus, which he then slid open.

Standing in its opening, he again handed them their passports, this time though he placed a folder in each one.

'Listen carefully,' he ordered. 'When reach border of Laos,

wait. I give signal. You walk up to border and give passport to man I tell you. You not open passport.' His eyes lingered on each face as he went through the instructions. 'Understand?'

He waited for confirming nods.

'When man stamps passport, walk through. Re-join bus. Understand?'

The response came in soft murmurs and more nods – except for Angel, who asked, 'Do we carry our bag with us?'

Mr Wang gave her a withering look. 'Yes.'

His patience seeming to have deserted him, he pointed inside the vehicle.

Angel smirked and, once on the bus, poked out her tongue. 'Mr Grumpy,' she said to no one in particular. Princess nudged her with her elbow. Rose's jaw dropped at the girl's daring, not to mention her lack of respect. Marisol, on the other hand, ignored her, instead took a mirror from her handbag, pulled a few stray hairs into place again, and touched up her lipstick.

Rose now sat opposite Marisol. 'Have you left family behind?'

'Yes. Only the younger ones are at home. Well, except for my oldest brother. He has a job at a call centre for an airline company. His English is really good. That's how he got that job. He's married with two kids. The other older ones are all working as waiters and house staff in Dubai.'

'Why not Dubai for you?'

'This is a lot closer. They only get home once every couple of years. This way I should get back more often. Besides, one of my sisters who works in a private home is treated really badly. I know she gets a beating if she does something that displeases them.' She touched her hair again. 'Sometimes they even withhold food. I don't want that to happen to me.'

'Why she doesn't move?'

'Oh no. The agency wouldn't allow that,' Marisol said softly.

'What are her work conditions like.'

'She says the house is like a palace,' Marisol obliged, still keeping her voice low. 'Her job is to keep it clean and tidy. There are different sitting rooms for men and for women. She must always be covered and can only clean the men's section when they are out. She has a hot stuffy room at the back underneath, and they only let her have Saturdays off.'

'Sounds harsh. One thing about our waitressing work; we should be in comfortable work conditions,' Rose mused. As an afterthought, she said, 'Are you a Moslem?'

'No. Catholic. You?'

'Same. I think we all are.'

They reached the border and for ages sat quietly in a parking area in the van, whispering snippets of information about themselves. Eventually, one at a time, Mr Wang called their names and they followed his instructions. Rose was told to go first and was directed to the third booth along from the vehicle lanes, these booths only for those on foot or on bikes. Rose had already seen the man lean out and give Mr Wang an inconspicuous wave and headed towards him.

The heat radiated up from the roadway as she made her way, but Rose took little notice, kept one hundred percent focused on this lone venture. Her eyes widened when she saw a stack of green US dollars inside the envelope in her passport — they disappeared into the border officer's pocket. *So that's how it works. But why is cash needed? Are they doing something illegal since the officer needs to be bribed?*

Once they'd reboarded the bus on the border's other side, they drove south through Laos for several hours. Angel continued to ask about the work ahead.

'I wonder if we will start straight away?'

Princess added, 'I wonder how big the tips will be? I'll make sure I make them so happy they'll give me huge ones.'

Rose's thoughts were more practical. 'We'll have to learn the local money. It's called baht. And they use credit cards. They'll have to teach us all about it.'

They fell silent then, thinking of the practical side, until Marisol broke in. 'I wonder where we will live? With other waitresses? In a hostel?'

They sat in an air of anticipation, the loss of families now at the back of their minds as they talked and surmised how their futures might unfold. Mr Wang, still up front with the driver, ignored the chatter. None of them queried what had gone on at the last border control. Perhaps they didn't notice the same thing Rose did.

Rose forced her mind off it. 'Next to me, who is the oldest?' she asked

'Me, I think,' Maria said. 'I'm twenty-two.'

'I beat you by a year,' Marisol said.

Rose already knew the two young ones' ages. Princess had her thick black hair piled on her head with a bright, red-spotted, decorative bow holding it in place. It reminded Rose of Minnie Mouse and made Princess look like a teenager.

Rose felt ancient, tired, and against the other girls, frumpy. She'd just stopped breastfeeding a few days prior, and had drunk buckets of black coffee to ensure her nipples were no longer leaking. She wondered why she qualified for selection with this group. *Maybe they need a mother figure. I certainly fitted the role.*

As though mind-reading, Marisol asked, 'Are you younger or older than me?'

For the first time, Rose smiled. 'Thanks for the compliment. Older, much older.'

They continued to drive across Laos from north to south, with only one brief stop. When they reached the Vientiane border crossing into Thailand, the same bribery process was followed without a hiccup. A tired group reloaded their bags and climbed back into their vehicle. The driver pushed on, heading southward into the night, the girls now quiet and leaning against each other, or propped against the bus walls as they napped for kilometre after kilometre. Rose awoke when they stopped for fuel, after which Mr Wang climbed behind the wheel. And on and on they travelled.

Light filtering through the windscreen woke them. Rose realised more than twenty-four hours had passed since she had left Annlyn's. She tried to push back the parting scene of yesterday, promising herself she'd only look forward. But those thoughts countered the promise. *Little Aaron — has he adapted to his Aunty? Jasmin — her Jazz — will she be a role model for Iris and get herself ready for school on time without prompting? What are they doing right now?* Her stray thoughts were interrupted as though Mr Wang guessed where her mind was.

'One hour time difference,' he yelled back at them. 'Going straight to house.' He deftly pulled the vehicle up in front of a high fence. 'Grab bags. Follow.' Taking a key from his pocket, he unlocked a padlock on the gate, and held the gate open for them to enter.

All eyes darted left and right and up and down. A concrete block fence surrounded the property, giving it privacy. The timber house beyond, painted a dark crimson, appeared solid. The ground floor looked like an addition to the older building, with sliding glass doors in an aluminium frame. They followed Mr Wang up the stairs to a solid timber door where he inserted a key in the lock and threw the door open. 'In,' he commanded.

Hauling their bags, they tumbled through the door into a sitting room. He pointed towards the back of the house. 'Two rooms. Work it out.'

Rose grinned slightly. They were going to be left to sort themselves out. *Mr Wang is certainly a man of few words.* She watched him insert the key into the front door's internal lock and relock it. She scowled. *Is it so dangerous here he needs to do that?*

Nevertheless, for her first act, she sent a message to Annlyn saying they had arrived safely.

The girls' spirits lifted as they worked out who would sleep where. It was certainly a step up for each of them to live in such decent accommodation. Rose found herself sharing with the stylish and fashion-conscious Marisol, even though all the room contained a large mattress with sheets and a fan in the corner. With its plain cream walls, the room was relatively clean. The other room was similarly furnished.

'We'll manage,' she said to Marisol as she moved to open the window. It had bars on it. 'Must be dangerous here,' she said, as she put her hand through, unlatched the window and pushed it open.

'Today, rest; tonight work,' Mr Wang called out before disappearing into a third bedroom at the front of the house. Rose noted he too looked exhausted. On exploring, they discovered a bathroom the five of them would share. *Mr Wang must have his own*, Rose guessed. *Or maybe he goes downstairs.*

The kitchen held some basic supplies of food in an old cupboard, including a plastic container half filled with rice, and half a bottle of soy sauce. Six non-matching chairs surrounded a laminated table, and a drawer beside the sink held cutlery and cooking spoons. The shelving underneath it was open, holding adequate pots and pans. With little else to explore, they all fell onto their mattresses and slept soundly – regardless of the daylight.

Chapter 4

A thunderous knock woke them.

'Out here now!' Mr Wang ordered.

Another gentleman had joined him. He had quite similar facial features to Mr Wang, but his skin was smoother and younger, his hair cut incredibly short and rather badly. He appeared neater and cleaner, and slimmer.

'Sit down!' the newcomer ordered. 'I am Mr Wong. One of us will always be here in attendance,' he said in much more accurate English. 'Now here are the rules.'

Rose and the others had gathered together on the beaten-up green sofas, Angel sitting with one leg tucked beneath her. They waited expectantly for the rules.

'You will keep forty per cent of what you earn. Out of the forty percent you must pay your share of rent here, your food, your taxi fare, and any other expenses you have. You will have Sundays off. You will be escorted on that day to send money home through Western Union and do personal shopping. The rest of the time you will be working, or you will be here.' He pulled a packet of cigarettes from his pocket and slowly lit one with a gold lighter, nonchalantly blowing smoke into the air.

'We recommend you work the bars in the hotels we've selected along and close to Kaosan Road.' He grinned and nodded to them in response to their startled looks. 'Kaosan Road is where you will find the up-market and wealthier clients to service. Saeli is your taxi driver. He will teach you and recommend for you.'

Marisol clutched Rose's hand at the back of the couch, and squeezed hard. Anxiety flooded through Rose's body like hot water pouring from a kettle. Her brow creased. 'Where are we waitressing?' she asked, knowing unconsciously she sounded naive. Air momentarily stopped flowing to her lungs, almost choking her, and bile rose to her throat. Her temples started pounding.

'Don't be ridiculous. You all know perfectly well why you were coming here.' He sneered as his eyes moved to catch each of theirs in turn. 'You all have the ability to earn big dollars with your good looks and charm. Be glad. Go clean yourselves up. Saeli will give you advice if you need to know how to approach customers. Or how to charge for what services. You will make all your arrangements through him.'

Sweet, petite Angel shot up from the couch. 'No, no! I want to be a waitress in a hotel restaurant and wear a uniform.'

Mr Wong walked up to her and, gripping her right shoulder, shoved her back on the sofa. 'Anyone else got any dumb questions?'

Princess put her arm around her sister's shoulders.

Rose whispered from her seated position, 'I'd like to go home please.'

Mr Wong let out a long dry laugh. 'Yes, of course. When you pay us back for all the expenses of getting you here, we'll consider it.' He pulled five passports from his pocket and waved them at the girls. 'You're all illegal immigrants. You cannot go to the authorities. They will lock you up. Besides, I have friends in the services and in your Embassy who will let me know, and I will simply bring you back and you will be severely punished – and I mean severely. And what's more – your families back home will suffer too.'

With that threat, he turned and strode off to the room Mr Wang had occupied, turning first in the doorway to face them again. 'And from now on, if you speak with Mr Wang or me, you will address us by our name.' He shut the door after him.

Mr Wang, their first escort, who'd been silent the whole time, said, 'I send Saeli in. Give instructions.' He unlocked the front door and after re-setting the lock, walked out.

The girls wailed. Rose found herself cradling and rocking Marisol. Her mind shut down as she closed her eyes and imagined she held baby Aaron instead of Marisol. Then she opened her eyes. The nurturing came naturally to her as she pulled down Marisol's skirt which had ridden up to reveal too much thigh, all the while continuing the rocking movement.

'Tell us what to do,' the now not-so-tough Maria said through her tears as she looked at Rose.

Rose shook her head. Home was the only word running through her mind. Angel and Princess clung to each other, wailing.

The front door clicked, and they sniffed and turned to see an ageless, smooth-skinned Asian entering. *This must be Saeli.* A huge grin spread across his round, friendly face.

'Girls, girls, don't be upset. Nothing to worry about. I will take care of you.'

Among themselves the girls spoke Tagalog. Their English, when they used it, was imperfect, and flavoured with an American accent like Rose's. Saeli's English came with another accent which held a lilt; it came across as soothing and calming. 'Now, tell me your names, my lovely ladies.'

After introductions, the crying ceased.

'I'll take you tonight. Drop you off one at a time. You all have cell phones?'

Through tears and hiccups, they nodded. Saeli gave them his number to enter into their phones. 'You call me when you are ready to pick up for home.'

'We need new Sim cards so they work here in Bangkok,'

Maria said.

'Anything you need I'll get for you. I keep accounts. You'll pay me back. You might need an adaptor for power points for charging phones too.'

Rose whispered, 'What are we expected to do to get money to pay back and go home?'

'Ah, Rose Petal, you have humour. Let me tell you all about how to earn big money. American dollars are best. You have all been chosen because you are beautiful women. Hmm-mmm …' He licked his lips and smiled as his eyes travelled from one to another. 'Those looks will make you rich. You will not be working on the street or in cheap bars. You will be working in classy hotels where wealthy men go.'

Rose felt as if she would pass out; she realised she'd stopped breathing again, then her entire body trembled from the great gulp of air she finally raked in. She didn't look at the others, but kept her eyes squarely on Saeli.

'You walk confidently into the bar, and casually look around for men on their own. Take in their dress, their shoes, their grooming, even the watch if you can see it. This will tell you it's a good mark. Now I will demonstrate how to approach the mark.'

Saeli encouraged Maria to sit on a dining chair. 'Pretend she's a man drinking at the bar.' He pulled a chair up beside her and turned to her. In a soft voice, he said, 'Hi, my name is Rose Petal. I see you're all alone.'

Rose's world spun around her. She wished she could disappear into its vortex. She'd just been betrayed by a husband she thought she could trust, and the last thing on her mind was to take lessons in flirting with a man.

Saeli continued by touching Maria's upper arm and smiling into her face. He turned back to the others. 'You all know how to flirt. Keep it going. The man will take over. He may offer you a drink, or a proposition, or a rejection. In that case, move away a little and order yourself a club soda while you look for your next mark.'

Bile returned to Rose's throat, and Marisol continued to squeeze the life out of her hand, yet she felt nothing. The sisters, Princess and Angel, stared at Saeli in disbelief. Maria, she noted, tried to shrink into a tiny ball beside Saeli.

Unfazed by their reactions, Saeli said, 'Now, the most important thing is to get the money up front. American dollars are worth the most. And the more you offer of yourself, the more money you earn. An all-night stand, where anything is possible, earns the most. And for you that means only one customer to service. Oh, and you can buy your condoms and sex toys from me.'

He reached into his pocket and pulled out a folder of condoms.

'You can carry a variety of styles once you get familiar with your work.'

Saeli pulled his chair back and away from Maria and smiled at them. 'Any questions?' He looked straight at Rose.

Staring at the dangling condoms and shaking, she found courage as the words tumbled out of her mouth. 'Please, I would like to be a waitress. I don't think I can do this work.' She fiddled with her silver bracelet, her only tangible connection to family.

Saeli spoke kindly and softly. 'Just take your wedding ring off, Rose Petal. You'll be surprised how well you'll do. You look like a school girl. Maybe later we'll even get you into a school uniform.'

Rose realised she should have sold the wedding band back in Manila, but marriage vows before God meant she'd always be married no matter where her husband was. Divorce didn't exist in her faith.

'Can we please go together,' Angel asked, clinging to her sister who had almost chewed her nails to the quick.

'Brilliant. You will charge your clients double for double the pleasure.'

'We do massage. We don't need to do anything else.'

'I am not concerned with what you do, you beautiful children, just make sure you earn enough for your keep and for your family at home.'

Marisol and Maria were next. Saeli's eyes shifted to Marisol. In spite of her fear and the tears streaking her cheeks, she still looked stunning. 'Please, Mr Saeli, how much to go home? My brother might pay for me to go home. He works in a call centre.' But her brother had a family to support, and she didn't exactly sound hopeful.

'Maybe after you work till Sunday we look at the finances and we can discuss.' Again his tone was kind. He turned to Maria, who continued to sit on the role-play chair. 'Have you any questions, Maria?'

'This should not be happening. We were lied to. When our families hear of this you will all be in trouble.' She sat upright, her voice strong, her teeth clenched.

Saeli chuckled. 'You can certainly let them know you are a valued member of a high-class prostitution club. That goes for all of you.' His voice, still monotone and patient, somehow changed, Rose detecting the coldness now in it.

He knows of our shame, she realised. We're all good Catholic girls. None of us could or would ever tell anyone. Not ever. We've been well-chosen, easily duped, in our own desperation to work.

Her thoughts were interrupted by Saeli. 'And if you think of running away, the police and your Embassy are already aware of your presence, and they will simply notify Mr Wang and Mr Wong and you will be returned here – with shocking consequences for you and your family.'

The words, already heard once before, sent a shiver down Rose's spine. The situation seemed hopeless and she felt helpless at the moment to change it, and the others did too.

'Now I have something special to give each of you.' This time he pulled a vial of pink pills from his pocket. 'This is a special free treat just for tonight. It will help you to relax.' He stood and walked around, giving one to each of the women, who automatically put out their hand to accept.

Like the others, Rose stared at it in the palm of her hand.

'I'll take you two children first,' Saeli said to Angel and Princess. 'Be ready at 7.30. I'll come back for you others later.'

Placing his hands together under his chin in the prayer position, he bowed with a smile, took a few steps backwards, then turned and walked out, again setting the locks on the door from the inside.

'They must stay downstairs,' Maria suggested, slipping the pill into her pocket.

A stunned and chilled silence engulfed the room after Saeli departed. Rose willed herself to take some deep breaths to control her breathing again, the thousand thoughts rushing about in her head bumping into each other. Nothing connected. Nothing made sense. What could she say in a message to her cousin, the only family member who worked? But he rode his tricycle for a living and didn't earn much. How could he help? She couldn't even tell him where she lived. *Where are we? What do I owe? Yes, that is the first step. Find out the amount.*

Slowly, she sensed the grip on her hand from Marisol had lessened. She turned and looked her in the eye. Marisol grasped her hand hard again, a signal of desperation, but said nothing. Maria was the first to move. Rising from the role-play chair, she walked over to inspect the lock on the front door.

'We are in trouble,' she said superfluously, turning back to the group.

Chapter 5

At 7.30 when Saeli returned, Angel and Princess were dressed in black three-quarter length pants and matching Disney Frozen tee-shirts. 'We're only doing massages,' they reckoned.

'Come, show me what else you have to wear.' Saeli entered their bedroom to wait for them. When they appeared back outside, Rose saw they'd changed into bright-coloured plain tops. Princess had added a matching bow in her hair, and Angel wore a glittery head band.

'Come, come,' Saeli said as he headed for the door. Glancing back, he added with a smile, 'And you three be ready when I get back. Don't forget to take the settle-me-down pill.'

'I'm not going anywhere or taking anything,' Rose said, while watching Marisol change into a plain black dress.

'I'll go along,' Marisol said, 'but I'm not going to do anything.'

'Find out where we are?'

'Yeah. I'll check out a few things.'

Maria stood in the doorway. 'I'll come with you. We'll find a way out.' She looked smart in a simple back skirt and top.

When Saeli returned, he went into the bedroom to fetch Rose. She had placed herself on the mattress, pillow against the wall behind her, with her knees in front of her and her arms wrapped around them. She refused to get up. Rose knew Saeli's patience might run out soon, but it appeared not yet.

He put out his smooth, ringless hand to help her up. 'Come, my Rose Petal. You need to be able to send money home to your sister for your children.'

Shocked, Rose said, 'How do you know that?'

'I have read all your files. We know you all have family back home relying on you. You can't let them starve. Pop the happy pill and let's go.' His arm remained outstretched to help her up.

'No!'

Saeli shrugged, turned his back on her and faced the other two. 'Let's go, lovely ladies.'

Marisol and Maria followed him. He stopped by the bedroom door to the right of the front door and knocked. Mr Wong opened it a fraction. They spoke in a monotone for a couple of minutes, then Saeli and the two ladies left.

Rose couldn't sleep. She had a shower and changed, fearing all the time Mr Wong, the one on shift right now, might interrupt her. Nothing. Saeli hadn't yet provided an adaptor. She tried plugging her phone charger into the socket and sighed with relief when it fitted. But if she sent a message to her sister, or to her cousin, what could she possibly say? Her parents lived on an island in nothing much better than a hut. She couldn't turn to them either. If Marisol or Maria escaped, or got help, would they think to come back and get her? But they didn't know where to come for her.

Legs tucked under her, she sat in the lounge with her partly charged phone and found a photo on it of Jasmin, Iris and little Aaron, taken just after Aaron's birth. Then she stared at the locked front door. *Oh, dear God, they are so far away and I'm supposed to help them from here doing something so awful and so shameful. It sucks.* More than that ... she was trapped. *No. Never give up.* She returned to the photos. Flicking through her collection, she steeled herself to stay strong, promising herself she'd find a way out.

Eventually, she nodded off sitting up with her phone in her hand, and woke when the front door opened. She heard Princess's and Angel's voices. They were laughing and dancing together.

'What happened?'

'We earned heaps and heaps of dollars. Saeli's looking after it for us.'

Skepticism embraced Rose. 'What did you have to do?'

'Oh, don't worry. It's not so bad. One big happy fellow. Lovely room he had. He fell asleep. We got him to pay up front just like we were told. But then we took more money from his wallet after he fell asleep and we left.'

'Come and sit down and tell me how you did it?'

But Rose saw they were unable to sit still, and were talking loudly and quickly. 'You took the happy pill, didn't you?' *They really are just children*, she thought.

'Oh, don't make a big deal of it, Saeli's little Rose Petal. It's fun. Get out and try it.' Angel had tried to imitate Saeli's way of saying Rose Petal – no malice. 'We danced for him, like this.' And they hummed and intertwined and giggled as they moved. 'And then we helped him undress. He had this enormous flabby belly.' Angel used her hands to shape a bulge in front of her and pretended to wobble it. 'We painted patterns on it with moisturiser from the bathroom and massaged it in. We sat on him and made him happy.' They threw their heads back and laughed.

The mother in Rose came out when she stood up and tried to coax them both to their bedroom. But she doubted they would sleep that night.

She returned to bed instead, but was woken soon after by Marisol tip-toeing in and shutting the door. Rose sat up against the wall. 'Turn the light on, Marisol. Now tell me what you discovered.'

When she took in Marisol's appearance, she saw she had been crying. Patting the mattress beside her, she invited Marisol to sit close. Marisol climbed down, put her head on Rose's chest and big noisy sobs erupted. Rose patted and gently rocked her till the sobs turned to hiccups. She waited patiently for Marisol to speak.

'What is wrong with those two outside?'

'Oh, they're off their face on happy pills. Now, what about you?'

'Oh no. Not me.'

'No, I didn't mean that. I mean what did you do tonight?'

'Saeli was kind. He took me to a really nice hotel. I shook so much he came in with me and took me to a bar and talked to one of the barmen. He looked after me and introduced me to a man.' Marisol's waif-like body shuddered. And words tumbled out. 'I went to his room and did it.' The tears trickled down her cheeks.

'Did he hurt you?'

'No, I don't think he meant to'. She stopped talking for a bit. 'I stayed for ages and he paid me in American dollars. Saeli has it all.'

Rose wondered about the safety of everyone's earnings.

'Do you know where we are?'

'About half hour from the main part. But I only spoke to the barman and my client. That's what Saeli calls them – clients. And this one wants me back again.'

No-one heard Maria come in, but she appeared late the next morning as they sat around the kitchen table to compile a shopping list as though nothing out of the ordinary had happened.

Pen in hand, found in a drawer with some used envelopes, Rose quickly realised none of the group had sufficient knowledge about cooking, about quantities or about healthy eating. It seemed their mothers had provided for them. And that, she grasped, was most likely why some of the mothers might have suggested a trip to the agency in the first place. They needed both to support themselves and to help their family.

Rose had already found basic ingredients in the kitchen. There would be no option to shop daily here like there was back home, so their list began with rice – the staple, naturally – and they agreed on fresh vegetables, eggs, and of course, coffee. None of them had experienced much meat in their diet, so it didn't make the list. Other individual favourite foods, like special biscuits, were written down. They settled on equally sharing food costs and cooking, but would pay separately for personal hygiene products.

Rose so wanted to ask Maria about her night's experiences, but discussion of anything other than food they deliberately avoided, for the time being. 'And,' she added, as she moved to the kitchen cupboard, 'we can tell from the leftover items someone has been here before us. 'I wonder if they were trapped like we are? I wonder what happened to them?'

'I had a good chat with Saeli last night,' Maria offered. 'The Chinese business has run this house and a couple of other houses for ages. There's a boss man too. Not just Mr Wong or Mr Wang.'

Marisol whispered, 'Is it as bad as they make out?' She reached for Rose's hand again, but Rose simply patted it and continued writing.

'Best we concentrate on what we need here,' Rose said. The domestic conversation developed further as they moved on to how they might manage their washing and ironing.

'We can have a roster so we don't waste soap and water,' Rose suggested, standing up and placing her hands on the bench now the list was complete.

But Marisol wanted Maria to tell them more. 'Business? What do they mean business?'

'Saeli reckons we have to work our way out of this. He says compliance is the easiest route. Mr Wang and Mr Wong do twelve-hour shifts, and sometimes they have to drive when Saeli is busy. Mr Lee, the boss, steps in and relieves them when needed. Saeli said awful things might happen if we try anything.'

'What does he mean?' Marisol asked, frowning.

'Well, when someone before us went to the police and complained, they brought her back to the house, and the men drugged her and made her a drug addict, but she still had to work, and then she had to pay for the drugs too, till they eventually threw her out onto the streets.'

Rose's heart rate soared again. She pressed her hand hard on her chest as though she could calm its pace. Her temples throbbed. *So the threats are real. Or are they?* Her mind raced as she wondered what had happened to the remainder of the last group of women in this house. Were they too thrown out on the street when they'd outlived their usefulness to earn for the Wang-Wong-Lee consortium?

'Let's just put some more food into the house,' Maria deflected, deftly texting Saeli the shopping list. It seemed to Rose the friendship she'd struck up with him might be useful in more than groceries and driving.

Angel and Princess went back to their room to catch up on lost sleep. Rose found some empty cardboard boxes on the rear enclosed veranda and converted them into clothes storage in the bedroom. Food arrived. Rose cooked. The evening fell heavily upon them too quickly.

Rose watched as the sisters accepted their happy pills again, with a reminder they would now be paying for them, and departed. Maria and Marisol were next to dress up and leave. Simple black seemed the most acceptable attire. Again, Rose sulked in the bedroom, surprised and shocked Maria and Marisol had accepted their situation so readily.

But this night did not proceed as the previous one. Mr Wong barged into Rose's room without knocking. He wore an open neck, white button-down shirt with neatly pressed trousers. No coat. No tie. 'Get up, bitch!'

Rose shrank into the corner and curled up in a ball, peered out from under her arm at this brute in the doorway. When he came towards her, she folded her arms over her head to protect it. He kicked her in her exposed back. She groaned.

'Get up, I said.' But Rose, paralysed with fear, couldn't move. 'I will sell you to a monster. Then you'll have something real to complain about!' Mr Wong leaned back against the wall for a moment, before taking a big breath and marching over to her again. This time he grabbed her with two hands around her neck, attempting to drag her upwards into a standing position. She couldn't breathe, so allowed herself to be pulled up.

'I'll take it from here, Mr Wong.' Rose heard Saeli's steady voice through the fog.

'Just get the bitch out working.' He stormed out of the room bumping Saeli's shoulder as he did.

Rose fell to the floor again, gasping. Saeli crouched beside her. 'Slowly, Rose Petal, slowly. Get your breath back.' He sat on the floor and leaned back against the wall, his soft and soothing voice continuing. 'Now, Rose Petal, you have family back home waiting for support from you. I will start you off gently. I know people at the hotels, and they call me when they have a client looking for a young girl. You can pass for a youngster. You are tiny and delicate, just like your name. I will ask them for a gentle man who is looking for company tonight. You can go straight to his room this time.'

Rose uncurled herself, and sat up. With her knees under her chin, she leaned back against the adjacent wall. She wanted to vomit, not just because she'd almost been strangled, but from the realisation that she was well and truly trapped.

'Come, come, get yourself ready while I line this up.' Saeli stood and offered Rose his hand, which she reluctantly accepted.

He left the room and closed the door quietly behind him.

Mindlessly, Rose pulled on Annlyn's straight black skirt and black and white top before slipping her feet into Annlyn's black, tiny-heeled sandals. The last time she'd worn these clothes had been to the job interview. This time though she felt like she was going to a funeral. Tonight would be the emotional death of her. After being abandoned by her husband, she could not comprehend her life could get any worse.

As she sauntered to the bathroom, she noticed Saeli talking on his phone. He gave her a thumbs up, which made her more nauseous. But, instead of throwing up, she washed her face, brushed her hair and applied lipstick. In the mirror, she acknowledged just how tiny she was, and understood how she would appear to others as young and vulnerable.

Saeli smiled warmly when she emerged. 'A touch of colour you need. Do you have a scarf?'

She nodded, and went to retrieve a red one to wrap around her neck, which had begun to discolour.

'Now, lovely Rose Petal, please take your happy pill for me.'

As though in a trance, as if this world she now found herself in wasn't real, Rose complied – her fighting spirit had deserted her. Some other spirit now inhabited her body and it marched itself to Saeli's car on its own. She began to feel warm and lively.

'What was it, Saeli?' She stood at the car door.

'Ecstasy. You'll feel wonderful now.'

She did feel highly alert. Without a care. He placed her in the back seat and chatted all the way in the slow traffic to a hotel. Parking the car, he escorted her inside, spoke to the concierge and slipped him some money. He then gently took Rose's hand and guided her to the lift. She found herself floating through a dream; a very luxurious dream with thick carpets, glittering chandeliers, padded lounges and pretty people.

They took the lift to the seventeenth floor. On the way, Saeli said, 'Now you call me when you're done and ready to go home. Take the lift down, and wait outside for me. Do you understand, Rose Petal?'

As they exited the lift, she nodded. She bounced along the corridor with Saeli still holding her hand till he knocked on a door. A smiling fat Japanese man opened the door and bowed. Saeli bowed back. He gently shoved Rose through the door, backed out with another bow, and closed the door.

The man bowed again to Rose and said some words in Japanese. She bowed back, as she'd seen Saeli do, but had no idea what Mr Japan had said, yet he indicated she should sit on the lounge. He fiddled with his laptop and suddenly the melody of *Dancing Queen* flew out of its speakers while the words appeared on the screen. Mr Japan, as she'd called him in her befuddled head, came and took her hand. He sang in stilted English, 'You are the dancing queen, young and sweet, only seventeen ...'

He actually wanted to dance with her. Well, she could do that, and with lots of energy too. Through hand movements, he encouraged her to sing. Her happy pill gave her courage as a strange combination of a dancing and karaoke evening began. She found the tension exiting her body like a shadow disappearing at sunset, and began to take in her surroundings. The room appeared as sumptuous as the hotel lobby as it folded in around her. The lighting, she observed, all came from subdued lamps. Nothing bright hung from the ceiling, like the bare globes back at the house. She couldn't sit down, but instead wafted around the room touching various objects, stroking the lamp shade, and rubbing her hand along the back of the soft sofa.

Mr Japan opened the liquor cabinet and the mini fridge. Rose had never experienced the consumption of alcohol, but since her host showed such politeness, she decided to comply. He popped the cork on a bottle labelled Champagne. She had never in her life been so close to such a thing. With her first sip from the flute, the bubbles tickled her nose; she screwed up her face and rubbed her nose with the back of her hand. Mr Japan laughed so much his tummy wobbled. He patted his thighs, gesturing to Rose to sit on his lap even though most of it was taken up accommodating his belly. She baulked at this suggestion, but his frown intimidated her, so she balanced precariously on his thighs and knees, champagne flute still in hand. He took it from her and placed it on the coffee table before wrapping a pudgy arm around her tiny waist.

Drug influences or not, she instantly froze. *No, oh please no.* But her body didn't seem to care – it almost responded. *Has the ecstasy kicked in to that extent?* She detected the stale odour of cigars on his breath.

She turned and faced him, her eyes pleading for him to stop. But he misunderstood the signal and spoke excitedly. She had not the slightest idea what he said as he inclined back on the lounge and pulled her on top of him.

The words of Angel and Princess reverberated in her head. *Massage a fat tummy.* Maybe she could get away with simply the massage. She smiled, pointed to the bathroom, and struggled up. Mr Japan sat up, watching her with anticipation. Rose inspected the range of bath and skin products and chose a lotion for the massage. Coming out, she held it high and smiled at him as she danced back to the music. He laughed again. She felt light-headed and somewhat optimistic she could champion this situation.

She signalled to him to lie down again; continued to experience the out-of-body experience as she undid the buttons of his shirt. Very quickly, she learned the massage translated as foreplay to him.

But she survived. Her mind detached itself from her physical body and visited somewhere else while her body moved into automatic response. Her disconnection took her into the painting of the temple on the opposite wall where she lost herself inside the rich colours, especially the vibrant red with gold leaf. She imagined herself there wearing robes in those colours. She found herself dancing elegantly outside the temple, with her elbows pointing and fingers showing long nails stretched. Her headpiece matched those in the painting.

And then …

The return of consciousness struck her like a slap in the face. Reality hit hard.

She was in the bed with Mr Japan. And it was over. Her awareness washed her temple dream away as she watched him roll over and fall asleep. *Oh, no, I didn't collected payment first.* She blamed the omission on her anxiety on arrival. She had no choice but to wait till he woke. Saeli's donated ecstasy prevented her from dozing off. It prevented her from staying still too, so she found herself still fully conscious when Mr Japan stirred and climbed on top of her again. So focused was he on himself, he had no idea she felt repulsed by him, even though she responded to him at the time. Right now, the red-hot fury she felt towards him forced her to imagine him on fire. She could have stood by with a full bucket of water and watched him burn to a crisp. She superimposed Ramil's body on her fantasy and watched with imaginary satisfaction as he writhed in pain. In the meantime, Mr Japan satiated himself.

When the ordeal was over, she rose, shut herself in the bathroom with her clothes and showered to scrub the degradation away. First, she stood in awe. She'd never in her life seen such a shower. Back home, it consisted of just the outlet on the wall, and the hole in the floor if you were lucky enough to have plumbing. She congratulated herself when she worked out how to get the temperature right with the mixer tap. After scrubbing herself till her body turned red, she picked up the fluffiest of towels. Of course, she'd seen all this on TV, including a phone in the bathroom, but could never have imagined she'd experience it first-hand. And never in these circumstances.

Fully clothed, she re-entered the bedroom. Mr Japan now wore a bathrobe so large it actually went right round his rotund torso.

With a big grin, a flow of words and hand signals, which she couldn't understand, he escorted her to the door. How could she ask for money? She couldn't leave without it. She hoped it would be enough so she could transfer money back to Annlyn for her children.

With huge relief, she watched him reach into the bathrobe pocket and lift out a bunch of folded American dollars. *Yes!* She couldn't take her eyes off them, and quickly reached for them.

He opened the door for her, and she fled along the corridor, stuffing the cash into her handbag on her way to the lift. She left the hotel and rang Saeli. It occurred to her while she waited, she could pocket some of the money and he'd never know. *Or would he?* She decided not to try it this time.

Saeli attempted to converse with her on the drive back, but she remained silent. Back at the residence, Saeli sat behind the wheel of the vehicle and counted the dollars Rose passed to him. 'Oh, congratulations, Rose Petal. You've done exceptionally. I knew you'd be right for him.' His grin went from ear to ear.

Morning had not yet dawned when he escorted Rose into the house and relocked the door. No way in the wide world could she sleep, even though she felt physically and emotionally spent. Marisol slept soundly, yet she'd taken the same drug as Rose. Rose curled up on the mattress on the floor beside her, eyes wide open, absorbing the cool air from the fan in the corner and trying to still her racing mind and pacify her vengeful thoughts.

Over a late breakfast that morning, the girls compared

experiences. Angel and Princess, or the Disney twins, as Rose now mentally referred to them, babbled happily. They seemed to be enjoying themselves, as though they were on some holiday adventure. Rose almost envied them, but couldn't relate to them on any level.

Maria, on the other hand, seemed in a permanently peeved mood, snarling at them when they dumped their plates into the plastic bowl in the sink. 'Who do you think you are? Who do you think is going to clean up after you?'

The two young ones giggled in response.

Rose might normally act as mediator, but not this time. She noted Marisol chose not to buy into the clash either.

'How did you go last night,' Rose asked Maria, trying to defuse the hostility.

'I didn't get to count the money.'

'I mean other than the payment.' Rose tucked her knees up under her chin, and wrapped her arms around her legs, trying to relax.

'Oh, the first one only lasted a little while, but the second one lasted longer and paid more.'

Rose gasped. *No.* More than one customer a night was beyond her ability to process. She remained silent, not wanting to know any more details.

'What about you?' Marisol countered. 'I can see you took your happy pill.'

'Yeah. I can't sit still.' She placed her restless feet back on the floor. 'I can't sleep. I can't think properly and, when I have thoughts, they're wild. But I only had the one customer. I think he paid well. I gave the money to Saeli. When do they pay us?'

'In a couple of days. We can send money home with Western Union. Do you know how to do the transaction?'

'No. I trust Saeli will show us.' *At least I will have some money to send,* yet she preferred not to contemplate earning more.

That night, Saeli said to her, 'You must have made a big impression, Rose Petal. The Japanese client has asked for you again.'

This time, Rose felt less stressed. She knew now what to expect. At least, she thought she did.

'Do you want to buy a happy pill? They are not free anymore.'

'No. It makes me feel funny. It hasn't worn off yet.'

The Disney twins lined up for some, and so did Marisol, but not Maria.

Chapter 6

Rose felt reassured when the night with Mr Japan began somewhat the same as the previous one, but it quickly moved to other games – games involving handcuffs and ties. An electric shock ran through her and she wanted to run, all her instincts telling her to get out, but when she worked through beyond instinct to practical, she froze and couldn't leave.

Mr Japan's excitement rose even more when Rose began to tremble and quiver. Without the full influence of the previous night's drug, Rose remained consciously alert, and overcome with terror. Dealing with her highly animated Mr Japan, she caved in, finding no other working response.

In the wee-small hours, he finally finished with her and she departed, visibly shaking. He seemed oblivious to it as he verbally expressed something and smiled. Rose interpreted the communication as gratitude as he pressed even more American dollars into her hands, and lingered at the door to hold her close.

Saeli's fist punched the air with delight at the financial windfall Rose dropped in his lap, and he did not bother asking how she'd earned so much.

'Never again to him,' she demanded, teeth clenched, from the back seat.

'We'll see,' he said passively and non-committedly.

The following day, Saeli worked out a running summary of their accounts. He sat them at the kitchen table and handed them each a piece of paper outlining income and expenses.

'That's not fair,' Maria complained, looking at the small amount she'd earned. The others muttered in agreement when they saw the figure in front of them.

'If you all do a good job tonight, there'll be plenty to send home,' he told them, smiling a smile devoid of emotion. Then he left.

Maria waved the paper about. 'How dare they! Look, they've already deducted rent, transport, food, phone SIM cards, and all our private purchases. We've not even had a full week of work yet.' She dropped the single sheet of paper on the table and hit it with her open hand.

The Disney twins added, 'They are charging too much for our happy pills.'

Rose saw the suitcase cost had been taken out of her two nights of work. She nodded sadly to the others. 'I've got so little left.'

'Fingers crossed for us all tonight,' Maria wished openly.

Mr Wong, the tidier and more intolerant and more demanding of the two Chinese men, was on duty.

'What's this mess?' He waved his arm over the kitchen, and then the rest of the house. 'Get onto it.' He turned to return to his room but stopped. 'And when you go out at night you need to look well groomed. Not as if your clothes have just come out of a suitcase. Get that sorted too.' He turned, but turned back to face them with his afterthought. 'We have a reputation to uphold with the class of workers we provide.'

Rose judged the others as clean and well-groomed, but they were not good at caring for their clothes. She instantly recognised an opportunity and put a proposition to four of them. 'I will cook and clean, and I will wash and iron your clothes too. These are chores I'm used to doing.'

She had inspected the facilities thoroughly. The back veranda was enclosed with open lattice work allowing a flow of air. There was no way to exit the rear of the house. Brooms and mops and buckets were stored out there under the strung-up ropes acting as clothes lines. Her familiar domain.

Their relief and gratitude showed through their expressions, which Rose quickly halted by adding, 'Here are the charges for these duties; house cleaning and cooking costs I'll share out equally, but washing and ironing is per garment.'

'Okay, okay,' the Disney twins said almost in unison. Maria and Marisol mumbled agreement.

Keeping busy during the day, and earning a few baht appealed to Rose. Maybe Mr Wang and Mr Wong would see her talents as a housekeeper were stronger than her night-time skills.

She decided she would ask both the men if she could clean their rooms and do their washing and ironing. She would make herself indispensable. For the first time since arriving, her spirits lifted and the tension in her shoulders slightly lifted. It felt good planning something familiar. But then evening came, with the same expectations as the previous evening. Her energy levels diminished somewhat as she dragged herself to the car.

'This time,' Saeli said, 'you have to go alone and pick up your customers at the bar.' Any optimism she might have experienced instantly disappeared at the thought, but she was determined to make it through the night, motivated by being able to send money home tomorrow, not having to work tomorrow night, and putting her housekeeping plan into action.

Saeli dropped her at the same hotel Mr Japan stayed at. She walked into the stunning reception and lounge area, across the uniquely patterned carpet, under the magnificent chandelier, past the towering floral arrangements and into the bar on the right, just as Saeli had instructed. She kept her chin up, walked with a poise she didn't really possess, and hesitated in the entrance, her eyes slowly assessing the potential targets, or, as Saeli called them, clients.

Yes, that one will do. Older is better he said. This one balding, wearing glasses, a tad overweight, but well-groomed and wearing an open neck business shirt. He was drinking at the bar from a large glass of amber-coloured spirit in which floated a few chunks of ice. He appeared to be western. His eyes were focused on a game of some kind of football on one of the screens above the bar. This analysis and subsequent decision Rose made in less than twenty seconds. She glided silently across the carpet to the vacant stool beside him.

Her hands were shaking, and she clutched them together so her anxiety wouldn't show, climbed on the bar stool and faced him. His head turned towards her when he realised she wanted his attention, and a smile hovered around his mouth.

'Whatcha drinkin', honey?'

Heavens, is it this easy? 'Club soda, thanks.'

'You've gotta be kiddin'. Nah.'

Catching the eye of the waiter, he nodded. 'Glass of Prosecco, thanks.' He turned to Rose and raised his eyebrows. She smiled in acceptance but, not having heard of Prosecco, had no idea what she would be drinking.

'What's your name, sweetheart?'

'They call me Rose Petal.'

He grinned. 'And I'm Chuck. What's the accent?'

'Manila … in the Philippines. Where are you from?'

He grinned again. 'Guess.'

An easy and relaxed conversation ensued and Rose felt relief when her drink arrived in a champagne flute. This she could manage.

A few drinks later, Chuck said, 'Well, sweetheart, how much?'

Rose realised this would be American dollars again. She named an exorbitant amount, but he didn't hesitate.

They slid off the barstools together and he guided her to the battery of lifts where they travelled upward, midway, to his room.

Chuck immediately ordered a bottle of wine from room service. Rose wasn't sure how she'd handle more, but said nothing.

'So, tell me Rose Petal from Manila, what brought you all the way to Bangkok?'

Sitting on the edge of the bed, Rose clutched her throat, the look of horror washing over her face making him add, 'What's up, sweetheart?'

Rose launched into her incredible tale of being held against her will and threatened, but room service arrived, interrupting her story. An ice bucket with wine and two glasses, along with a container of French fries sat on the round table. Chuck tipped the waiter, which reminded Rose she hadn't collected the fee up front yet again.

He poured the drinks, and said casually, without hearing Rose's whole story, 'You just need to go to the police with your story, sweetheart.' He passed her a glass of wine. 'Here, this'll make you feel better.'

He sat beside her, his thigh pressing against her thigh, and downed his drink in one hit. 'Down the hatch, atta girl.'

Rose took a sip and coughed.

'Never mind.' He took the glass from her and placed it on the table before turning on her. 'Now, how's about it?'

With a silent prayer, Rose endured, wondering briefly how her god could let this happen to her, or to any woman. She again focused on a framed scenery print on the wall, and told herself she was by the water with a cool wind blowing under the shady trees in the picture. Chuck threw her light frame around as though she were a rag doll. When he finished with her, he rose from the bed, put on a hotel bath robe and paid her. She clearly got his message. At least he paid the agreed amount. He didn't acknowledge her again, so she quickly dressed and left. She wondered if offloading her so quickly could be blamed on her inexperience or perhaps he disliked hearing her incomplete tale of her predicament. *Well, none of it will stop me from telling everyone who will listen about my circumstances. I will tell it until one of them takes notice.*

She had no idea what clients expected. *Did one get lessons in sex games? How gross.* She determined not to find out. She stepped out of the lift on the ground floor. If she rang Saeli to go home, he'd simply tell her to get back to work. Maybe she could just hang out and pretend all the money came from two separate clients.

Just shy of midnight, she made her way back into the bar, tucked herself in a corner and ordered a club soda, breaking into the cash in her handbag. She shook her head at the few men who attempted to connect with her. *Do I look so obvious?*

She felt embarrassed by her ability to act like a magnet. *What is it about my appearance? No men back home would have given me a second look. It was as though 'Prostitute' was tattooed on her forehead. But how can I justify knocking back the opportunity to earn? Those dollars are my family's food and shelter.* She decided she must say yes to the next offer.

And so she went through the motions of acting the role of a prostitute twice more by switching her mind into neutral and her body into mechanical robot. She justified her actions by convincing herself she'd be sending more money for her children.

On the way home with Saeli, Rose said, 'Saeli, will you ask Mr Wang and Mr Wong, on my behalf, if they'll give me the opportunity to clean and wash and iron for them? I'm charging a small fee and I'm going to do it for the others.'

Late the next morning, Saeli reported her housekeeping offer had been accepted. Mr Wang, the man of few words, was on duty. 'Come, change sheets and towels,' he commanded, standing at his door and holding it open. 'I give money Saeli.'

With trepidation, she slipped past him into the front bedroom. There were two proper beds, on legs, a bedside table, a chest of drawers, a small desk and chair, and a wardrobe. A bathroom with an actual toilet adjoined – no hole in the floor for them. As she stripped the bed, she noted the top drawer of the bedside table sat slightly ajar. But it wasn't open enough to decipher the items inside. *Passports?* Would she dare? *Not at the moment.* Mr Wang hung about outside. She'd come back to dust and check out a few more things. *But even with a passport, what can I do? Could fleeing with a night's takings and a passport to the airport get me home?* She had no idea the cost of a ticket. But she'd begin planning.

She hummed gently to herself while pegging the sheets and towels on the lines strung across the back veranda where a hot breeze blew. A hint of hope that her earnings would increase gave her motivation. She might even find more opportunities for earning that did not involve selling her body.

The following day, after a night off with the girls watching TV and eating popcorn, and avoiding talking about work, Rose sent the first lot of money off to Annlyn. Saeli even gave her a few extra baht to put in her purse. Rose sent a message with the money with the code for collecting the cash from a Western Union agent.

A short time later, her phone buzzed, and Annlyn appeared on a video-calling app. The hairs on Rose's arm rose when Annlyn lashed out.

'Rose, listen to me. This is nowhere near enough!' she yelled. 'We're about to move into a house in Project 11 and we need to put some furniture in there. More mattresses too. What are you doing?'

Dear God, Rose reeled. *Imagine if I told her.* Instead, she said, 'What's the house like?' Rose envied them. But foremost in her mind was a sense of safety for her family because then the

Wongs and Wangs wouldn't be able to find them at the new address, so wouldn't be able to carry out their threats of hurting them.

'We'll have three bedrooms. Mum and Dad are coming to move in with us to help with the children, so there are more mouths to feed. Aren't the tips big enough at work? What are you spending all the money on?'

'Oh, I'm so sorry, Annlyn. I truly am. It's only been a couple of days. I'll see if I can get more waitressing shifts.'

She could never ever tell her family what had become of her. Although alone, she felt herself blushing at the thought and the shame of being discovered. And she was mortified at being given orders, along with the others, to buy some spicy, sexy underwear. Such a waste of precious money, and the cost of such frivolousness would be deducted from the next week's takings.

'But how are my beautiful children? And yours too?' Her heart fluttered as she visualised them.

Annlyn's response shocked her. 'All the children need new school uniforms, and shoes soon too.'

Tears of disappointment formed. In a firm voice, Rose said, 'I'll go and do my best for you all.'

And so time and work progressed in both jobs for Rose; the home front housekeeping and the client-based servicing. She held to her own newly established principle; just one customer per night. This self-promise, though, meant she now earned considerably less than the others, even with the housekeeping fees added. If Annlyn knew she wouldn't be happy. But Annlyn could never know the truth.

Annlyn had moved everyone into a government-provided townhouse where they now needed to pay rent. She sent photos to Rose but complained constantly about the lack of financial support from her. Annlyn's favourite saying was: 'The trees around here don't produce pesos, and neither do you.'

Rose felt crushed by the constant badgering, not just from Annlyn, but also by the two Chinese men regarding her meagre income. Even Saeli chastised her till their tolerance could last no longer.

Sombrely, Saeli said, 'There's a meeting downstairs with the boss, Mr Lee. Follow me.'

As they went together down the stairs, Rose began to sweat and her hands shook.

Saeli slid open the glass door under the house, and Rose got her first glimpse into the downstairs interior. Saeli shoved her into an office furnished with desk, computer and filing cabinets with linoleum on the floor. The place stunk of cigarettes with the stinky air circulated by the slow-moving overhead fan. All three Chinese were present, with Mr Lee sitting behind the desk. At least that's who Rose assumed he was.

A fleeting thought about her passport being here flitted into her mind, as she'd ascertained earlier during cleaning it wasn't in the men's bedroom upstairs. But much more serious matters were at hand.

'I am Mr Lee,' he said from behind the desk. 'We are going to help you.' His cold, abrupt manner scared Rose. Turning to Saeli, he added, 'Bring her in here.'

With that, he rose and opened another door off to the side of the office. Rose cringed and refused to move when she saw a raised bed furnished with leather straps. She quickly took in a nearby cabinet. It appeared to be covered with medical paraphernalia. Her knees trembled so much Saeli grabbed her arm to support her as he pushed her into the room.

'Get her on the bed.'

Rose instinctively turned to flee, but Mr Wong and Mr Wang grappled with her, then dumped her roughly onto the bed where they started strapping her arms and legs to the rails. Rose cried out; flung her head from side to side as she tugged at the restraints.

'Still, you crazy bitch!' Mr Wong snapped, slapping her face before moving back against the wall.

Rose drew a sharp breath of terror when she watched Mr Lee preparing a syringe. 'No, no. I will do anything you ask!' she screamed, still struggling. 'Anything at all.'

Ignoring her, Mr Lee addressed Mr Wong. 'Hold her arm steady.' He tied a tourniquet above the elbow, slapped her inner elbow, found a vein and plunged the needle into it.

Saeli walked over and stroked her hair. 'There, there, Rose Petal. All will be calm and easy now. You'll see.'

Slowly Rose felt her insides begin to smile at the world. Her body felt heavy and warm with relief. *All will be well.* 'What was that?' she mumbled in wonderment.

'A pick-me-up, sweet Rose Petal. You'll be fine now.'

Somehow, with her brain crying out no, no, it became overridden by a new euphoric feeling of knowing she could achieve anything, overcome anything. She'd become a champion and that belief conquered all logic.

Chapter 7

Behind his desk, Bob bowed his head and rubbed its smooth shiny surface with both hands. The sales figures were not looking good. *More advertising? Cheaper pricing? Better staffing?*

Bloody staffing. Most of them were millennials. Cared more about themselves and their rights. Give him the good old days when passion and dedication, ambition and money reigned. But his daughter fitted the gen X category, and she constantly reminded him nothing could be gained from living in the past and it was best to meet the staff where they were at. He hated to admit it, but she was probably right.

His offices were located above his store in Chatswood, on the northern side of Sydney Harbour. It was his first store. Over the years, both the store and the offices had been renovated a couple of times. He had three other stores around Sydney he visited weekly when in the city. This store, though, had become home to him.

Bob studied the comparative columns from the four pages of printout on his desk. He jotted some notes in the margins. His jottings were becoming tiny and almost illegible, even to him. He put an asterisk beside the Chatswood store because it was the only one pulling its weight. Maybe he'd swap some better-performing staff with the poorest-performing optometry store which happened to be in the heart of Sydney. He drew arrows on the pages, before looking up and staring at his Pro Hart painting of a dragonfly hanging on the wall opposite. *Such vibrant colours.* He never tired of appreciating its artistic intricacies, the detail. Its purchase represented his reward, his personal luxury spend after some magical profits decades ago, just years after his first opening. It symbolised his success. He'd added to it over the years with more pieces, but nothing brought him greater pleasure than the first taste of success. A smile flickered across his face with the memory of the joy of those early days when hard work returned big rewards, when staff earned bonuses. Now they seemed more interested in working less hours than in earning commissions.

His long-serving personal assistant, Georgina, walked in without knocking. She was family – not related – but she'd been around so long it felt that way. Bob's eyes feasted on her neat, trim figure clad in a black tailored suit set off with pearl earrings and a pearl brooch to match. *Classic. What happened to classic? Look at those kids on the floor downstairs. Just a hodgepodge of colours and styles.* Georgina's make-up was immaculate too. Not overstated. Then he spotted the wrinkles around her mouth and the ever-so-slight jowls developing. *When did she start ageing?*

'I'm making your bookings for Bangkok next month. Same as usual?' she said casually, wandering around behind him to see what he'd been working on. 'Oh, they're not great this quarter, are they?' she added. She'd printed them out in a large font and left them on his desk, so she knew exactly what they contained.

'Not great for the third quarter running, Georgina. I'm thinking of switching floor staff around between Chatswood and the city store.'

'Hmm. I'll get HR to bring in the files and help you go through them if you like?'

'Not right now. I'm searching for an edge. What do you reckon is making us different from all the competing franchised optometry stores now? Anything at all?'

Totally at home, Georgina moved around in front of him and sat in a guest chair in front of his desk. 'Well, they've all got designer frames. So have we. They've all got competitive prices. So have we. They've all got great locations. So have we. They've got good turn-around in supply and service. Ditto.'

Bob bowed his head and massaged it again, this time with his fingertips. 'Maybe we need to market the Bob Marks brand differently. Or maybe we need to experiment with a new range of frames. Maybe we do all three. Change staff, change marketing, change stock. Do a survey?' He sat upright. 'I'm going to see our suppliers again next month in Bangkok. I'll talk to them about new designs. Nothing we can do about the lenses they supply. There's no room to cut costs there. But just maybe the frame makers can start a new fashion. It's time to take a risk.'

Bob had been in this game all his life. His profitable stores provided him with a comfortable lifestyle but Bob was never satisfied with the status quo. Pleased with his latest decisions, he leaned back in his high-backed leather chair and interlinked his fingers behind his head.

Arriving home from work late as usual, he headed straight to the liquor cabinet and poured himself a Glenfiddich then dropped in a couple of ice cubes. He removed his tie and suit coat and threw them on the back of the lounge before settling in his favourite chair overlooking the pool in the backyard. The open French doors allowed the balmy evening to creep in.

His wife Denise wandered in barefoot, wearing a long fashionably-crumpled white linen shirt over her bathers. Her bleached blonde hair was so short-cropped she could simply run her fingers through it and it looked fantastic.

He glanced down at his beer belly and wondered, not for the first time, how she could stay so slim and glamorous, while he continued to grow larger and sloppier.

'Good day?' she asked as a simple greeting.

'The usual. But sales are down again. How about you? Don't

you miss going to your private counselling business every day?'

'Ah, semi-retirement agrees with me.'

Pouring herself a glass of wine from a bottle in the wine fridge, she said, 'I picked the grandkids up after school and took them to music lessons.' She parked herself on the arm of the lounge and sipped the wine. The clinking of ice from Bob's glass caught her attention. His hand shook slightly although Bob seemed not to be doing it deliberately.

'Bob, what's wrong?'

'Oh, nothing. It just does that voluntarily every now and then.'

She'd already noticed Bob's walking had slowed considerably; his steps much shorter than usual. She'd put it down to his weight and age. She said nothing more about the tremor while they chatted about the family. But she watched him carefully as he took the glass to his mouth. His slow hand movement showed deliberation. She contemplated how she might approach this issue with him. Not now, though. They rarely talked about their own health to each other. Most conversations revolved around their daughter and the grandchildren. Over the years, while both were busy with their diverse businesses, they'd grown somewhat distant from each other, with Bob not understanding Denise's work nor what drove or inspired her. She, however, felt compelled to show a degree of interest in his work in optometry and retailing since she sat on his Board of Directors.

'You've got your Lions meeting tomorrow night, haven't you?' she asked.

'Uh huh. I'll be late in.'

'What's different?' Denise shrugged and smiled at him without malice. It would be another evening she wouldn't have to cook a meal. Not that she minded cooking, just that his diet, if you could call it that, was the opposite of her more healthy one. He loved anything sweet. He bought dark chocolate regularly. He didn't bother to hide them anymore and she didn't bother to chastise him anymore.

Bob rubbed his head again, this time with just his left hand, before placing his empty glass on the table and levering himself out of his chair. 'What's for dinner?'

With U2 playing on his in-car stereo system on his drive to work next morning, Bob waited at the umpteenth red light. He lifted his right hand from the wheel and stared at it. No, it didn't shake. He could concentrate and control it.

'Georgina,' he said, stopping by her office on the way to his own, 'have you noticed any change to my handwriting?'

She chuckled. 'And good morning to you. Can you even read your own writing? I can't anymore.' Seeing the concern in his eyes, she said, 'Are you worried about it?'

'Nah – forget it.'

But he didn't forget it. In the privacy of his office, he made an appointment to see his old mate from school days; his doctor, Suresh Patel. He told no one of his intention and early the next day he fronted up at the surgery, explaining to Suresh what he'd noticed.

'I'm going to refer you to a good neurologist,' Suresh said, looking down as he hit the keys on the computer keyboard to produce the referral document.

'But what do you reckon?'

Suresh glanced up. 'Something neurological, Bob, that's for sure. You worried?'

'Of course.'

Picking up the phone, Suresh said, 'Then let me see if I can skip the queue for you with a mate of mine.'

And so it was done. He'd see the neurologist on the following Tuesday.

Bob said nothing to Denise nor to Georgina, and certainly nothing to any of his mates at the Lions Club meeting that night. The format of the evening followed the usual format, and Bob felt comfortable with the friends he'd made over the years.

The after-dinner guest speaker's topic was youth suicide. He began with an anecdote of a young man who'd become withdrawn and had shown signs of depression, which was noticed by his workmates. But suddenly one day he arrived at work with a great positive attitude, laughing and joking. He brought in a book he'd borrowed from a friend and returned it, told his mates he would pay out his loan with the bank at lunchtime, and went for drinks with them after work. His mates, the speaker said, were pleased their old work colleague was mentally back with them.

'Next morning,' the speaker continued, 'word raced around the office that their workmate had jumped from the fifteenth floor of his apartment block and killed himself.'

The guest speaker hesitated, looked around his Lions Club audience with anticipation, and asked, 'So, if they'd realised he had actually exhibited signs of being suicidal, what might they have said to him?'

One bright spark yelled, 'I would have said, "Move to the ground floor, mate".' Bob stifled an inappropriate laugh.

The poor guest speaker was left speechless and took a step back from the podium for a few seconds, but recovered well. When the evening finished, Bob stood around chatting with friends when one of them said, 'So Bob, you've been pretty quiet lately. You travelling okay?'

'Me? Quiet? Nah, I'm fine, mate.' Bob knew his mind had been on other things, like business and health, but was surprised others were picking up on it.

At golf the following Sunday, he met up with his usual three golfing buddies. His swing and his balance were shaky as he teed off with his wood. He struggled to keep up with them as they walked down the fairway to his ball. At least the ball landed in the middle of the fairway, even if he hadn't hit it far. He wondered if they'd noticed. He became quiet as he analysed and obsessed over each movement he made.

'You okay, Bob?' one of them asked over post-golf drinks.

'Sure, why?'

'You're not playing your usual game. You seem a bit off?'

Avoiding a response, Bob changed the topic. He summarised in his mind who noticed his condition: Georgina at work, Denise at home, colleagues at the Lions Club and now his golfing buddies. Roll on Tuesday when he could see the neurologist and maybe get some answers.

He felt a mixture of relief but also trepidation when he finally fronted up at the neurologist's surgery – relief because the time had come for facing the truth, and trepidation for what exactly the truth would be for him to face in the future.

After a fairly extensive interview, the doctor put him through a number of physical tests, first with his eyes open and then closed. His balance, he conceded, was cactus, as was finding his nose with his index finger with his eyes closed. The doctor called his condition bradykinesia. Bob practised the word in his head so he'd remember.

'So does that mean … it's Parkinson's?' he asked, using the word out loud for the first time.

'It means slow and decreased movement. You don't tick enough boxes to call it Parkinson's. We can treat it and it may not progress much, or it may develop into Parkinson's disease. There's a neurotransmitter in your brain called dopamine, and it's not sending your body the signals as it should. But we have a drug that will help.'

Bob vaguely remembered his Uncle Stan, his father's older brother, who had shuffled about stooped over. His dad had called the condition Parkinson's. Bob hoped Parkinson's wasn't in store for him in the future. He didn't think he could handle it or the pity that went with it.

He arrived at work mid-morning. Georgina immediately pounced on him. 'Is everything okay? I tried calling. You didn't answer.'

If only Denise showed so much concern. 'Sorry, Georgina. Just a little shopping to take care of.'

Georgina's taste in clothes impressed Bob yet again. Today a deep red pants suit with a crisp white shirt was set off by a patterned silk scarf tucked inside the suit collar. He lifted a menswear store bag up to show he'd been shopping. 'Anything urgent here?'

'Show me what you bought first.' Georgina peeked into the bag to see it contained a plain blue business shirt. Nodding indifferently, she said, 'HR has some recommendations for possible staff transfers. I think you'd be doing some of them a favour, especially since they live closer to their new place of work.'

'Let me take a look.' He'd made no decisions staffing-wise when he left the office early.

He arrived home to find it had been invaded by his two grandchildren and his daughter. The twin girls rushed at him, hugging his legs. 'Got any surprises for us, grandpa?'

He put an arm around each of their shoulders. 'Whoa. Let me take my jacket off. Now, let's go into my office and look in the cupboard.' Denise had set up a box when they were little, and placed it in a cupboard in Bob's study. She added several knickknacks to it each week to encourage the grandchildren to spend time with their grandfather in his study. Bob had no idea what the box contained till the girls opened it. He sat in his leather chair, watching them as they tipped the entire contents on the floor, inspecting each item and talking to each other.

'So, what have you decided?'

They almost always chose identical items. Denise almost always bought two of everything.

'These stones, we think.' They held them up.

'Oh, they are beautiful samples. You like them?' *If they drop them on their foot, they'll end up with a broken bone. What has gotten into Denise?* He held out his hands so they could tip the rocks into them.

'We're collecting rocks, Grandpa. Do you collect rocks? We've got a whole box of them now with a separate place for each one.' Their mother, his daughter, nurtured a broad range of interests for the twins. He'd noticed pretty hair clips had sat in the box for months untouched, and the clothes they wore were often not frilly or feminine. The movies they chose to watch were not about princesses, but about villains and about justice and kindness. He only knew this because Denise told him.

Bob adored his conversations with the twins. Or rather, listening to them talk and tell him of their adventures.

'We go rock hunting in the mountains. Last time we found ochre next to a big rock, and we pounded it up on the rock into a powder and poured some water on it and painted with it.'

The call to dinner interrupted their time with him. This was not the time for Bob to talk about his visit to the neurologist at the table. He'd wait till later. Let the medication kick in and see if Denise noticed the result. Then he might talk about it.

Chapter 8

Because he travelled often, Bob had developed his own style of packing, just as he'd developed his own style of dressing. All his suits were dark colours. All his shirts were either white, blue, grey or pink. All his ties were diagonally striped silk. His socks matched his shoes, which were black. They all went into the suitcase in the same way each time. He travelled in casual pants and a sports jacket.

His carry-on bag contained not only his blood pressure tablets and cholesterol tablets but now his new Parkinson's medication, together with a letter from Suresh, his doctor, explaining why he carried these drugs. While he meticulously packed his clothes in his suitcase, he chucked his medications, still in boxes and bottles, haphazardly into the carry-on. With the carry-on and his black leather briefcase, he presented himself at the Qantas business lounge.

'Welcome back, Mr Marks.' The lounge attendant scanned his electronic boarding pass. Bob's ego appreciated this recognition at his clubs and the restaurants he frequented as well.

The ten-hour flight overnight, coupled with the three-hour time difference, meant he could have a meal on board, sleep on a bed and wake refreshed to breakfast on the plane, then on to the hotel to have a shower and shave after being deposited by the hotel complimentary limousine service.

'Welcome back Mr Marks,' the hotel doorman said, instructing an underling to carry his luggage. Bob always carried a stack of single and higher denomination American dollars for tips. The Thai people much preferred this to their own Thai baht. Bob tipped generously.

Faithful to his travel routine, he showered and changed, and ordered a car to deliver him to Arthit, his supplier.

'So, you want some new frame designs?' Arthit said.

'Something really different, like we discussed. What have you come up with?'

Arthit and Bob had become more than business acquaintances over the three decades they'd partnered up. They'd holidayed in each other's countries and met families. Through all of this, they maintained a healthy degree of business formality. Like many Asians, it was impossible to pick Arthit's age from his appearance. Bob guessed they were a similar age. Where Bob had begun losing his hair at the age of about thirty, Arthit displayed thick black hair for decades, but the hairline had begun to recede.

'See you're heading for a hairstyle like mine, Arthit. Save on haircuts.'

Arthit laughed as he produced a huge sketchpad. 'Now, Bob, you did say different.' He pointed to the open page. It held sketches of spectacles showing a bar running from the centre of one lens frame to the centre of the other. 'We're back to aviator spectacles. What you do think?'

The sketches of nose bridges were decorated with a variety of shapes, one of which depicted the easily identified Sydney Opera House.

'Good heavens, Arthit. That's extreme.'

'I thought it might be the kind of thing you might have in mind?'

'Oh, ten out of ten for creativity.'

The next page showed the temples, otherwise known as the wings. They went from the frame to the ears, with similar decorations.

'Not so fussed on them,' Bob commented.

Arthit pushed on. 'The frames themselves would need to be made of carbon fibre. Strong but lightweight. Expensive,' he added, glancing up at Bob, who nodded his acceptance, and waited impatiently for more, undeterred by costs.

'Now, the bar must also be carbon fibre. We have a few choices. Either just the bar from middle top frame to middle top frame, like this sample.' Arthit pointed to the sketch of the Sydney Opera House drawn in above the bridge. 'Or … the bar could go all the way across and extend left and right of the frame so a decoration could be placed on the outer frame, instead or as well.' He tapped another sketch.

'I like that.'

'Now, what I'm thinking is, your clients could choose a basic frame of a shape of their preference, just as they normally do. Then they select the extended bar or just the middle bar.'

Thoughtful, Bob nodded slowly in agreement again.

Taking in Bob's positive demeanour, Arthit continued. 'And the clip-on decorations could then be chosen. Any shape and any colour and any number. Again, in carbon fibre. It could be, for example, a series of red hearts. It could be a name, or the name of their company – in silver or in gold if they so wished. Just the colour I mean, otherwise it would be too heavy. The parts clip on easily.'

Arthit's speech sped up, and his eyes grew wider. 'We could supply samples for the clip-ons to choose from, but it wouldn't be limited to just them. Fashion is so conservative at the moment.'

'You're excited by this, aren't you?'

'This is adventurous. I am so tired of the same all the time.'

'I'll stay with the conservative range as well for the conservative customers,' Bob said quietly, almost to himself. 'But to have this line exclusively, hmm.' He hesitated again, rubbing his head with one hand. 'You know, Arthit, I don't want to share this with anyone. It's ours. Yours and mine. It needs its own name too. And we need to give the naming some thought.'

Bob would have to patent the design back in Australia.

Discussions and sketches went on and on. Bob grabbed a 2B pencil to express himself on paper, but when he tried to draw what he had in his mind his hand didn't go where he wanted and he tried to cover it up. He muttered 'Stupid' to himself.

'What's wrong, Bob?'

'Ah – just a shaky hand. Nothing to worry about.' Everyone had begun to notice. 'Let's take some time out for lunch.'

Talk over lunch revolved around wives, children and grandchildren and their achievements. Photos on phones were produced, and stories expanded.

'I'll fly back home tomorrow. Will you manufacture some prototypes to take the attachments, and a couple of the attachments as well? Costings are going to be important. Any ideas yet?'

'I'll get straight onto it. Exclusivity costs, my friend. Want me to contact you online when I have something to show you?'

'No. I'll come up again. It's good to get away sometimes. Oh, and I want to take some sample gemstones home for the girls. Can you recommend somewhere?'

Late the following evening, Bob arrived home with extra weight in his bag. Pleased with himself, he transferred the special rocks into the grandchildren's surprise box in his cupboard before he went upstairs to bed.

Chapter 9

A few hours after her first drug dose, Rose exerted her newfound power and marched boldly out to Saeli's car, with Marisol and Maria following sedately. She sat in the front seat with Saeli – not her normal behaviour. But then neither were her other actions.

A heightened awareness of her surroundings overtook her – a vividness she would have struggled to explain. Awareness of her own sexuality had never been so dominant. She wallowed in it, unconcerned. Light rain fell on the windscreen and windows. Grinning, she puffed 'huh' on the inside of the glass and drew circles, glancing across at Saeli for approval.

'Look, look,' she said, grabbing his thigh as her circles slowly disappeared.

Maria leaned forward and said in Saeli's ear, 'Is she going to be alright?'

'She'll out-earn both you ladies tonight,' he chuckled, giving Rose a return pat on her thigh.

And his prediction wasn't wrong. Each of the women were dropped off at different hotels, with Rose being the last. She always frequented the same place. The bar staff and concierge knew her and sent business her way, thanks to Saeli's tips which were deducted from Rose's income. The two younger sisters had been taken to work earlier. This had become the regular pattern.

Rose swung herself out of the car and, head high, shoulders squared, strutted through the doors the doorman threw open for her. Swinging her hips, she sashayed across the foyer into the bar, pausing in the doorway before picking a target. She sauntered up, smiling all the while.

Her child-like and innocent appearance and nature, two of her major earning attributes, had been replaced by a raw sexiness within her still child-like body and demeanour. She didn't care. She wasn't fully aware of what had happened to her; she acted out of her drug-induced self. Her target spoke only broken English, but an instant mutual understanding occurred.

In his room, she turned to him and stroked his beard. 'You are my Leo – with your ginger hair and beard you are my lion.'

Whether or not he understood, Rose didn't care. He grinned broadly. She sniffed Leo's face, then rubbed her face against his beard. 'Hmm, delicious,' she said, her eyes just inches from his.

Already aroused, his grin remained, and he allowed Rose free reign. She needed no help. She danced and sang for him – Rod Stewart's *Do ya think I'm sexy*. She didn't know all the words, but it seemed irrelevant. She just hummed, interrupting her outburst of song and dance to remove his pale blue business shirt, slowly, button by button, her knuckles caressing his hairy chest as she worked sitting astride his lap. She sang softly into his ear, '*If you want my body and you think I'm sexy, come on, sugar, tell me so.*'

With Leo's shirt removed, she backed off and danced again, using his shirt as a prop and continuing, in a husky voice, '*If you really need me, just reach out and touch me, come on, honey, tell me so.*'

The grin remained on Leo's face while he waited patiently. Rose's alluring accent had a tantalising affect.

Next, she pulled her black and white top over her head and draped it loosely around his neck before falling to her knees to undo his shoelaces. She slowly slipped the shoes off, reached under the trouser legs, snapped off the socks and threw them over her shoulder.

Still humming the parts of the song she didn't know, she slid out of her black skirt, and discarded her shoes. There she stood in lacy black bra and panties, completely uninhibited, swaying her way towards him again.

Rose felt driven by a single focus, and that focus was sex. Insight into her actions had deserted her.

Leo hadn't said a word. He leaned back, arms outstretched along the back of the sofa, almost in a trance. Rose knelt again, this time to undo the belt buckle. She slowly dragged the belt out from its loops and ran it sensuously under her nose. 'Beautiful leather,' she declared, gently stroking it before putting it aside.

Leo's patience expired. He reached forward and cupped her breasts, still encased in her bra. He slid forward and caught her up effortlessly in his arms, one arm under her knees, and the other across her back. Cooperatively, she placed an arm around his neck and kissed his red beard.

She succumbed freely as he placed her on the bed before unzipping and dropping his trousers and jocks. Seeing how prepared he was, Rose could barely wait. She herself stripped off her bra while he dragged off her panties. She giggled. He climbed on the bed, knees between her legs, looking down at her expectant face.

She stroked his chest before her hands moved quickly down to capture what lay between his legs. He in turn used his fingers between her legs. Rose needed no further foreplay. She was more than ready. She was hungry. Hungry for sex. And she had not a care in the world at that moment, apart from appeasing her own hunger. Fireworks of all colours exploded in her head. Blood rushed through her veins. This was an experience like no other.

Afterwards, she curled up beside Leo the lion admiring the trailing vines in the wallpaper while stroking the hairy forest growing out of his chest.

It wasn't long before they started all over again – and again.

Dawn had broken when Rose, sufficiently satiated, left the hotel and rang Saeli. 'Home, Saeli.' She threw him a bundle of cash. It fell about his seat and the floor. She didn't know the currency, nor did she care. Saeli laughed loudly.

And so it went on, night after night, although Rose lost interest and energy every four or five days. She'd then seek out Saeli for another drug fix. She'd almost stopped eating. Food didn't interest her. Sex did. But, somehow, she kept up the housework and the cooking for others, albeit somewhat sloppily at times.

Marisol hovered around Rose as she scrubbed the floor with gusto, humming Destiny's Child's *Say my Name* over and over.

'What have they done to you, Rose?'

The girls, though, well knew what had happened to her.

Marisol pulled Maria aside. 'She'll kill herself. We have to do something.'

Maria agreed. 'But what? How?'

Rose still sent money home; more than before, but it was never enough for the support needed by her own children, her sister's family and her parents – the cost of her meth addiction ate into her earnings big time. The Disney twins were blitzing it by using the cheaper MDMA, and both Maria and Marisol seemed to do well by simply acquiescing. When her longing for family life tried to overtake her, Rose worked hard to stifle it by sweeping and mopping floors. Dreams, when she was able to sleep, constructed scenes of her children clambering on her and holding her tight. The dreams were not helpful. She'd wake in a sweat, confused and stressed. She somehow continued to go through all the motions of functioning but now avoided looking at the photos Annlyn sent of the children. The remaining fight within her couldn't see the way out but her highs from the drug let her cope day to day.

Maria marched into Rose's bedroom, propped her hands on

her hips as she watched Rose energetically cleaning the floor again. 'You can't go on like this. You're going to end up dead,' she warned, 'or on the streets,' she added. 'Right now, you're working like a mad woman. And look at your arm, Rose. We've got to get you over this. You know you're addicted?'

Rose closed her eyes and rocked back. It was all too hard.

Then Marisol came in, knelt beside her and rubbed her arm. 'Will you let us sort it for you?'

The rare act of kindness struck a chord in Rose's psyche and she responded with a brief nod, but no words.

The following night Rose spent several hours debasing herself again with a client but, in her drugged state, she no longer cared. When this latest client had finished with her, she collected her fee, and turned to him with her usual spiel in her imperfect English. *What was his name again? John, yes, John. Weren't they all?*

'John, I wonder if you help me? I have family in Philippines and just want to go home. But I held here by a gang and they not let me go.'

In spite of her drugged state, she never stopped trying to get her message out.

John's mobile rang. He looked at Rose, turned and looked at his mobile on the bedside table, then walked across and picked it up. Turning his back on Rose, she heard him say, 'Hello, my darling. How did your meeting at the school go?'

Rose left the room. She would never give up trying to get help. Never. She returned to the lounge bar where the staff recognised and ignored her. She felt quieter and calmer tonight, coming down from her high. The barmen still received regular payments from Saeli to send customers in Rose's direction. Looking directly at one of the bar staff, Rose shook her head, signalling she wasn't looking for another customer yet.

Tonight, an attractive female singer dressed in a long deep-red gown stood by the piano singing Celine Dion hits. Rose decided to sit and listen.

In spite of her addiction, Rose remained polite and respectable, but somewhat extraverted compared with her usual introverted self. She often smiled at complete strangers, but right now she put even that on hold as she courageously took out her phone, and finally looked at the latest photos sent by Annlyn of her own two girls and a healthy happy growing Aaron. Taking a deep breath, Rose confirmed in her mind all her actions were to help them and she would find her way home eventually.

Her eyes were closed when she heard a familiar voice say her name. When she opened her eyes, she reckoned Marisol, who stood right in front of her, could look stunning wearing a hessian bag, never mind the plain but classy black dress she always chose.

'I'll join you?' She perched on the vacant bar stool beside Rose. 'You don't look as though you're touting for business?' Marisol whispered.

'Nor you. You're not usually in this hotel?'

'You don't mind?'

'Of course not. There could be half a dozen of us and still plenty of clients to go round.'

They shared their earlier experiences in whispers till a tall, good-looking man approached Marisol. 'Come, dance with me,' he said in a heavy accent, purposefully taking her hand.

The pocket-handkerchief size timber dance floor provided just enough room for couples to hold each other and sway back and forth to the music.

Rose watched them till another man, much older, maybe in his fifties, caught her eye; he took the stool beside her, and smiled. *Oh no, here we go again*, she thought. But just as he was about to speak, the tempo of the music changed and the dance floor emptied. Well, almost.

Marisol and her man commanded the middle of the floor. Rose had no idea of Marisol's talent. All heads turned. *You'd guess they'd been dancing partners for some time,* she thought.

'Very impressive, your friend. My name's William, by the way.' The stranger held out his hand.

What is going on? This didn't seem the usual way men propositioned her. But Rose hadn't been in this game long enough to know what constituted usual. It simply registered as unusual in her repertoire.

She automatically reached out her hand, smiled and said, 'Rose.' Fairly quickly she cottoned on he simply wanted company, and didn't realise her profession. He just wanted to talk to her, and it felt like a compliment. A few minutes wouldn't do any harm.

He was fluent in English. 'Where you come from?' she asked.

'South Africa, and you?'

'Philippines. What brings you here?'

'Diving. I'm off to Phuket tomorrow. Let me buy you a drink?'

Rose ordered a club soda and William respected her choice. Another tick for him. Here was her chance to tell someone of her predicament – someone who wasn't compromised in any way by her occupation. She bided her time as they watched, listened and relaxed till after the music and dancing stopped. She waved to Marisol as she disappeared with her dance partner. William moved with Rose to two comfortable lounge chairs with a low round table between them.

'What brings you to Bangkok, Rose?' He placed her drink on the table, and waited for her to sit.

'I know what brings you, William, but what you normally do for a living?'

'I'm a doctor. A general practitioner.'

Here we go, Rose thought, somewhat optimistic, and launched into her tragic tale.

William's eyes grew rounder while she talked, but he didn't interrupt, even when fresh drinks were put in front of them. When she told him of the injections of methyl amphetamine, his lips thinned and he shook his head.

She concluded by pre-empting his predictable suggestion of going to authorities, explaining about the corruption. It was impossible to circumnavigate the authorities.

Finally, he spoke. 'I think I might know a way to help with the addiction. But you'll just have to try to trust the authorities for getting back home. Or I can let them know. I just don't see any other way but to risk it. Do you have an address?'

But Rose didn't know where she lived.

'Would you like me to escort you now to the police?'

'No, no, no!'

She reiterated her understanding of the corruption, and the very real threats to herself and her family. 'They already got me hooked on drugs. They very powerful.'

Again, he shook his head in disbelief. 'Well, come up to my room and I'll write down some information for you. It's up to you what you do with it.'

Rose's short-lived optimism plummeted. *Damn.* He wore the same man-cape as all other men she'd met. *One track mind.* Oh well, she might as well bring in some more dollars, or whatever currency this man provided. Deflated, she rose slowly from the chair and accompanied him. Once they'd entered his room, he took a pad and pen from his briefcase and began writing notes as he spoke. Rose stood stock still in amazement.

'Since your addiction hasn't been going on for too long, you might have an easier time withdrawing. But you must do it. And you will need support. Have you got any?'

'Two of my co-workers,' Rose confirmed.

'These notes will be for them as well. You'll become weak.

Physically and mentally. When times get tough – and they will – you must look at the pictures of your children.' He paused. 'Show them to me now.'

Rose passed her phone over, open at the family collection.

'Hmm. Three beautiful children. Worth fighting for. And it will be a fight. Are you up for it?' His voice held warm compassion.

This was the kindest man she had met in her whole life. *Too good to be real.*

He went through the notes he'd written. 'You're going to suffer withdrawal symptoms in about three days. You'll beg for more drugs. You'll feel depressed, exhausted and just want to sleep. It won't be pleasant.'

'I can't sleep. I must work. They will not let me sleep at night. Right now, I should be working.'

'You are. You are working to get well.' William fossicked around in his bag. 'Here, take these with you.' He passed over a blister pack of medication. 'When you feel anxious or depressed, after day three most likely, take one of these a day. Keep these notes and make sure you share them, so they'll know why you are behaving erratically. I don't think you'll be able to work.'

'Why you are being so kind to me?' Rose verbalised her innermost thoughts, confused he didn't ask for sex in return for the favour.

'I'm a doctor. I want to see you well. But since I'm leaving tomorrow I can't follow up on your imprisonment, and I'm not sure how I can help you if you can't go to your embassy or the police.'

'You have truly done enough, and I thank you.' Rose stood up, and tucked the written notes and medication in her bag.

William escorted her to the door and pressed some foreign currency in her hand. 'This will make up for what you didn't earn tonight, and hopefully give you the rest of the evening free?'

Without much inhibition, due to her drugged state, Rose threw her arms around him and kissed him on the cheek, smiled and walked out. In the lift, she shuffled through the notes, adding them up. Nearly 8,000 rand. She had no idea how that converted though.

Reaching home, she asked Saeli if he would work out the conversion.

'It's more than 400 US dollars,' he said after checking his currency converter. 'Well done, Rose Petal.'

Rose showed the hand-written notes to Marisol and Maria. 'Will you help me?'

It didn't take Rose long to come crashing down. A couple of days later she couldn't drag herself off the mattress.

'Can you ask Saeli to come to me, Marisol? I need an injection or I'm going to die.'

But Marisol, with Maria's support, kept guard, reading the advice from the notes that explained what would happen and what to do. Just as predicted, Rose became utterly exhausted. With the help of the medication, she slept around the clock in a thick film of perspiration and desperation.

'She is very sick,' Maria reported to Saeli. 'She just cannot work.'

'What's wrong with her?' He stared at her prone body covered in sweat.

'Terrible fever. We'll keep our distance but watch over her. Can you tell the bosses?'

'Just make sure she's back on deck quickly, or they'll throw her out on the street and replace her.'

Whatever Saeli said to the Chinese men worked because they left Rose alone to recover.

Just as Rose had consoled Marisol, now Marisol returned the kindness. When Rose cried, and rambled on, and begged for meth, Marisol showed her the photos of her children, saying, 'This is why you're doing this, Rose. You are strong. You can and will do it.'

Marisol held Rose in a frail embrace, then she gave Rose one of the tablets left by the doctor, and Rose fell into a deep sleep again.

The next day, Rose awoke and again begged for drugs, and when her request was refused, she said to Marisol, 'I hate you! I hate you! You are a nasty, wicked witch.'

Marisol ignored the comments and made her drink more water, this followed by chicken soup.

When Marisol came home after her night's work, she was repulsed by the sour odour of her bed-mate. But Marisol and Maria continued to nurse Rose towards health. They cooked and cleaned for a few days, but drew a line at washing clothes for Princess and Angel, who were beginning to appear ragged around the edges with dark circles constantly appearing under their eyes.

'They've become reliant on the MDMA stuff,' Maria told Marisol as they poured a cup of coffee each in the kitchen. 'They're more interested in having a good time than in taking care of themselves. I've tried to tell them, but they don't listen to me.'

Hearing a door open, they turned. Having dragged herself out of bed, Rose came across the room and plopped into a chair at the table. Her hair had become greasy and tangled, and she stank of stale sweat and something else unpleasant.

'Sorry, everyone. My mouth tastes like I've been licking the bottom of a bird cage,' she proclaimed. 'I can only imagine what I look like. How long have I been out of it?'

'Looking pretty good, Rose Petal,' Marisol lied affectionately. 'You've only missed five nights of work, given you slept through our night off. Now, time for a shower and shave and clean up.'

Rose gave them both her best smile. 'I'm back. Thank you both. I have not enough words to describe my gratitude. I hope the bathroom doesn't reject me because of my stench.'

Marisol high-fived Maria as they watched Rose amble off for a major overhaul. She fronted for work in the evening.

'Free condoms for you as a gift, Rose,' Saeli greeted her and dangled the pack for her to grab.

She clenched her teeth, straightened her shoulders, and slid into the car, sequestering the condoms in her bag. She would charm the socks off the wealthiest guy in the bar tonight and charge a fortune.

She would find a way home too. Somehow.

Night after night Rose worked. She suffered humiliation much of the time, role-playing a dog, an angry teacher, belting her client, allowing herself to be struck, and whatever else they demanded of her. She sucked it up. She got slapped, tied up, bullied, and occasionally, just occasionally, treated decently, as decently as was possible when someone paid to use her body, but she had learned to separate her mind from her body. *They can hire my body*, she told herself. *But not my soul.*

She began talking to Annlyn weekly. 'I can't earn bigger tips. This is as good as it gets,' she lied to her sister, who constantly complained of the shortfall of funds she received. Rose continued to pay off all the drugs she'd relied on over her addiction weeks. She said to Annlyn, 'I have to pay for all my own uniforms, and rent and food too.' This was not far from the truth. 'And please don't put the children on the phone,' she begged. 'It kills me to see what I'm missing.'

'Jasmin and Iris just got their latest report cards. I can send a photo of them. I told them you'd be very proud of them. Are you sure you don't want to tell them yourself?'

Rose would rather not even talk to Annlyn once a week,

never mind anyone else in the family. *If only they knew. But they can never know. Not ever.*

Rose and the four other working girls gathered around the kitchen table to eat the healthy stew with rice Rose had prepared. The Disney twins were as animated as ever.

'We've got exclusive rights at a really good hotel. We are private night time masseurs. And then we get paid lots more for all the other favours,' they bragged. 'How about you, Marisol? You making enough?'

'Yes, thanks.' Marisol maintained her privacy, sharing little.

'And you?' The twins said, turning to Maria.

She put down her spoon. 'Yes, thanks,' she responded sarcastically.

'And you?' to Rose.

'Here, have some more food,' Rose said ladling more of the stew on their plates.

When the twins returned to the television, Maria and Marisol huddled around Rose.

'I can't earn any more. I just can't.' Tears welled up in her eyes. She squeezed them away. 'Saeli says I'm earning just over half of what you all bring in even with the housekeeping money. And I'm not supporting my family enough. They are constantly complaining.'

They shook their heads in sympathy, but could add nothing.

Chapter 10

Sunday afternoon. No more golf for Bob. He'd swing himself off his feet if he tried. Lunch, a buffet by the pool at home, had been a chaotic affair with their daughter and her twins, the children yelling and screaming – happy yelling and screaming though, he acknowledged – as he bit his tongue when his instinct told him to demand they stop.

The girls had found the rock samples in the box he'd brought home from Bangkok and proudly traipsed out to show them off to their granny and mother.

'Let's throw them in the pool and dive for them,' Sarah, one of the twins said, holding a handful above her head.

Bob didn't hold back; he jumped up, stumbled, grabbed the table for support, gasping. The girls turned.

'No! No throwing any rocks in the pool, thank you,' he recovered.

Some hours later, after the departure of the gang, he sat under an umbrella by the pool and poured a glass of wine for Denise as she pulled herself out of the pool. There were steps, but he admired her shape and athleticism as she swung herself up and out even though they were the same age. She lightly towelled herself dry before pulling a white linen shirt over her bathers. It accentuated her tan. Bob silently passed her the filled glass after she sat down opposite him.

Raising it up, she murmured, 'Chin chin.'

'And to your health too.'

No time like the present, Denise decided seeing the word *health* had been mentioned. She'd been sitting on her thoughts for some time. 'Talking of health, Bob … are you noticing your tiny tremor?'

Bob was in the process of carefully manoeuvring his glass to his mouth to take a sip. 'Hmm. You noticed. I knew you would. Yeah, I'm on it. Saw Suresh. Then saw a neurologist.'

Surprised this breakthrough came so easily, she added, 'Well, good for you. And?'

'I'm taking a form of dopamine. Seems to be helping. I'm fine.'

It was a rare and precious time for them to be alone and relaxed. It was rare and precious for Bob to share something personal.

'I've been concerned. It's Parkinson's, right? Are you okay travelling up to Thailand?'

'Good heavens, it's nothing. He hasn't called it Parkinson's yet. It's under control. Now, what about you? What have you been up to?'

Typical bloody Bob, Denise thought. *Deflection, denial.* But she humoured him. 'I'm taking up a bit of part time work. My brain needs a bit more than grandchildren to keep it going.' She reached over and pushed a stick of celery into the guacamole dip left over from lunch.

'I'm not surprised. What, where?'

'Giving lectures on counselling techniques and suicide intervention at TAFE. I start next semester. Just pulling all my notes together now to fit the course outline.'

'Retirement didn't last long.' He grinned.

'You giving any thought to it?'

He looked serious. 'What? Retirement? Why? I'm just in the process of sorting staff, upgrading and introducing that whole new line of exciting products.'

'The business must be worth a fortune. Have you given any

thought to selling it? And don't you want to do other things now in case you get worse?'

Bob just stared at her. 'What do you mean … get worse?'

Denise had gone too far. *Too much too soon*, she realised.

'I'm doing all the things I want. I'm back up to Bangkok next week to see all the new samples. Just wait till you see them. Interchangeable accessories on the frames. They have to be specially designed to take them. I'll take them to the Board for approval then.'

Denise read the excitement in his voice and his body language as he leaned forward in his enthusiasm, with hands waving.

'So explain it,' she demanded of him. She sat on the Board together with Georgina, but she rarely involved herself to any extent. Mostly it filled a statutory formality. Georgina ensured the legal requirements were met, and Bob had always been the creative one.

Bob had been solving a Sudoku puzzle in the Sydney Morning Herald. He took up the pencil – he always worked in pencil so he could erase an incorrect number, or clear if he spilled over the line – and he began sketching frames on a blank margin. While he could usually fit a number in a square of the puzzle, he couldn't seem to get his hand to sketch his ideas. Tiny squiggles appeared. He scoffed and thumped down the pencil with impatience.

'Just tell me,' Denise said, to save his discomfort.

When she began to understand the concept, she said, 'You know, you could put advertising across the top of the frames, or political slogans even.'

'Yes, yes. That's the idea. There's no limit, apart from keeping it tiny and lightweight. I don't have a name for it yet.'

'I'll give it some thought too.'

The next morning Bob showered and dressed for work. 'Damn

buttons,' he muttered, fiddling to get the tiny things in their holes. Maybe he'd go casual and stop wearing a tie too. He hated all the fumbling. And as for tying shoe laces – well, his lack of balance leaning forward meant he occasionally found himself on the floor on all fours.

Georgina greeted him when he arrived at work. She followed him into his private office and waited till he sat down behind his leather-topped desk. 'You'll be happy to hear all the staff changes have been made. We got it right, and they're all settling. What about re-introducing bonuses in some way now, Bob?'

'Yeah, I thought of setting targets for each store, and sharing excess profits relating to hours worked. What do you reckon?'

'Clever. It should make them pressure each other to look after their customers and tout for new ones.'

'But I want to wait till the new range comes out. Big incentives then to promote it. I'm off to see the prototypes next week and bring some back. We need to get the staff geed-up about something special coming without saying exactly what, till we have a big launch.'

'Ooh, exciting. That'll be my job. The launch.' Georgina sat down with her iPad.

'We'll bring in an agency for you to work with, Georgina.'

She looked up at him. 'That big? What time frame?'

'Well, we've got to have enough stock. Big outlay to cover all the stores. Several months from when I get up to Bangkok and approve the manufacture. And it would be great to be out for Christmas.'

'When are you going to Bangkok?'

'I thought next week. It's early, but Arthit will be ready.'

'Do you want me to come?'

'And why would I want you to? I've never asked you before.'

She hesitated. Her brain told her to shut up, but her mouth decided to operate independently. 'I thought you might do with an extra pair of hands?'

Woah, this woman has strong intuition. Should I accept some help? He knew he had become slower and more deliberate in his movements, but he managed, and no, he would not admit he might need help.

Just one week later he asked for help for the first time. Bob had always meticulously folded his shirts to pack in his routine way into his black leather suitcase laying on the bed.

'Denise?' he called, hoping to find her within earshot.

She appeared in the doorway. 'What's up?'

'Do you mind folding these shirts?' He held them out on hangers.

Silently she took them from him and within minutes deftly presented them back to him in a neat pile. 'No problem, Bob. Anytime.' The action symbolised moving into a new stage.

Bob arrived in Bangkok more tired than usual, but keenly looked forward to viewing the new line of frames the following day. His routine was to head down to the bar for a nightcap before turning in.

'Welcome back, Mr Marks. The usual?'

'Thanks, Enzo.'

The Glenfiddich with ice appeared on a napkin coaster in front of him. As Bob reached for it, someone touched his shoulder. He turned to see a youthful female on the next bar stool, dressed simply in black with a plain silver bracelet on her wrist. She honoured him with a warm smile.

'Hello, Sir. I see you are alone.'

'I am. Can I buy you a drink?'

'Club soda?'

Bob nodded again to Enzo who took the order.

'You don't drink?'

'Well, I prefer not.'

Enzo placed a glass in front of her, and she bounced the lime wedge with her finger against the chunky ice cubes then sucked her finger slowly and sensuously. In a sultry voice, she knew worked well, she said, 'My name is Rose Petal.'

'Where are my manners? I'm Bob. And what a pretty name. You're from the Philippines?'

'Oh yes. You pick my accent? All my family there.'

'So what brings you to Bangkok, Rose Petal?'

She'd never had such a perfect opportunity, and was tempted to answer with the story of her situation, but sensed it was not yet the time or place. So, with regret, she ignored his direct question, and replied instead, 'Mister Bob, can I be of service to you tonight if you all alone?'

Bob drew in his breath sharply. *How naïve am I*, he thought. *As if she'd just want to talk to me.* He brushed his head with the palm of his hand. Of course, he'd been propositioned in the past, but it had been quite some time since it had happened. To cover his surprise, he picked up his glass and held it to his lips for a few seconds. 'You seem so young, Rose Petal. Is that really your name?'

'My working name, Mister Bob.'

'Well, I'm flattered by your attention, but I'm not sure I'm up for anything tonight. Stay and talk to me for a while.'

'Oh, but I must earn money for my family. I so sorry but cannot sit and talk, Mister Bob.' Disappointed, her eyes strayed around the bar.

'Here's the deal. I'll pay you to sit and talk to me. You can tell me about yourself and I can listen to your pretty accent and look at your pretty face. How much, Rose Petal?'

Rose hesitated. This had never happened to her before. She was on a steep learning curve. Boldly she said, 'One hundred American dollars each hour, Mister Bob.'

He chuckled. 'Well, I'm not American, but I'll give you one hundred Australian dollars. How's that sound?'

Having no knowledge how much Australian dollars were worth, but being able to earn something by just talking appealed to Rose, so, mustering the widest smile, she said, offering a handshake, 'Deal, Mister Bob.'

'Let's move over to a more comfortable setting.' He picked up both drinks, but stumbled awkwardly from the stool. Rose reached out to help. He regained his balance by standing still for a few seconds.

He laughed. 'And I haven't even finished one drink.'

Seated in the richly upholstered chairs in her little black outfit, legs crossed, Rose felt in the moment, like a princess. When she launched on her story, she felt the weight of her occupation immediately strip her observation away.

After Rose finished her tale by relating how she overcame her drug addiction, Bob, who had not interrupted, nor touched his drink, rubbed his bald head a couple of times. 'Shit, Rose Petal, you've been sex trafficked,' he blurted.

She looked bewildered. 'What those words do mean, Mister Bob?'

'You've been stolen and forced to work as a prostitute. That's terrible. Shocking.' And then Bob presented a range of options, none of which, Rose told him, could be considered an option.

'Tomorrow I'm meeting with a business associate who's a local. He'll know what to do.' Barely suppressing a yawn, Bob felt suddenly overcome by tiredness. Business deals he could handle with ease, but highly charged emotional stuff, well, that belonged in Denise's domain. If only she were here. He scratched his ear, then finished his drink.

'I so sorry, Mister Bob. You pay me for my company and just go *blab blab blab*. I do not ask you about your business. What you do?'

Bob stared at this not-so-innocent but very child-like-looking companion who spoke in clipped English, and realised all he wanted to do was to escape and go to bed.

'Rose Petal, I'm exhausted from travel, and have a busy day tomorrow. Let's meet here around eight tomorrow night and I'll have more information for you.' With arrangements made, he opened his wallet and withdrew three fifty-dollar notes. 'I hope that helps a little.' He stood. Rose did likewise and offered her hand for him to shake. 'Till tomorrow night,' he responded before slowly heading for the lifts.

Rose strolled back to the bar with her unfinished drink.

'No go there?' Enzo queried.

'He's too tired. Maybe tomorrow.' But Rose knew tomorrow wouldn't happen. Men were terrified when they heard of her circumstances and never re-appeared.

Chapter 11

Bob arrived at Arthit's factory in an industrial area via the hotel limousine. Having bare concrete floors, unlined walls and cheap light partitions, the factory wasn't fancy, but it was clean and organised. Arthit's main office was in a high rise in the city, but all the manufacturing took place out of the city. Bob had been here several times before over the years, and knew the two senior staff and supervisors who welcomed him warmly. While being escorted through the factory to Arthit's office, the workers' waves and smiles greeted him from all corners. He felt the excitement and buzz of electricity in the air – more so than normal.

'Come, come, Mr Marks,' his main escort called, rushing ahead. Bob couldn't keep up, but the surrounding excitement propelled him as he carefully climbed the narrow wooden staircase with sharp risers to Arthit's office overlooking the workshop, holding the rail all the way.

Arthit's desk was smothered in an array of frames of all shapes and colours. Sitting atop display boxes were the sample decorative attachments.

Arthit grinned widely. 'Well, my good friend, what do you think?'

Nodding approvingly, Bob said, 'Arthit, you've done it.' He picked up a bright yellow carbon fibre frame at random and passed it to Arthit to clip on a row of tiny yellow and green boxing kangaroos, one at a time, with one on each end as well. 'Put them on, Arthit.'

Arthit complied.

'Unbelievable. Fabulous. And you can produce any colour frames? What about footy colours, or foot mascots? The choices are endless. And you can choose to wear just one of two, or fill the whole row.' Bob took off his own spectacles, and donned the yellow ones. The frames, together with the accessories, felt lighter than the ones he'd taken off.

Arthit passed him a hand mirror.

'Superb, Arthit. Superb.' Bob grabbed Arthit's hand and shook it vigorously, then smiled smugly. 'But I haven't come up with a name yet. Any ideas?'

'Well, the frames can simply be *Bob Marks*, or *BM*, or even *Marks*, and then the clip-on accessory could be *'On your Mark.'*

'You've been giving it some thought, haven't you? I like it. I like it. Yes. Even *On the Mark* instead of *On your Mark*. Hmm, clever. Now, next, how do we package the accessories?'

'I think presentation is really important. They can be given as gifts separately. Maybe something like a jewellery ring box in a velvet bag for luxury, or both.'

Arthit dismissed the rest of the staff once Bob congratulated them individually for their creativity and production skills. Then he poured over Arthit's new sketches. Arthit passed the pencil to Bob, but he declined. 'Can't draw any more, mate. Parkinson's has got me.'

Arthit stopped, held the pencil in mid-air and said, 'I knew it. I knew there was something going on. Doesn't seem to be stopping you too much?'

Bob nodded, ignoring the opportunity to expand. 'Back to the sketches.'

Satisfied with a great morning's work, they rose to go off to lunch to celebrate.

Bob had been so absorbed he'd forgotten to take his medication, and his feet were not obeying his brain. They simply froze to the floor. He dug out his little dispenser from his pocket and threw a pill down his throat. He arrived at the top of the steps, and, holding the rail, watching carefully, thrust one leg out in front and let his body drop down.

Seeing the problem, Arthit said, 'No, no. This will never do. Let me get some of my men to help.'

Gripped by embarrassment, Bob realised he wasn't going to be able to do this alone. With one heavyweight guy in front of him and one beside him, whose shoulder he held, he continued down with his thrust-and-drop pattern knowing he'd be caught if he stumbled.

Once they reached the bottom, he shook his helpers' hands.

'From now on, I'll bring everything into my city office and we'll meet there. You're a very brave man, Bob.'

'It's not bravery Arthit, it's necessity. Now where are we going?' he said determinedly.

They climbed into Arthit's Mercedes and arrived at an exclusive Thai restaurant.

As always, Bob let Arthit do the ordering. On this occasion, the head chef came out and discussed the fresh seafood with Arthit. These Thai meals were often highlights of Bob's visits. Today, though, much more occupied his mind.

'Now, I've got something to ask you,' Bob said with his head bowed, and elbows on the table as he rubbed his temples in a warm-up. He then sat up straight and related, in full, the previous night's experience and Rose's dilemma of being held against her will by a Chinese gang of three.

Arthit sat motionless, totally attentive as the situation revealed itself.

After a long silence, Bob said, 'Well?'

'Hmm. I recommend just leaving it alone.'

Bob raised his eyebrows, not just for the comment, but because of Arthit's neutral tone. But he would not be deterred.

'You must know a straight cop? Or someone she can turn to for help?'

Bob hoped Arthit might even volunteer himself. He picked up his wine glass and slowly raised it to his mouth, not taking his eyes off Arthit's face.

Arthit sipped his orange juice in a wine glass chilled with ice blocks. He put it down, leaned forward and said in a serious, low tone, 'You're dealing with the Chinese Mafia, my friend. Don't go there. Just don't. Now, I don't want to hear any more. It's too dangerous – for both of us.'

A series of dishes arrived at the table and the conversation returned to business after an explanation of the aromatic cuisine for Bob's sake. Although shocked, Bob decided this would not be the last attempt, only the first, to try to help Rose.

Arthit returned to discussing business.

'I'll make another trip up in the next couple of weeks. But you know what's required now. Plus some sample display stands or cases?'

After lunch, Arthit competently weaved and dodged his way through heavy traffic of all shapes and sizes to drop Bob back to his hotel around five o'clock.

Bob was pleased to hit the room, take off his shoes, lie on the bed and turn on an American news channel. In a few minutes, he'd dozed off. He woke with a start. *Where am I? Oh, yes.* And he had a date in the bar. But first, he took out his laptop and made notes on the morning meeting, and the lunch meeting. Pity he could no longer understand his own writing; he rather liked sketching and jotting.

After a shower and a change of clothes and much muttering over the effort he had to exert to tie his shoelaces, Bob headed down in the lift.

Enzo made a beeline for him as he climbed on the bar stool. 'The usual, Mr Marks?'

His tumbler of scotch had just been placed in front of him when he glanced towards the door.

Rose caught his eye and smiled broadly, relieved he'd kept his word. He gave her an encouraging smile as she walked towards him.

Once they were settled at a table, Bob said, 'I asked my friend, but he reckons it's the Chinese Mafia, and you don't mess with them?'

'Your friend is right, Mister Bob. I am stuck.'

'How much to buy your way out?'

Rose paused, her thoughts scattered. 'I don't know. I can ask, but I don't think they would let me go, now I know what I know.'

'You're probably right. But see if you can find out. What is it you need? I want to help but I can't think of a way.'

'As long as I earn enough to make them happy, and enough is left over to send home – but there is never enough left over.' Rose blushed when she added, 'I can't earn like the others. I am not good at this job.'

'How much do you send home each time?'

When Rose told him the amount in Thai baht, he took out his phone and used the calculator app. 'That's just over one hundred dollars Australian per week.'

'I don't always send enough, and sometimes my sister, Annlyn, she say she need money for school uniforms, for medicine for our parents living there in the house with them — all kinds of things.' Rose's heart rate shot up, driven by admitting all these stresses out loud. *I carry so much responsibility,* she thought. *But is there hope? Why would he ask this kind of detail?*

'And how do you send the money?'

'Every Sunday Saeli give us some cash. We go to Western Union agent, and tell them where to send money. Then I message Annlyn the code so she collect at another Western

Union agent there.'

'It sounds simple enough. Maybe we can go to a Western Union agent now and you could show me how to send some money?'

Rose thought quickly. Could this be a trick? But how? Why would he?

Tentatively she said, 'I do not know where agent here is.'

'I'll ask Enzo'.

He went to stand up, but fell unsteadily back into the chair, just as Rose panicked. 'No! no! He is in on it too.'

'Shit! Okay. Bloody hell!' Bob glanced up at the bar. People weren't always what they seemed. 'What if I get some baht from an ATM and give it to you to send home?'

'Then they take sixty per cent, plus all my other expenses. Rent, food, taxi fares with Saeli.' She hesitated, but then added, 'And for the drugs I am still paying off. There would be almost nothing left, Mister Bob.'

Taking another swig of his scotch, Bob just stared at her, and saw her blushing again.

'Can't you hide the money if I gave it to you?'

This was too complex for her to consider. 'Too dangerous, Mister Bob. I sorry. I don't think you can help.' Rose felt a prickle behind her eyes, but she determined she wouldn't cry in front of him. It was becoming apparent to her there would be no relief, no escape, no hope.

'Okay, let's try another tack. What say you give me the details of where you send money, and how to contact your sister to tell her it's there?'

Again Rose hesitated. Could she trust this relative stranger she'd just met? 'Annlyn think I a waitress.' Her hand flew to her mouth as she coloured up yet again. 'What would she think of man sending money?'

'You could tell her I'm your boss and I'm paying you directly.'

Rose flopped back into the soft chair. Her shoulders dropped along with the tension as the concrete block of despair that had been crippling her lifted. Hope rose with the released weight. She sighed, realising this could actually happen.

'These ATMs only allow me to get the equivalent of a few hundred out at a time, but I see no reason why I can't do a couple of withdrawals each time while I'm here.'

'I don't know about such things, Mister Bob. I so grateful.' Even if he did this once, Rose realised, it would ease the situation back home. 'You incredibly kind. I not know how to thank you.' She looked at him directly, expecting an answer. Instead, Bob took out his phone and passed it to her so she could type the required names and places to do the first transfer.

Rose spoke with an American accent, and her English was far from perfect. Sometimes she used the wrong verb, or the wrong tense, or left words out.

'Your English fascinates me. Where did you learn it?'

With a soft laugh, she said, 'We all must learn at school. And I watch American TV.'

'Ah – and your favourite show?'

'America's Got Talent. Your favourite?'

This time Bob laughed. 'Not that.'

Bob had one more day in Bangkok. He decided he'd not use the hotel's limo, but an ordinary taxi to take him to an ATM and then a Western Union agent, so there'd be no risks, no rumours. He would fly out the following night but wanted to meet with Rose briefly to ensure the money he sent was received.

He'd been shocked by Arthit's response, but it also validated Rose's story. He couldn't figure out why she'd tell him such a wild tale if it wasn't true. What could she hope to gain from it? It wasn't as though she asked him to send money to her family. It was a considered response on his part to offer when all other avenues of assistance seemed thwarted. But it was only a temporary fix.

Bob's day with Arthit, after the uncomplicated and successful transaction of forwarding the funds to Rose's family, was one of meeting with other designers in Arthit's office where a few designs were trialled.

'Are you happy with the name *On the Mark*?' Arthit checked.

'Well, to fit on the box, why not go with the abbreviated *OTM*?' Bob responded. And the label on the frames can be simply *Marks* or better still *BM*.'

With a bag of samples and design sketches, he returned to the hotel, having extended his stay for a late departure.

Bob had grown up being reminded constantly by his father of the motto: *Good, better best, never let it rest, till the good is better and the better best.* His father had also insisted that no room existed for failure, and Bob should celebrate each success. But he'd also balanced it by saying: *He who never made a mistake never made anything.*

A grey cloud of doubt travelled across Bob's thoughts. *Could this new line be a flop? No, never.* He was on a winner.

And then his thoughts turned to Rose. The bubble of elation he'd revelled in during the day burst. He detested not solving her problem. Yet, apart from financial assistance he offered, he could see no way out for her. Next month when he travelled to Bangkok, he'd take her out and buy her things for herself as well as send money to her family.

Rose floated across the lounge and into the bar grinning widely. 'It got there,' she said before she even reached him. She put her hands together in a prayer position under her chin and bowed to him. 'I so very grateful, Mister Bob. And so my family.'

He smiled. He was dog-tired and had only a few minutes before he needed to depart for the airport. Her charm was hypnotic. 'I expect to be up here in a few weeks again, Rose.

We'll do it all over again. I can send you a text when I arrive so we can meet. And I'll carry plenty of cash to transfer. I look forward to our next meeting.'

Rose believed him. They walked together to the bank of elevators where she spontaneously gave him a hug.

She turned to try to pick up a client in the bar.

'Oh, no,' Bob said, realising he'd forgotten to pay her. 'No work for you tonight,' and he dug into his wallet and shovelled all the notes into her hand.

Rose hugged him again.

For Bob, the following days and weeks back in Sydney were filled with secrecy surrounding the new product. Georgina, too, was thrilled to see samples, but no staff could be included in the secret until the patent became registered, and then progress could be as rapidly as manufacture in Thailand allowed.

He often thought about Rose and was genuinely keen to see her again.

For Rose, the following days and weeks blended into an ugly routine. There were no criticisms coming from her sister, and that was a rare plus. Her one event to look forward to was the next visit of her Mister Bob.

Chapter 12

Rose told no one of her fairy godfather, Mister Bob. She settled into a sense of control she hadn't felt for a long time. If her children were being well-cared for, and Annlyn had sufficient funds, then perhaps all her earnings could be put towards buying her freedom.

She approached Saeli when he was alone. 'How much do I owe?' she queried.

'Too much. Why do you ask?'

'Maybe my family get me home,' she lied with ease.

'I will check with Mr Wang,' he replied.

Within hours, Rose was called to the downstairs office. With no preliminaries, Mr Wang challenged, 'You steal. You keep money from us.'

'No, no.'

'They say you not send much money home.'

Lie again, Rose. Lie again, her brain yelled at her. 'My family have got good jobs right now. They don't need my money, so they want to pay my debt so I go home.' She held her breath.

Mr Wang, the man of few words, leaned back in the chair behind the desk, while Rose's legs trembled. 'You do?' he scoffed. 'Not happen.'

'What you mean?' Now Rose found herself responding in his signature telegraphic speech.

Mr Wang looked up at Saeli, standing by the door. Gruffly, he muttered, 'She go.'

Rose swung around and looked frantically at Saeli. *What did he mean?*

'Come, my Rose Petal. You can drown your disappointment with work. Meet some nice men instead.'

So at least the word *go* referred only to leaving the office. Still, now there was no positive response, Rose took a dive down into the darkest depths of her mind. Her whole body screamed to gear up, to rear up. She turned, tears in the corners of her eyes, 'How about some rocket fuel to help me, Saeli?'

They were halfway up the steps, with Rose a few treads above him. He stopped. 'I'll ask. You will go further into debt.'

'What does it matter? If they won't let me leave.' Then she wondered whether her Mister Bob would continue supporting her family if she were all fuelled up all the time – or worse still – dead. Dead sounded like a good option right now. The fear, the pain, the humiliation – all would stop.

Rose fell onto the mattress in her room and curled up into a tight ball, trying to figure out how she could end this futile existence. A hotshot would mean she'd need access to drugs. Mr Lee controlled them downstairs. But she could buy some on the job. *Or – cut wrists – no, always too many people around to save her.* Rose fell asleep from emotional exhaustion and from the effort of trying to find an accessible method to end the pain.

She awoke to the gentle shaking and Marisol leaning over her. 'Come. Work calls us.'

'How do you do it night after night, Marisol? Do you know you'll never get out of here?'

'I'll keep being kind to my clients. I'm waiting for one who will help me so I can go and live with him. I will be his servant. It will happen, you know. Now, up and tidy yourself. You can plan the same if you keep up your appearance.' Marisol stood up.

Rose stared up at her. She was truly beautiful, long-necked, with poise and elegance. Rose firmly believed Marisol would pull off her escape. But she didn't hold out any similar hopes for herself. After she'd showered and dressed, she looked at herself in the mirror; smiled an artificial smile. It came from a very dark place. Her only hope lay with Mister Bob but she couldn't even advise him of how he might go about rescuing her.

Saeli dropped her at her usual hotel base. Occasionally a client didn't want to take Rose to a room in the hotel. Tonight was such a night. An older guy, a local, approached her. First he spoke in Thai. She'd picked up enough of the local language to recognise it, but not enough to understand much of it or speak it.

'English?' she suggested.

'Enzo say you come,' he said in broken English, pointing outside. 'My car.'

They discussed the hourly rate. Rose couldn't afford to refuse anyone referred to her by Enzo. He was yet another male who had power over her.

Rose excused herself on the pretext of freshening up in the bathroom. She sent a text to Saeli to track her movements. She never felt safe leaving the hotel on her own. She never felt more disgusted than when she had to perform sex acts on a so-called client in a car either, as was the case tonight.

With a sense of numbness and neutrality, Rose went through her daily and evening actions, week in and week out, the only break being the day off. Contact with Annlyn had become regular, but Rose refused to look at the photos of her children growing up without her. She clung to a morsel of hope. Would her Mister Bob keep his word and send her a message when he next visited Bangkok?

And eventually he did. The text asked her to meet him at the bar at seven that evening. Her heartbeat quickened at the thought. *Of course I will.* She could be honest enough to tell Saeli this was a special request for an early meet from a regular customer.

Rose hesitated in the entrance to the bar, scanning the room for him. He glanced up and gave a small wave when their eyes connected with more than just recognition. While she made her way to him, Bob gave a signal to Enzo to bring drinks to the table.

Normally Bob would rise to greet any woman, but the slowness of pulling himself up defeated his good intentions.

Rose smiled warmly. 'So good to see you, Mister Bob. Tell me what you been doing.'

Bob was again mesmerised by the intonation in her accent along with the clipped words and returned the smile before he told her of his mission. 'But more importantly, Rose, I've brought some American dollars with me for your time tonight. And tomorrow I'll transfer more funds to your sister.' After a quick stroke of his bald head, he rested his hands on his belly. 'How are things going for you at your …' He was about to say brothel, but caught himself in time. '… home.'

In a pragmatic tone, Rose launched into a summary of the refusal by the boss to allow her to pay her debt. 'So I am trapped,' she concluded, still showing no emotion, but feeling hope rising because Mister Bob cared.

'Oh my God, Rose. No. No. I won't accept that. There has to be a way.' Bob had believed if he paid for the family expenses back in the Philippines, then Rose could and would pay her way out. 'Did they give you an amount?'

Rose shook her head, and sipped the soda Enzo had placed in front of her. 'They won't even discuss with me,' she said, putting her glass down. 'I don't understand. I don't earn enough for them anyway. You'd think they'd be happy to let me go.'

'What if you ran away and I rented a little place for you, Rose?'

'They would kill me if they found me. And anyway, how would I live? … and support my family? But enough of my troubles, Mister Bob. Tell me about living in Australia? Do you see kangaroos all the time?'

In spite of Rose's dire situation, Bob chortled. 'Not exactly. But some of the spiders in the garden are pretty ferocious. And the snakes. Well, we host some of the most venomous in the world.'

From the puzzled look on Rose's face, he simplified his last statement, and added, 'But they rarely attack. Now, tell me more about Manila and your family.' Bob had to stifle a yawn. It was his first night back in Bangkok, and tiredness had caught up with him.

Rose, perceptive to his needs, said, 'You are too tired, Mister Bob. Maybe next time we talk.'

He didn't put up an argument. Before excusing himself, he handed her a bundle of American twenty-dollar notes. 'I hate to think how much these bastards take from this. Rose, do try to get a pay-out figure from these pimps. Don't give up. And smile. You have a beautiful one.'

The next day, after a busy and productive morning with Arthit going over samples and making decisions, this time in the central city office, over lunch Bob again brought up Rose's circumstances and put forth some potential ideas. Again, Arthit refused to discuss Rose's situation.

'This is dangerous territory, Bob. Leave it alone.'

Bob frowned; he had never seen this side of Arthit. *Is it really this bad?* Bob sent Rose a text that night. KEEP YOUR SPIRIT UP. He refused to give up on her rescue.

The following day was consumed by more choices and more decisions on OTM clip-ons and BM spectacle frames, together with displays and presentation boxes. He wished he'd brought Georgina with him to make some final decisions. But he would take home an extra suitcase of samples to make the final selections anyway. First, he'd analyse them with Georgina, then he'd see if Denise, and even his daughter might give their opinion.

Finally on the plane home, Bob relaxed. The effort to move around all the official requirements demanded at the airport terminal, including filling in forms requiring legibility *and* walking significant distances, had taken its toll on his fatigued and unsteady body.

Chapter 13

Rose's spirits rose when she received a text from her Mister Bob a few weeks later, saying he was at his usual hotel and hoped to see her. He'd be waiting in the bar.

She was in agony from a tooth-ache but nothing was going to stop her. She arrived in her usual sleek black dress, but held her hand across the bottom of her face covering the ugly swelling. As she walked in, she saw him trying to stagger to his feet to greet her.

But instead of a welcome greeting, he frowned. 'What happened?' Anger welled inside him. He thought someone had hit her. She moved her hand and he saw the swelling.

Her eyes were moist with pain and she struggled to say, 'Tooth-ache, Mister Bob. So sorry.'

'Well, why are you here? Why not at a dentist?'

'Never been to one. Saeli gave me pain killers and some oil of cloves to put on it.'

'For god's sake, Rose. Sit down. Stay there.' His frustration level rose as he went over the bar. 'Enzo, can you find me an after-hours dentist?'

'I'll call the concierge.'

A few minutes later, the concierge arrived and Enzo directed him over to Bob. 'Can you call us a cab?'

'Come with me now, Mr Marks, and I'll call ahead for you.'

'It's actually for this young lady.'

Eyebrows raised, but the discrete concierge just nodded.

Rose didn't know whether to be pleased or mortified.

Watching the confusion on the faces of the hotel staff confused her too. She sat in the taxi and texted Saeli that she was leaving the hotel with a client. She found it difficult to talk, but hoped Bob would pay her, as she would find it hard to explain if she arrived back without her earnings. But then again, the hotel staff would surely fill Saeli in, and she would not be chastised.

Bob waited while the emergency dentist filled the cavity. If he charged his work credit card, Georgina would ask questions. If he put it on their shared credit card, Denise would ask questions. What the heck … he could have had an emergency on arrival himself. *Problem solved.*

Rose came out of the surgery with a crooked smile and a half numb mouth. She put her hands together under her chin and bowed. 'Thank you, Mister Bob.'

'Hrmph,' he barked. 'That's a first … being thanked for taking someone to the dentist. You probably don't feel like going for something to eat now? I don't blame you. I'll take you back to the hotel and you can arrange to be collected. Come on.'

Bob fell in a chair with relief when he arrived back to his room. He'd passed a hundred US dollars to Rose in the taxi on the way back, and arranged for dinner with her the following night, promising he'd pay for her time again.

Next morning, he dressed in an open neck shirt. He'd abandoned ties altogether, and now getting socks on had become a bit of a problem. 'Bloody things,' he complained, trying to pull the heel into place. 'Bloody shoelaces too.' He leaned back and took a break.

Business with Arthit progressed in the morning, with pricing locked down, and orders and timing locked in. Over lunch at the Thai restaurant, Arthit checked with Bob, 'You're not still caught up with that prostitute, are you?'

Bob felt the blood rush to his head as he took a deep breath. *Calm down,* he told himself. *This is your business associate. Be polite.*

He pressed his lips together to hold back the words desperately wanting to tumble out.

'Do you know about the size of the sex trafficking business in this country, Arthit?' he retorted.

Arthit smiled his inscrutable smile. 'Let it rest, my friend. I shouldn't have raised it.'

They continued to talk business amicably through lunch, and Arthit dropped Bob back to the hotel early. After he took a quick nap, Bob sent a text to Rose.

She arrived at the hotel smiling.

'How's the mouth,' he asked her.

'Good now. Thank you.'

When she smiled again, he added, 'Okay, so now let me take you for dinner in the restaurant.'

Rose's eyes widened. 'Oh, no Mister Bob. Please.'

'We can talk about how to get you out of this pickle.'

'What you mean *pickle*?'

'Oh, sorry … how we get you back home.'

'We can talk here, please?'

'What are you afraid of, Rose?'

'I never been in a place like that. So sorry.'

'Oh, Rose, let me help you. Come.'

Rose felt unable to refuse when he stood and held out his hand to her.

They were seated by a waiter. Rose understood when Bob nodded to her to wait as the waiter deftly placed a starched napkin in her lap. Never in her life had she been treated like this. The waiter then poured water into their glasses. She was happy to let Bob take over, watching and learning as he ordered drinks for them both before opening the food menu.

'What's your favourite food?' He smiled across the table at her before suggesting a few things. 'Fish or meat?'

'Fish.' Rose squirmed, feeling decidedly uncomfortable and

unsure.

Bob placed a simple order for grilled fish with steamed vegetables. Noticing her concern when the waiter changed her cutlery, he said, 'That one's just a blunt-ish knife for fish.'

She wondered why she couldn't just cut the fish with a normal knife. But it got even more complicated as Bob proceeded to point out the different sized glasses and the cutlery. Then, as he offered her a bread roll, he explained she might use the butter knife to place some butter on her side plate. She thought it might be easier to forget the butter till she watched him lead by example.

'Now, tell me what's been happening since I last saw you.'

Rose blushed. 'Just more same same, Mister Bob.'

'Tell me about the other girls.'

'They all come from my neighbourhood back in Manila.' Rose felt reluctant to divulge details of her friends. Even the crazy Disney twins deserved protection.

'I've already sent more funds through to your sister, so you can relax about how they're managing. Do they make you go to work all the time?'

She tried not to show her discomfort by sitting completely still. She hated these questions, but felt obliged to Mister Bob to respond. 'I go six nights in a week, Mister Bob. But thanks to you, I only see one client every night.' She blushed again and fiddled with her napkin.

"I'm so sorry. We need to find a way where you can stop working altogether. These people you work for sound very powerful.'

Rose put a finger to her lips. 'Shhh ... this place is part of it too.'

'I'm so clumsy. Sorry. Next time we'll go somewhere else so we can talk freely.' He reached for his wallet. 'I should have done this ages ago.' He withdrew a business card. 'Have you got an email address?'

Rose nodded.

'Then email me so I have it. And as soon as I've worked out an escape route, I can email you, just in case I can't get here.'

Rose looked him in the eye. She saw concern below his frown. 'I hope you think of something, Mister Bob. I don't even know my own address here.' She sparked up. 'Tell me about living in Australia.'

'I'll tell you about the last time I arrived home? There was a bit of family drama.'

'Yes please.'

'I got in late and Denise – that's my wife – was waiting up for me in the lounge. That's not usual. And she was dressed in her day clothes with her handbag on the table. I knew something was wrong.' Bob paused to drink the wine he'd ordered.

'It was our daughter, Charmaine. She'd been rushed to hospital. Turns out it was an emergency appendix situation. The long and the short of it was that she had surgery and is now okay. But the interesting thing from that night was the twins. Charmaine's kids. Her husband works overseas.' Bob had been spreading butter on his dinner roll and stopped talking to take a bite.

Rose sat enthralled by Mister Bob's sharing. 'How old the children?'

'About seven. See, I'm not good with detail, or with little children, Rose. They were asleep upstairs and Denise had waited for me to arrive to mind them so she could get to the hospital. I'm pretty useless, you know.'

'I do not think that.'

'Good with business. Not good with emotional stuff. That's Denise's domain. But there I was in charge. Denise rang me from the hospital at four in the morning to tell me Charmaine was in ICU.

Rose tilted her head.

'Sorry … that's the Intensive Care Unit. That was scary news.'

Their main courses arrived at the table, and both were silent as they watched the pepper being ground over their food.

'What happened next, Mister Bob?' Rose watched Bob pick up his cutlery and begin to cut, so she did likewise.

'You would have laughed to see me try to get them breakfast. Mind you, I still can't tell Lola from Sarah. And to make it even more impossible, they wear identical clothes. I tried to talk them into having cereal and milk, but they were in revolt. Pancakes, they reckoned.' Bob stopped to cut into his fish fillet. He chuckled. 'They started chanting together, demanding I cook.' He stopped to eat before continuing. 'I can barely boil water, Rose. Me, cook pancakes – now there was a challenge. So I told them I couldn't cook. Guess what. They opened the pantry cupboard and got out a plastic bottle of pancake mix. "This is how Granny makes them," they told me.'

'That is so funny. That you are so clever at so many things, but you can't cook?'

'Oh, it gets worse. So now they've had their pancakes. They've got honey all over their faces, their pyjamas, the kitchen bench … everywhere. I don't know what I'm supposed to do. I know I can't disturb Denise. She said she'd ring me as soon as there is a change in Charmaine's condition. So I rang Georgina – she's my personal assistant in the office. I was kinda hoping she'd offer to come and help. She helps me with everything – usually.'

'She didn't come?'

'She laughed at me. She thought it was a joke. So I sent Lola and Sarah up to wash themselves and dress. I had no idea if they could do it.' Bob saw the amused grin on Rose's lips. 'You think it's funny too.'

Rose ran her hand comically across her mouth to wipe the

smile. 'No, no. Never,' she said irreverently. 'I just know what little girls can do.' It had been a long time since she'd been treated so well and so respectfully; so long since she'd had a humorous conversation. Her faith in him grew as he shared his personal life with her.

'So there I am, wondering what I'm supposed to do with the two of them. They come downstairs all dressed. But then they hand me elastic bands for their hair. "Piggy tails" one of them says. So here's another test for me. I failed.'

Bob stopped talking for a while as he ate and drank. He nodded and waved the waiter away when he checked they were happy with everything.

'Did you like the fish, Rose? I should have asked first.'

'Thank you. What are these green things?'

'Capers. Salty, aren't they?'

'So much I don't know.'

'You're learning. I'd love us to do this more often. But we must get you away from ...' Bob was about to say *Chinese Mafia* and then realised he was not necessarily in a friendly environment. 'You know what I mean,' he concluded.

'You must finish this story, please?'

'Hmm. So, up to my usual standards, I couldn't do their hair. They found a brush, and I did brush it though. Then I thought I'd let them watch some TV. They were pretty chuffed about that. Till I couldn't work out how to use the remote to find kids' channels. I was terrified, Rose, that I wouldn't be able to keep them occupied all day. They were so demanding.'

The waiter came to clear their plates and refresh the drinks. Rose wanted the waiter to hurry so Mister Bob would continue his tale.

'And?' she said encouragingly, once they were alone again.

'Not so funny anymore. Denise called. She'd arranged for the children's other grandmother to come and get them, and I got my instructions to get to the hospital.'

'Oh no. Bad news.'

'You think I'm not good with kids, Rose. You gotta see me in a hospital.' He shook his head at the memory.

'But how was your daughter? It doesn't sound good.'

'No. She was still in ICU. Denise thought I should be there. But I'm more trouble that I'm worth. You should have seen me. They escorted me through to the ICU lounge. I felt sick. The smells, Rose. All those smells.

'Denise got cross with me. She told me I was not allowed to be sick. Huh! You can't order that. She ordered me to hold it together. So next thing I know, I get up to rush to the bathroom and end up on the floor.

'I was mortified. I realised I'd forgotten to take my Parkinson's medication with all that had been happening. Next thing I know they've got orderlies picking me up.'

'Oh, no. And did you get to see your daughter?'

'Eventually. You should have seen her. It was awful. They've got these swing doors into the ICU. I had to brace myself. I pushed the door inward.'

As Bob took a sip of his red wine, the waiter reappeared to hand them the dessert menus.

'You got a sweet tooth, Rose?'

'What you mean?'

'Ah – do you like sweets?'

Rose had no idea what half the items on the menu were. 'Yes, I like sweets.'

'Perhaps the crème brulee?'

She smiled. He nodded to the waiter. 'Two, thanks.'

'So how was your daughter when you saw her?'

'So many machines. So much clicking and clacking. So many tubes. I could barely see my little girl through all that.' Bob shook his head to shake off the memory.

Rose rested her chin on her interlinked fingers. For the time being, she had escaped the lonely money-sex dominated world she was enclosed in. This man's life was so distant from anything relatable to her, but she was fascinated.

They sat in silence in their own thoughts for a bit.

'Sorry. I talk about myself too much. Denise tells me that. She sent me home from the hospital. She knows me so well, Rose. She calls me a sook.'

'Sook?'

'Woos?'

'Woos?'

'You know,' he said, laughing, 'weak and pathetic.'

'No, that's not you, Mister Bob.' Rose dropped her hands back in her lap, smiling.

'I can't cope with seeing blood either. Anyway, Charmaine and the girls are staying with us while she recovers fully. But all is well, and that's why I was able to come to Bangkok again. My business is growing.'

'Tell me more.'

'Enough self-indulgence for now.'

Dessert had arrived. Rose looked at Bob, eyebrows up.

'Ah, "indulge".' He picked up his spoon and plunged it in. 'It means let's indulge in this.'

Chapter 14

Rose fell onto the mattress after another night of work, but when she awoke around ten in the morning, Marisol hadn't returned. She heard the buzz of male voices outside. Grabbing a wrap, she walked out.

'Where she is?' Mr Wang demanded of Rose, who cringed because he was standing too far inside her personal body space for comfort.

She trembled, and shook her head, 'I truly don't know, Mr Wang.'

He raised his hand to her, but paused when Saeli shook his head and said, 'I dropped her off at her regular place. I'll go and talk with them.'

Rose showered and dressed and waited with a cup of coffee till Saeli returned. Again he shook his head at Rose and frowned.

'What?' she asked.

'She has run away with a client. You will all be punished.'

Rose's heart raced; her hand went to her throat. So Marisol had carried out her plan. *Well, good for her*, she thought. *But what will they do to the rest of us?* She didn't have long to wait to find out. She alone was summoned downstairs to stand in front of Mr Lee and Mr Wang. Saeli was also present.

'You've been cheating us for too long,' Mr Lee accused. 'I am selling you privately. Get some money back at least. Get your things together.' He pointed to the door.

Rose's legs gave way. Saeli grabbed her elbow and marched her out.

'Someone will come and pick you up soon. Pack up, Rose Petal.' He sneered. 'Wait for me to call you.'

'What will happen to the others?'

'No business of yours.'

Rose grabbed her almost-unused suitcase and threw her possessions into it, using a plastic shopping bag from the kitchen for the overflow of personal products.

The Disney twins and Maria awoke and wandered out to find Rose packed up and pacing the floor.

'Marisol has run away. They are selling me.' Tears escaped despite her effort to control them. 'They are punishing all of us.'

The twins clung to each other. Maria folded her arms in defiance. 'We'll see about that.'

Saeli came through the front door. 'Come.' He beckoned Rose to follow, but to leave her suitcase. Maria tried to engage him in conversation but he didn't reciprocate.

Yet another Chinese man, a stranger to Rose, stood just inside the downstairs office beside Mr Lee. 'Turn around in a circle.' He twirled his fingers at Rose. Terrified, she complied.

The guest turned to Mr Lee, nodded and shook his hand. 'She'll do.' A bundle of cash changed hands. The guest then said to Rose, 'You can call me "Sir".'

She nodded.

He turned and slapped her across the face. 'I said, call me "Sir"!'

Picking up on his meaning, she responded meekly, 'Yes, Sir.'

'Follow me.'

'Yes, Sir.'

Saeli loaded her suitcase into the car. She climbed into the front seat beside her new owner as directed, and glanced sideways, sneaking a better look at him. He wore a short-sleeve cotton sports shirt with long pants, was middle-aged, overweight and reeked of cigarettes. His narrow lips curved in a permanent smirk across his bloated face. They drove in silence while he mauled her thighs for about forty minutes. With no sense of direction, Rose had no idea where they were going. Her thoughts went to planning an escape by jumping out at a set of lights. But the same impossible challenges of survival alone in Bangkok stopped her from acting.

Sir pulled up in front of an average house in an average neighbourhood – *not vastly different*, Rose judged, *from the one I've just left*. She wondered if this was another prostitution business.

Getting out, Sir instructed, 'Follow me.'

'Yes, Sir.' She wouldn't risk being slapped again.

She climbed a few stairs. He opened the door and shoved her and her bag into a small bedroom on the right of the hallway, and promptly slammed and locked the door.

Rose stood in the middle of the tiny room and slowly turned a circle. *Are there other captives here? Is this a brothel?* Still stunned, she sat on the edge of the bed, and, before her mind totally shut down and became vacant, she noted the window was nailed shut.

After a while, she heard the door being unlocked.

'With me,' Sir commanded.

'Yes, Sir,' she remembered, and followed him into another bedroom.

'Undress.'

She began slowly. Another slap nearly knocked her off her feet.

Oops. 'Yes, Sir,' she mumbled too late, tears welling.

He pushed her over a stool and handcuffed her hands to the lower legs of the opposite side of the stool. The ensuing abuse made her cry out. Once spent, he uncuffed her, grabbed her roughly and threw her onto her back on the bed. Rose froze with fear. She tried to take some breaths to counteract the pain. The next thing she knew he had climbed on top of her again, and raped her violently, one arm across her neck so she could barely breathe.

Reaching out, Rose grabbed fistfuls of the crumpled sheet, and pulled hard; in all the time she'd been prostituted and abused, she'd never felt this much pain. Nor had she been treated so much like an object – a toy – not at all human. She screwed her eyes shut, not sure if she ever wanted to open them again. While she couldn't see anything, the stench of the male sweat repulsed her. And she felt his disgusting slimy body sliding against her nakedness. He'd not used a condom, but that was the least of her concerns. Although in pain, she dared not make a sound.

Suddenly, survival dominated. Tendrils of anger ripped through her mind. *Even dogs are treated better than this. How dare he!* She moderated her breathing, thinking beyond her anger and her fear. She needed to survive at all costs.

Once spent, Sir lay on his side beside her, one arm across her chest, one hand cupping a breast, and a leg across her legs pinning her down. Still in agony, she stared at the ceiling, hearing through the pounding in her ears a tap dripping rooms away. She felt the weight of his body parts slowly increase and realised he'd fallen asleep. Ever so gently, and breathing so shallowly, inch by inch Rose slipped sideways. Holding his arm, she placed it gently on the bed, before doing the same with his leg. Sir had not locked them into this room of torture. She snatched her clothes from the floor and quietly opened the door. Nothing stirred. She surmised they were alone.

Her bedroom door was open. She tiptoed in, pulled on her dress, grabbed her phone and handbag, and tried the front door gently. *Locked.* She would not be outdone. She had to get out.

She tried the room opposite hers. The door opened to a sitting room with beat-up old furniture. She crossed to the window and slid it up, fearing the thumping of her heart might wake him as she shimmied through it and dropped to the ground below. Rolling slightly on landing, she rose to her feet, brushed the dirt from her legs and clothes as she scanned left and right, then up and down the street. *A few cars, several bikes, some with motors, some without.* No one seemed to take any notice of her as she began walking, trying to appear normal, even though her bruised body hurt inside and out with each step. She threw her shoulders back. *I can do this. I will do this. I am free.*

She walked and walked, right through the pain. When she finally sensed she had travelled far enough for safety, she asked her way to the nearest shopping centre. *But then,* she thought, *that will be the first place he'll look.*

In her handbag, she'd cut the lining, and stashed some Thai baht along with Mister Bob's business card. They'd already exchanged one email in order to have each other's addresses. *But where is he now? What can he do?* He had given her the card to use in case she found herself in trouble. And she was. So she found a shop offering free Wi-Fi and sent off an email. But she couldn't rely on him to do anything. It was up to her now. She'd keep on the move. Maybe she'd see someone from the Philippines. Surely, they wouldn't turn their back on her.

She wandered aimlessly among the crowds in the small shops on either side of the street, scanning faces.

Screening potential TV ads with the PR and advertising consultants in the boardroom, Bob and Georgina listened to explanations of the appeal of each sample. When they broke for tea, Georgina went off to check Bob's email.

She returned and whispered in Bob's ear, 'Strange one has come in Bob, from a Rose at a gmail address.'

He swung his head sharply towards her.

She added, 'I think she sent you her email address a while back. She seems to be in some kind of trouble?'

To Georgina's amazement, Bob instantly pushed his swivel

chair back, excused himself from the boardroom and rushed, as much as his mobility would allow him, to his office and sat in front of his monitor.

Rose's email read:

> *Mister Bob. They sold me to a bad man. Very cruel. I escaped. I don't know where to go.*

He instantly emailed her back.

> *Well done, Rose. Have you got your passport?*

After a short wait she responded:

> *No, just phone. No charger.*

So buying a plane ticket is out. Besides, they'd be watching airports for her anyway, if he believed everything he'd heard about this Chinese Mafia mob. Arthit would refuse to get involved. He'd made it very clear.

'Georgina …' He looked up at her standing in the doorway. '… I need you to postpone this meeting. Try to set it up for tomorrow? Apologies from me. Then come back in here.' He leaned forward, put his elbows on his desk and rubbed his bald head over and over as though the repetitive action would release solutions.

Soon enough Georgina sat opposite him, curiosity written all over her face. Bob said, 'She's a trafficked woman I met in Bangkok, and I sort-of promised to help get her back to her family. I don't know what to do next, Georgina. She's escaped from her latest owner, and she's petrified and wandering the streets with nothing.' He looked at her anxiously. *Georgina always fixes things. But this thing?*

'What does Denise think?'

'I've never told her.'

'Are you kidding? This is her area of expertise. Get home now, and see what you can sort out together? Or is there more to this?' She pursed her lips.

'There's more. But not what you're thinking.'

'I don't care. Go sort it now.'

Give me business decisions, he thought, not these emotive ones. Then what will Denise's reaction be? She's worse than Georgina. Pair of bullies they are. Before he left the office, he flicked off another email.

Charmaine still lived with Bob and Denise, even though she'd fully recovered from the earlier surgery. The twins were home from school and in the pool. Bob usually enjoyed all the activity, but he wanted to be alone with Denise. Then he realised with a start Charmaine was no longer a child, and she could afford to hear Rose's story. In fact, being only a little older than Rose, she might be able to add something relevant.

He found Denise in the kitchen putting a snack together.

'I have something urgent and important to discuss with you and Charmaine,' he said dramatically. 'Can you come outside?'

Denise wiped her hands on the towel and, saying nothing, followed Bob, Charmaine close behind them. She sat quietly while Bob related an abbreviated version of Rose's story to both women.

'Oh, Bob, you silly man, you've been conned,' Denise said. 'It's just her way of earning money for nothing.'

'No, no. This is legit. Trust me on this.'

'Trust you? Trust you?' She raised her voice. 'You've been sending money overseas? You've been consorting with a bloody prostitute? Trust you?' She drew breath. 'How long has this been going on?'

'Steady on, you two,' Charmaine intervened. 'I believe Dad.

We have a trafficked woman in trouble, Mum. You fight for women in trouble. You're good at this. Let's try to deal with it first, then you can chew Dad's head off. What about all your contacts in Bangkok, Dad?'

'No go. They're terrified of the Chinese Mafia.'

'Who else can we contact there?'

Denise's face lit up. 'I know. I know. Sissy. Remember Sissy?'

Charmaine looked at her strangely. 'Sissy, our au pair from decades ago?'

The twins climbed out of the pool. 'We're hungry,' they said in unison, dripping water all the way to their mother.

Denise jumped up. 'I'll just grab their platter. Back in a second.'

Bob waited impatiently while Charmaine towel-dried the girls. 'You can have a picnic under the tree over there,' she suggested to them. She took the plate from her mother and set them up on their towels.

'Yes, Sissy,' Denise continued, once they were alone again.

'What's she got to do with this?' Bob asked. 'Charmaine was at primary school when Sissy lived with us. Is she in Bangkok now?'

'She heads up a religious order based in the States. They look after homeless women in South East Asia.'

'What? Really? How do you know all this? I thought she returned to Paris after her spell with us to go to university,' Bob said.

'She did. She got a degree in Theology and another in Social Work. Then she tootled off to work with Mother Teresa in Calcutta for a bit. Then she joined a small mob called Sisters of Good Grace in Los Angeles. I've stayed in touch all these years.'

'You never ever told me,' Bob accused.

'You were never around to tell,' Denise retorted.

'Holy crap! Enough, you two! So, Mum, have you got a phone

number for her? Can we call her?'

'I don't have it, but I can look it up. Best I talk to her first.'

Denise disappeared inside, found the number online, but realised it was almost 10 pm in Los Angeles. Regardless, she rang. When the number answered, she said, 'I'm so sorry to call so late. It's an emergency and I wonder if I may speak with Mother Simone?'

'One moment.'

'Mother Simone speaking,' the next voice said.

'Oh, Sissy.' Denise could not bring herself to call her au pair from years ago Mother Simone. 'It's Denise here. Denise from Sydney. We have a problem I'm hoping you can help with.' With no initial pleasantries, Denise launched into a summary of Rose's situation in Bangkok. 'You have people there, don't you?'

'I haven't heard from you since last Christmas, Denise. But we can catch up with family later. I'm so glad you thought to contact us. Now, yes, that's right. We have offices in Thailand, both lay and religious workers. Let's get down to some detail.'

Sissy's French accent had not faded over all the intervening years. 'Hang on, Sissy, and I'll put Bob on. He's the full bottle on it.'

After a long discussion, Bob hung up, brought Denise and Charmaine up to date on possibilities and hurried off to his home office to send an email. He wrote:

> *We need to pinpoint where you are, Rose. We can send a Sister Bridget from the Sisters of Good Grace to meet you. You can trust her. She will be wearing a beige habit with a big white collar. You must approach her and ask if she is Sister Bridget. But first, we need to know where you are. She can take you somewhere safe. Please take care. And keep smiling.*

Denise and Charmaine were busy with the twins when he

returned. He waited till dinner time to ask more about Sissy.

'I can just see her as a bossy nun. She was a bossy nanny,' Charmaine laughed. 'I was in year four at school and you two were never around. But she did fun stuff with me,' she added.

'What do you mean … we were never around?' Denise said defensively.

'Never mind. Well, you were both working. But how did you know her? Did you just find her out of the blue?'

'Her father and I were friends,' Bob explained. 'Same business. Don't you remember our French holiday when I went to a conference? You met her then.'

Bob had brought his phone to the table. Usually, Denise forbade phones at dinner time, but they all understood he constantly needed to check for a reply from Rose. They looked at him expectantly each time, but he shook his head. 'Nothing.'

'Yeah, I was, what … nine years old then?' Charmaine continued. 'I must admit I liked her even then. I always felt safe with her. She seemed like a giant to me at the time. So tall. So big. She taught me stuff I'd never have learnt otherwise.'

'Like?'

'Oh, you know. Stuff like caring for the environment, and even what a European Christmas is like. Mum, you kept up some things she did after she went home … Advent candles lit every Sunday. The Advent Calendar tradition she started that you now do for my girls.'

Denise smiled at the memories. 'I taught Sissy a thing or two as well. She wanted to come with me on one of the demonstrations.'

'What demonstrations!'

'We had a spate of suicides. The Government didn't fund counselling support back then, so we gathered outside Parliament House with banners and tee-shirts that were numbered, each representing a person we'd lost. Sissy fell right into it, even back then.'

Charmaine looked at her mother. 'Well, you are a surprise.'

Bob glanced at his phone again. Hours went by. He refused to go to bed.

It was late at night for Rose. While it wasn't cold, and there was plenty of lighting and movement of people, she remained frightened. And tired. And sore. She needed to find somewhere to rest.

Up ahead was a multi-storey shopping place. Seeing a sign offering free Wi-Fi, she made her way there. When she read Mister Bob's latest email, she leaned against a pillar to absorb the contents. *Is this real? Am I really so close to being rescued?* Surely the Sisters from this Order she'd never heard of wouldn't turn her in? She replied briefly to Mister Bob's email:

> *Running out of battery. No charger. Will hide behind stall near Patagon Department Stores.*

She hit send. Her screen went blank. No battery power left, but it sent. She sighed.

Bob quickly responded.

> *Rose, see if you can pawn your silver bracelet and buy a charger. You will need one. Set a time to meet at the store that is safe and suits you. Describe the doorway to me.*

Bob googled *Patagon* and saw only one in Bangkok. That made it easy. He notified Sissy via email. More hours went by. Bob nodded off. Denise came and dragged him off to bed. By morning he'd still not heard a word from Rose.

'Maybe I should fly up there and look around for her near the department store?' Bob proposed, already dressed for work.

'Don't be ridiculous. Just let Sissy take control. This Sister

Bridget will go and look.' Denise was about to leave for work, and Charmaine had the twins ready to be taken to school.

'I'm worried. I hope the Mafia don't find her. I'm going to send Sissy an email now and make sure this Bridget woman is wandering around even if she doesn't know who she's looking for.'

Then, annoyed with himself that he hadn't considered it earlier, Bob sent an email to Rose:

> *Rose, if you can find a Western Union office near you I can send you money. Please get in touch. And watch for Sister Bridget.*

Chapter 15

Rose woke oblivious to the latest email from Mister Bob. Her body ached all over. She struggled to her feet and tried to tidy her appearance. She could do nothing about her body odour. Although it wasn't yet daylight, stalls around her were re-opening and the smells of food tantalised her. Maybe she'd find someone to give her a bowl of rice.

She began to wander up and down, hoping to see a woman in a beige habit with a big white collar as she followed her nose, doubting though that anyone would look for her in the badly lit laneways at this time of day, but it wouldn't be long till sunrise. She wandered further, stood looking at an older woman with an enormous rice cooker on her bench, and considered asking her for food. Her stomach rumbled.

Then a beige-clad woman appeared and said softly to Rose, 'You know Bob Marks?'

Sister Bridget was a short, middle-aged woman with eyebrows almost meeting on the brow of her kindly moon face. Her smile, which exposed crossed-over front teeth, still managed to convey warmth. Rose's eyes lit up when she said, 'Hello, Bob sent me.'

Sister Bridget had already said it to many other women in the area but they'd just looked at her blankly. She grasped Rose's hands and said, 'You're safe now. Come,' as she pulled a waif-like Rose into a hug against her mother-earth softness.

Rose stayed motionless and emotionless for some time within the embrace, till an awareness of her own smell shocked her. She felt disgustingly unclean, and not just from street grime. She hadn't showered or changed in forty-eight hours. She carried the weight of both the invisible shame and the visible bruising of the last couple of days.

But kindness oozed from this sombre-clad rescuer, and Rose gladly accompanied her once they broke from their embrace. Sister Bridget escorted her to their communal house where Rose washed and dressed in clean secondhand clothes before eating a meagre but welcomed meal of rice and soup. Then she was escorted to a small basic room furnished with a single bed, above which hung a crucifix. Over an adjacent chest of drawers hung a framed picture of the Sacred Heart of Jesus. The religious icons smothered Rose with feelings of security and relief, and the tension of fear began to exit her body and her muscles relaxed. She sighed deeply, realising this was the first time she'd been alone and felt safe for many years.

'Sleep. We'll talk later.' Sister Bridget closed the door gently.

After kneeling by the bed and giving thanks, Rose slept through to the next morning. Over a breakfast of rice and soup again, Sister Bridget said, 'We're going to get you a housekeeping job in a safe house, Rose, while we plan how to get you home. We can't hide you here for long. We'll need the room for the next person.'

'Thank you. Do you have a charger where I can charge my phone?'

'I'm sorry. It's probably too dangerous right now to make contact with anyone. Do you want me to contact your family? We can do that more safely for you.'

'I need to see if Mister Bob is continuing to send them money to survive.' An escalation of panic and shortness of breath gripped her. *What if he disregards me now? What if he thinks he's done his duty now?* She spoke rapidly. '… ad I want to know my children are okay. The … the …' Rose stuttered, not sure what she should call her kidnappers. 'They said they'd hurt my family, you know … if I tried to get away.'

'Do they know where your family live?'

Rose took a moment to think. 'No, my family moved after I was … um … employed. I never told anyone their new address.' And, she thought logically, *my captors sold me. So they probably recouped their outlay and they might not care anymore. But the new owner might care about his loss of the human goods he paid for. And he is a violent man.*

'We will try to check on them for you and let you know,' Sister Bridget promised.

'No, No! Let me talk to them. Please,' she begged.

Sister Bridget emailed Annlyn in front of Rose, reporting Rose's phone didn't work – well, it didn't, only because of a flat battery. She said Rose wanted to know all was well and said Annlyn could reply any time on this email address.

At work the following day, Bob constantly checked his email for messages. *Nothing. Damn it.* 'Georgina, can you book me on a flight tonight or first thing tomorrow? I need to know Rose is safe.' His voice wavered, overflowing with concern.

This was a side of Bob Georgina hadn't experienced. He always exhibited confidence and being in control, yet right now he seemed lost and unsure. *He* was usually the great problem solver, even though others carried out the solution. Sharply aware they were only weeks away from the launch date, with the Christmas trade to follow, Georgina said, 'If you found her, Bob, what would you do? Surely, you'd put her and yourself at risk?'

Bob thought about that. It rang true. 'I can't sit and do nothing.'

Georgina turned to leave his office, but paused in the doorway and slowly shook her head in concern. His mind, she saw from the vacant look in his eyes, was thousands of miles away.

Indeed, Bob stared at his computer screen. Finally, an email arrived from Sissy.

Dear Bob, Warm greetings across the waters that divide us. My father sends his regards from Paris. He is keeping well, and he hopes you are too. Denise tells me you suffer from Parkinson's disease. I am sorry to hear that, but it sounds as though you keep highly active.

You will be pleased to hear Sister Bridget has made contact with Rose. Sister Bridget tended to all the single women she found in the alleyways around that department store till one responded tentatively to the mention of your name.

On Sister Bridget's recommendation, we think it safest if you communicate through me and not direct with Rose. We will take care of her, and get her back to her children in the Philippines, but please realise this may take some time and also be quite a dangerous and expensive process. She has no passport nor any form of ID whatsoever. We will have to establish a background for her.

Bless you for the good work you have done to date. We shall keep you informed of progress.

The sign-off read quite formally. Bob leaned back in his chair, stroked his head with both hands, then clasped them together on the back of his neck as he clenched his jaw. *What? No, this won't do. Who the hell does she think she is, trying to take over?* He'd asked for help, yes, but this act was a step too far. He leaned forward and began tapping the keyboard, drafting a reply, and copying Denise in on it.

Hello Sissy. Thank you for finding Rose. But I do not agree with having me cut out contact with her. We have

Bob's image of Sissy in his mind's eye as he struck the keyboard was of a solidly built, six-foot tall teenager with long jet-black hair and a confident air, just as he'd last set eyes on her all those decades ago. He couldn't see her as the leader of a business, even if it was a religious one. And he resented being advised by her. *Little upstart. Make that*, he corrected, *a big upstart.*

Bob stared up at his dragonfly painting. It usually calmed him. Not this time. Instinct told him not to press the send button, but impulsiveness won.

The following week Rose began a housekeeping job for a family of four in their modest home. She'd been warned that, although nominated as a safe house, she was not to trust the family with any information. As far as the family was concerned, they believed her to be a permanent housekeeper who had been cast out by her husband, so needed the Church's support. She worked six days a week, but it was not too taxing. On her first Sunday off, she walked to the local church with her sponsor family.

After Mass, with a small remuneration from them, she purchased a phone charger. At last, she felt some control for the first time in a long time. She picked up the last messages from Mister Bob and also from Annlyn, and marvelled at the latest photos of Jasmin, now twelve, and Iris, now ten. They had gained in height and weight. Then there was little baby Aaron. He was not a baby any more. Her heart ached. Would they even know who she was? She messaged them all with a selfie, saying:

planning to come home soon.

But she couldn't bear the thought yet of talking to them. She needed to hold herself together and stay strong for a bit longer. The instructions from the nuns, from a safety point of view, were not to show too much emotion, which she found almost impossible.

The next priority saw her fingers, with some trepidation, create the email.

Hi Mister Bob. I am OK. How are you? Thank you for the help. You are so kind.

She paused in her message to ponder whether to ask if he had sent any money to the Philippines. Asking would be too presumptuous, she decided. *I am now housekeeper for nice family. I wait to go home. I will let you know when.*

That's enough for now, she thought. I'll wait to see if he replies.

Within minutes, her heart sang when her phone showed she had a response.

> *Oh, Rose, we have been so worried about you. I am very pleased to hear you are doing well, finally. You must tell me more. I am in touch with the Good Grace Sisters who are doing all they can to get you back to your family. In the meantime, I have continued to send money to your sister. My wife, Denise, and my daughter, Charmaine send their best wishes.*
>
> *Keep Smiling!*
>
> *Bob.*

Although surrounded by support and kindness, Rose longed for was home, even though she'd not seen the new one. She sent another message.

Rose stopped to ponder how she should sign off. She felt
close to Mister Bob, but didn't want to appear too familiar.
Finally, she decided she'd just say:

With a grateful hug.

Her request to him fitted in the safe territory to talk about, so
he expanded for her.

He thought more about what he might say, but already
considered it might make her sad. Denise had a hand-made
Advent calendar for the girls on which she tied little parcels
along with a special saying. He would save that story for later.

Every morning, once Bob arrived in the office, and regardless
of what else was happening, and whether or not he'd heard from

Rose, Bob emailed her: *Keep Smiling.*

It was months into the new year when Sissy phoned Bob from LA. After a few niceties, she continued, 'I'm not entrusting this to written messages, Bob. You'll be happy to hear we've now got documents for Rose. Don't ask what and how. She will become a Sister of our Order, have a new name, and fly out as one of us. By doing this, she can be escorted and kept safe at the other end as well. These gangs don't like escapees. Bad for their reputation. They'll be watching airports.'

'You're kidding!'

'No, I don't joke about such things.'

'I had no idea the extent they go to. Brilliant work. When is it happening?' Every time he spoke with or had email from Sissy, he visualised the tall gawky eighteen year old who had, for a year, become part of their family. He pictured her with her recorder sitting cross-legged in front of the Christmas tree teaching a very young Charmaine to play Christmas carols.

The responses to his questions came from this now mature and competent religious businesswoman, 'A couple of days' time.'

Does Sissy wear a habit? He couldn't imagine her in one. He still couldn't imagine what Sissy looked like now. *Mother Simone?* His mind couldn't cope with the image he tried to conjure up. 'Let us pick up all the costs, at the very least,' he offered, having already sent some money in the meantime.

'Very happy to accept,' she said. 'It's been quite an exercise. Not that each rescue isn't. You mustn't tell Rose anything. Too dangerous. We'll brief her last minute so she can't accidentally let anything slip or give anything away. Now my next question is – can you ask Rose if she has any communication with the other girls she lived with, and if any of them might like to make contact with us? It's dangerous for us and for them too, as I'm sure she knows, but we can't ignore them if there's something we can do.'

'What about Sister Bridget? She visits Rose. Perhaps she can ask?'

'Bob, we're aware Rose has complete faith and trust in you. Those virtues have not yet fully extended to Sister Bridget. Do you mind checking for us?'

'Of course not.'

Bob did as Sissy requested.

The email reply read:

> *Mister Bob, my room-mate ran away. I hope she ok. Her escape is what started the whole thing. The two young sisters are hooked up on drugs and not good, but do not want to leave. My other friend, I do not know, but cannot contact. She goes to a hotel two down from mine every night. Her name is Maria. That is all I can say. Sorry.*

Bob forwarded the email to Sissy.

Chapter 16

Rose sat demurely in the international airport lounge, dressed in the beige habit with the oversized white collar of the Good Grace Sisters, clinging to her passport and boarding pass. Her heart pounded and her shallow breathing scared her as she stared straight ahead. Another Sister sat beside her, saying nothing.

Three Chinese men walked along the row a few in front of them. Rose's already pumping heart almost shot out of her chest in fear. She wanted to grab at the Sister beside her, but she had strict instructions to follow. This was a risky time. One of the men glanced up and made eye contact with Rose, who looked down at her trembling hands. *No, no, no! Surely not.*

But when she glanced up, the men had moved on.

Boarding began. Desperately Rose tried to walk slowly and sedately even though the urge to run rose strongly within her. Still she and her companion did not speak. They took their allotted seats side by side. Then those same three men walked up the aisle past them and her heart raced again. Silently she prayed that her children had been taken to safety, all the while resisting the need to grab her escort.

The three-and-a-half-hour flight passed quickly enough. Her first action on board was to change from her religious habit to normal clothes. She returned the Orders' clothing to her escort before enjoying the food and drinks served.

Her thoughts strayed to the other time she'd been served on a flight. *I'm such a different person now*, she thought. *Not naïve any more.*

Once again, after disembarking, Rose ran the gauntlet of presenting her forged and stamped passport. It was readily accepted when she spoke comfortably in Tagalog to the officer, telling him, as she'd been prepped to do, that she had just returned from a work trip. Much to Rose's relief, there was no sign of the Chinese trio. Her Sister-escort led her to a mini bus with the Order's logo on the side, and the driver jumped out and hugged Rose.

'Welcome home,' she said warmly in their native tongue. 'I am Sister Hailee.' She then drove as though she were being pursued by the Chinese Mafia themselves through the heavy undisciplined and manic Manila traffic.

Rose asked softly, 'So what's been happening while I've been away?'

'How long were you away?'

'Since 2014. Nearly two years.'

'Biggest news … did you hear we have a new President. Rodrigo Duterte took up his new post last June.' Sister Hailee needed no more encouragement. All the way to Rose's new home she chatted about local happenings.

After an hour and thirty minutes, as they finally drew close, she turned to Rose while paused at traffic lights. 'I am here to support you in any way, my dear child.' She reached into the pocket of her habit and withdrew a business card. 'Any time – you just call me.'

The sun casting long shadows when they pulled up outside a block of five two-storey, newish, adjoining town houses. Rose sat in awe, looking through the window, as her two girls, Jasmin and Iris, came flying out through the doorless garage, closely followed by Annlyn, with a hefty Aaron balanced on her hip.

Rose could wait no longer; she almost fell out of the mini-bus in her rush to hug her children. She dropped to her knees, and the girls threw their arms around her neck. Tears flowed. Everyone spoke at once. Rose became aware of a pat on her shoulder and glanced around, nodding briefly at Sister Hailee who had lifted her bag out of the bus, and who then waved good-bye.

Reluctantly, she disentangled herself from her girls, turned and embraced Annlyn, wet cheek touching wet cheek. Aaron clung to Annlyn's neck so tightly Annlyn had to prise his fingers open. But there was no way he would allow himself to be passed to Rose.

Her heart felt instantly heavy, but she tried not to show the hurt. Rose looked beyond Annlyn, beyond Annlyn's two girls who stood in the front of the garage beside Rose's parents. Rose rushed to them, tears of happiness still streaming.

'Mum, Dad.' Her mother held Rose close. Neither spoke but Rose felt love flow in both directions. Her father simply patted her on the shoulder.

She was aware of being dragged into the house through the garage which housed no car, but instead an old table and chairs. Holding on to her girls – Aaron still showed no interest in her – she instantly noted the money she sent home – or rather that Mister Bob had sent – had made them comfortable. Up the stairs, and into the house Rose's father carried her luggage and placed it in the largest room, which, she noted was smaller than the one Marisol and she had shared in Bangkok. But unlike Bangkok, this was home. A queen size mattress lay on the floor, with a clothing rack against the wall along with a plastic set of shelves housing children's clothing.

The window was open; the air was still but there was a fan in the corner.

Rose soon learnt Annlyn and her husband had the next room, and her parents the one after theirs. All five children were to sleep with Rose.

'While you've been away, we've all had to care for the children. We figure it's your turn now,' her sister said.

Rose detected a touch of hostility and stood still, stunned into silence. Of course, she'd sleep with her three. She always had.

Over dinner, a simple meal of rice and a kind of spicy stew cooked by her mother, she was bombarded with questions. 'Why did the Sisters of Good Grace drive you home?'

Rose put her spoon down. 'They've been very kind to me. I was so alone. It was hard work.'

Annlyn scoffed. 'Hrmph. You think we had it easy here? And what about your Mister Bob?'

'He was a regular customer at the restaurant, and he always showed an interest in me and all of you here too.' Rose struggled with the lie and began eating again.

'Does he want to marry you?' Annlyn asked.

She looked at Annlyn sharply. 'What are you talking about? I am still married. Besides, he has his own family. He's a grandfather. He just saw my constant battle to earn enough even though I was working six days a week.' This statement flowed easily out of Rose's mouth since it wasn't a lie.

'Will he continue to support you?'

Rose hesitated. She looked around the table. The children had finished their meal and been sent off to play outside. 'I don't know. How long since he sent money, Annlyn?'

'Six days ago.'

'Well, we'll soon be able to tell.' Her phone pinged. Rose raised her eyebrows. 'Do you have Wi-Fi?'

'It comes and goes. We tap into one without security.'

Rose lifted her phone from her pocket to see an email from Mister Bob. 'It's him,' she said excitedly. 'I must read it and reply.' She pushed her chair back and walked out and down the stairs, where she sat at the rickety old table.

Hello Rose. The Sisters have been in touch. I believe

Rose hugged the phone to her chest, and stared thoughtfully into the cloudless but somewhat polluted sky. *What is this? Is it really happening?* She re-read the message. Considering the discussion she'd just been having around the dinner table, it was as though her Mister Bob had been listening in. She jumped up, ran back up the stairs, and burst into the crowded kitchen, holding the phone aloft.

'It's Mister Bob, it's Mister Bob! He wants to set me up in a small business so I can earn enough by myself. I just have to think of what kind of business.'

All the adults spoke at once. 'Hush. Let's just enjoy being together now. I'll go out tomorrow and check out this neighbourhood for places and ideas. Annlyn, will you come with me? We can take Aaron with us.'

Rose's body ached for her baby – toddler, she corrected her thoughts. But her intuition told her not to rush him. However, any time she could spend with him would help the re-attachment, she figured.

Annlyn sighed, but agreed to go with her. 'You can leave Aaron with me, though,' their mother offered.

Rose couldn't quite figure why Annlyn's behaviour was so strange. Kindness and enthusiasm seemed to have deserted her. Her husband sulked and avoided eye contact, and had said very little the whole time. Her own father seemed remote. Still, Rose wouldn't let it get in the way of the excitement of her first night home.

The four girls were called back in to clear the table and wash the dishes. Rose helped them, stroking and cuddling them one at a time. Aaron wrapped his arms around Annlyn's leg. *Patience*, Rose told herself, dying to pick him up, but knowing she had to wait to be accepted.

'What about selling food?' Rose's mother said, still seated at the now empty table. 'There are a few big buildings with call centres and other offices not that far away.'

The two men had moved downstairs to the old table setting, not able to see or hear the conversation.

'I wonder if there's already one there?' Rose mused, open to any ideas. As if being home was not a momentous enough occasion, trying to get her mind around someone buying her a business filled her head like an overstuffed cushion.

Her smart mother then said, 'Let's leave it till tomorrow. Rose, maybe you need to unpack and have an early night.'

Rose's new bag, provided by the Sisters contained just a few basics from her housekeeping life, and took only a few moments to unpack. The children watched and Rose realised they were hoping for some kind of gift. It had crossed her mind, but it had been more important to send all the money she earned home. But out of her handbag she lifted a small bag of sweets she'd been given by her employers as a farewell.

They all whooped with delight when she handed them over. 'Share nicely.'

Her first night at home proved a restless one, with Aaron fussing and wanting Annlyn, and the other little bodies constantly moving. Rose's brain raced from one idea to the next.

In desperation, and fearful no one would get any sleep, she said, 'Jazz, darling, will you cuddle him?'

Annlyn had showed no sympathy, no warmth towards Aaron. Jasmin, being the eldest had always been the responsible and compliant one and willingly took her baby brother. Rose kissed her head. The girls had school the next day and Rose wondered how they would all cope after such a momentous and disturbed night.

Movement outside their door woke everyone at 5.00 am.

Annlyn yelled, 'Come on, girls, bathroom first, in order.' All the girls had the earlier 6 am to 12 midday session at school, so the house was abuzz with line-ups and sharing a bathroom where cleanliness was paramount, and where a full bucket and dipper were the essential item for washing, flushing the toilet and keeping the floor clean.

Rose watched in awe as Jasmin brushed and tied back Iris's hair. Aaron sat at the table with a biscuit. All four girls, their long black hair brushed and tied back and uniforms neat, walked to school at 5.30 am after their breakfast, which their grandmother provided.

Little Aaron, after his night with all the children in one bed and being forced to touch his mother, began to accept Rose's affections. She was conflicted as to whether to take him with them. But he was heavy, and couldn't walk far or fast.

'I'll take you up on your offer to mind him, Mum, while Annlyn and I go and check the neighbourhood for business opportunities?'

Annlyn led Rose to a recently developed mixed business and

residential area about a twenty-minute walk away. Tall buildings housed not just apartments, but call centres.

'Lots of opportunities here,' she commented, sweeping her hand wide, showing a few shops with grilled barriers waiting to be rented. 'Tell me more about this man. Is he your sugar-daddy?'

Rose detected a hint of … what was it: bitterness? jealousy? anger? If only Annlyn knew. But she would never tell her sister the truth. 'Mister Bob is an optometrist and he does lots of business in Bangkok all the time. That's how we met.'

They came upon a shuttered-up corner shop in Bukidnon Street with a To Let sign hanging out the front. The few fittings they saw showed promise. 'Will you support me if I take on a venture like this? They'd be long hours. We could share the housework, the care of the children.'

Now Annlyn's voice held enthusiasm. 'We could do all sorts of things.' She started throwing ideas about. 'We could even make products at home and sell.'

Once home, Rose sent an email to Bob:

> *Hello Mister Bob. I am safe home. So very very good. We all cry with happiness. Today I look at shops. Popular area and not far away. I think sari sari shop is good. It is near offices and call centres where they work all night too. What do you think?'*

Bob, sitting at his desk, smiled with smug pleasure and enormous satisfaction from just the first innocuous sentence. Having met Rose and seen the challenge, his initial goal, he realised, had finally been achieved. He leaned back, stared at that first luxury buy representing his initial business success. Maybe he should mark this one in some way. So different, but so rewarding in its own special way. He sat up and tapped away at the keyboard.

So glad you're home safe, Rose. I wanted to hear it from you. Now you must download the app so we can talk about business. That was fast work. Give me time to talk it over with Denise when I get home. But tell me, what exactly is a sari sari shop?

A quick reply came.

It sell a bit of everything. Depends on the area. Maybe here, like, morning porridge or soup or rice in a bowl. Workers can eat on way to work. Can sell cigarette one at a time. Little packet of treats. Candies. Noodles. Maybe even cleaning products and clothing hangers. All that stuff. I am very excited.

Bob responded with:

I'll reply tonight, Rose. Keep Smiling.

That night, over their evening drinks, Denise said, 'You know I'm really supportive of what you're doing, but I am concerned for Rose's mental health, and you need to follow through.'

Bob cocked his head on one side. 'What do you mean?'

'She's at risk of suicide, possibly. Let me talk to you about what I teach my students. Suicidal ideation is associated with loss. Tell me some of the things Rose has lost.'

'Wow! Um, well, she just got most of it back, didn't she?'

'Well, yeah. In Bangkok, she lost her freedom, her dignity, her family, control of her life – just for starters. And add to that the sense of helplessness and hopelessness – other key indicators, not to mention the sense of being alone in it all.'

'Now you're talking like a lecturer.'

Denise laughed. 'I guess I am. But you get it, don't you? That last one, the sense of being alone would still exist, since you reckon she can't or won't share her shocking experiences in

Bangkok with anyone.'

'I should get the Sisters involved again?'

'I think Rose should re-take control of her life, but you can suggest. And, I'll be here if you need me. Now, let's go eat.'

After dinner, Bob retired to his study. He'd leave emotional stuff for later. He typed up:

> *Okay, I've spoken with Denise. She's with us. Her biggest concern is your wellbeing, Rose. When we talk on the phone I'll say more.*
>
> *Now let's begin to put together a business plan. I'll download a sample for you. Find out what the owners want per month for the lease and how long the lease. Work out if you need more fittings inside and cost them. Then stock. Make a list and cost it out after you've sussed out the neighbourhood and what they might need. Look at the competition. Then hours you need to work and wages to pay. Do you understand government regulations? Big job ahead. I know you're up for it.*
>
> *Keep Smiling.*
>
> *Bob.*

Chapter 17

Rose downloaded the Whatsapp phone app recommended by Mister Bob, and emailed to let him know. Before long, while she was washing dishes, she heard a strange new sound emanating from her phone. She dried her hands on the towel, and saw with excitement, it was her Mister Bob calling.

She listened to him explain a problem while she stood by the window.

'I took $1,000 in cash from the ATM to the Western Union Office, as usual, yesterday to send to you. But this time they refused to send it. "Your request has been rejected," the guy behind the counter said to me after returning from his back office.'

'I said to him, "What do you mean? Why?"'

'He said he had no idea. It wasn't his decision. He said I'd been sending quite a bit lately and maybe they thought I was laundering money.'

'Oh, that could almost be funny, Mister Bob.' But Rose wasn't amused. She was desperate to get his help as soon as possible.

Mister Bob went on. 'I decided to go home and give the cash to Denise. I asked her to try at another agency, but she met with the same response. So I have a solution. How about you open a bank account, Rose?'

'I have never had one,' Rose admitted. 'I have never even been in a bank.'

'Fund transfers may take longer, but otherwise, there's no

downside. You'll surely need one to run a business. What about tax, and registrations, and such things?'

'I will go and look tomorrow, Mister Bob.' Rose wondered how to choose one.

'Ah, is that your children I hear?'

Rose laughed loudly. 'Five of them. They make a lot of noise. But they are happy. Here they come.'

The rare sound gave Bob such pride. He'd not heard her this happy before. 'I'll let you go and play. Just email me the details when you open the account. I presume you can put a little cash in it to start?'

Rose took some deep breaths as she imagined the task ahead of her. Going into a bank on her own was intimidating. What if they laughed at her? *Maybe if I dress up in some of my sister's clothes I might look like a businesswoman?* she pondered. *I can act the part. I've done that before.* She shuddered at the thought of her past play-acting, realising she could act out anything, but then faced the thought she'd need to ask Annlyn for a few pesos to open the account. A sense of helplessness swept over her when she realised she had nothing of her own … except the silver bracelet which she didn't pawn in Bangkok and would never part with.

Bob interrupted her thoughts with his. 'It'll actually be a relief for me, I've got to admit. I can get the office to handle the transfers with internet banking. No more having to deal with cash, ATMs and agencies. Now, go and enjoy the children.'

The following morning, after a scolding from Annlyn because they would have to wait for cash to arrive, Rose, wearing her sister's plain skirt and pretty floral top, took a bus to the nearest major centre. Opening the bank account was paramount. Talking to the owner of the shop for the lease must wait.

Rose went through the automatic opening doors into BDO Unibank, looking up and around, reading all the signs. Tentatively she decided to queue for a teller, where she was finally given a form, and treated respectfully by other staff. One of the signs said FREE WI-FI so, once she had the account details, she emailed them immediately to Mister Bob.

After catching a bus back, she returned to the vacant shop and photographed the sign with details of the owner. But she had almost no money left on her phone, and the possibility of running out during a call to him appalled her. Instead, she messaged the man, asking if he'd call at his convenience re the possible lease.

Back home, Rose said to her mother, 'Thanks for minding Aaron again. I'm waiting on the call back now about the lease.'

'Rose, how soon do you think your Mister Bob will send money? We've only got rice for tonight.'

'Annlyn's husband hasn't got any work at the moment?'

Why is it always up to me, Rose considered, *that the money must come? It just isn't fair.* To distract herself, she started to fill in the business plan with pencil on paper, using the guide Mister Bob had forwarded. Her phone made its specific sound again, signalling support from her mentor from Sydney, as she now saw him.

'Did you get bank details, Mister Bob?'

'I've sent a couple of thousand Australian dollars so you'll have the security deposit and first month's rent for the lease, as well as money to survive on.' He went on to say, 'Whatever he says the rent is, Rose, you offer less.'

Rose held her hand to her heart and, bowing her head in silent gratitude, barely heard the advice. Her thoughts were more about everyone being able to eat properly again in a few days. She tuned back in to hear Mister Bob go on to teach her how to negotiate.

'Now, Rose, if this deal goes ahead, do you know anyone who can give you a good price for renovating?'

'My cousin, Joshua, Mister Bob. And he can deliver stock for me from warehouse too. All good price.'

'It's sounding promising, Rose. You can do this. I know you can.'

After their meagre meal, at which the women held back, so the children didn't have to, Rose's phone rang. She'd noted the two men – her father and brother-in-law – had filled their rice bowls, making no sacrifice. Disgusted, she left the kitchen and marched down to the men's territory in the garage for privacy with pad and pencil while she answered the call. She and the owner arranged to meet at the shuttered shop at nine the next morning.

Wearing her sister's clothes again, with a newly found confidence given to her by Mister Bob, and from opening a bank account, she watched the owner unlock and open the grilled roller door to the business. After looking behind the fixed partition at the back, which housed a sink in a bench of low cupboards, she took out her tape measure, borrowed from her father, and jotted down some dimensions. The frontage to the street was five metres, and the depth was seven metres.

'Hmm. Smaller than I thought,' she said with more confidence than she felt. This was the beginning of the negotiation. But she managed to get him to agree to knock a considerable amount off. She also became aware she'd need to place signage on the main road just along the way so trike and bike riders could easily pull off and drop in. The foot traffic, while they talked, was encouraging.

All she needed now was the deposit and the first month's rent, so she played for time by asking to take the documents away. She discovered that the call centre shift change mostly occurred around 6 am, so she'd need to open around 5 am each day. That meant asking for help yet again for her children, but this time everyone would see how hard she worked to support them all. Maybe they'd all step up and share the load.

The tiny cramped townhouse in the Project 11 area provided by the Philippine Government rocked with activity and voices when everyone was home. The four girls arrived home for lunch every day after their lessons had finished. Young as they were, they had their chores. But much to Rose's consternation Annlyn's husband continued to accept the free ride on Mister Bob's support. Aaron was on the move, and the floor needed to be kept clear of hazards. Rose walked in to see him trying to taste one of Annlyn's husband's cigarette butts he'd found on the floor.

Rose flared up. 'Go and do something with your life,' she retorted angrily. 'And clean up after yourself. You think we're here for you!'

Annlyn flew to her husband's defence, moving in front of Rose. 'You weren't doing much around here all the time you were away. We worked hard to keep your family and everything afloat, in spite of never having enough money. Don't you dare criticize!'

Rose's father, who never became entangled in family squabbles, retired downstairs to sit on an old chair in the shelter of the empty garage.

Rose signed the documents, and with her cousin and Annlyn, designed the internal layout and chose transportable counters, cabinets and hooks for the walls. They also wrote a list for the first delivery from the warehouses.

Rose's only time to herself was when, on Sunday mornings, she took herself off to her familiar old church, The Church of the Holy Rosary, while the children attended Sunday school. Although she followed the words and the never-changing rituals which comforted her, her mind often wandered back into her past. She marvelled at and accepted God's way of leading her. It must all have meaning: growing up in a family that didn't have much, marrying a man she thought she loved, giving birth to three healthy children, being abandoned by her husband, and living in poverty. That much she could accept. But being taken against her will and prostituted, after she sought only to work for her family was a circumstance she couldn't yet reconcile. What plan of God's could that possibly be, where she had no choice but to breach her and her church's moral code? *Why*, she asked herself, *did God abandon me at that time? And where, now, does my Mister Bob fit in all this?* Then she gave thanks for all she had and re-joined the Mass.

Rose's Place opened with balloons and twisted crepe paper hanging out front and blowing in the breeze. Her mother and her sister celebrated with her on that big day. Her mother then took little Aaron home.

Rose quickly established a relationship with regulars and expanded her stock to suit them. Light plastic storage containers stacked along the back wall sold fast. Minor medical supplies like sticking plasters and antiseptic cream were added to the stock along with many other bits and bobs.

'I think we should branch out into birthday parties,' Annlyn said. 'I can make cakes to order at home. All we need is a mixer. We can get a tank of helium gas and sell balloons too.'

Rose liked the idea. 'We need more working capital, though. And we need a fridge too, for ice blocks and ice creams. By the time I pay the rent here and at home, and electricity here and at home, and all the food and clothes we need, we're still short, Annlyn.'

'Oh, just ask your Mister Bob.'

'Well, he's still subsidising us as it is. I'd be too embarrassed. This is supposed to make us independent.'

Late in the night, after Rose closed the store at the usual 9 pm, she shot off an email to Mister Bob. *The shop continues to go well,* she wrote, before branching off into Annlyn's proposal.

Bob responded immediately.

> *Bakeries here have a picture catalogue of cakes and people pre-pay when they pre-order. I don't think you can go wrong. Nice of your sister is becoming part of the business. Do you need more money to begin her venture? What do you need to buy? Looking good, Rose.*
>
> *Keep Smiling.*

Following on from this development, Rose's mother began to make sauces, pickles and jams.

Christmas markets were about to begin. 'If you can keep the store going, Mum, Annlyn and I can open a stall at the markets too. We've got plenty of produce.'

Rose's cousin transported all the fresh produce for sale as well as other goods from the store, together with a few small display tables.

On the first day of the big weekend, after lunch, Rose said to Annlyn, 'Can you watch while I go to the restroom?' She unstrapped and passed over her cash bag. When she returned, she saw the panic on her sister's face. 'What's wrong?'

'The money's gone.'

'What do you mean?' Rose saw the empty cash bag she normally wore clipped around her waist sitting on a trestle, open and empty. With voice raised and tears about to break through, she said, 'What were you doing? Or not doing? How could you be so careless!'

Annlyn stormed off without a response.

The woman in the next stall beckoned Rose over. 'Couldn't help overhearing. None of my business, I know, but no one has actually been into your stall, only at the front.'

Rose read from the raised eyebrows what was meant. *Surely not*, she thought. *Not my own sister.*

In shock, Rose carried on alone for the rest of the afternoon. When security took over, Rose caught a bus home with the meagre takings that had eventuated.

'Why would you leave so much cash in that bag?' Annlyn chastised her when Rose arrived home. 'That was a crazy thing to do. We've been working our butts off to make all those foods. You can do it on your own tomorrow.'

Rose sat in the kitchen with her head in her hands. Little Aaron pulled on her shirt sleeve, and she dragged him into her lap and smothered him with kisses to alleviate her stress. He laughed at being tickled.

She didn't dare email Mister Bob about the failure of her venture. He'd be so disappointed in her. She had planned on putting the profits towards a secondhand chest-type fridge.

The next morning, Annlyn appeared at breakfast wearing matching cream shorts and top showing a bare mid-riff.

Rose's eyes flashed from the outfit to Annlyn's eyes and repeated the action. But she held her tongue. She knew she had stolen the money but she didn't know why.

Chapter 18

'Happy New Year, Mister Bob.'

'Happy 2017 to you, Rose,' he responded on the phone. 'And how were your Christmas sales? Have you had time to do the figures?'

She'd glossed over the disastrous weekend market results some time ago. 'The shop did really well, and how about you with your OTMs this year?'

'I'm excited, Rose. Listen to this …' It was evening his time, and late afternoon in the Philippines.

Rose had found the best place to sit and talk to Mister Bob on the phone app was to commandeer the men's downstairs space. The single low-watt bulb was too dim in the evenings for the men to play cards, or for Jazz and Iris to do their homework, but she didn't mind being interrupted by Aaron's need for attention which needed no light. He busily played trains by pushing and dragging boxes tied with string around the rough concrete floor.

'Go on, Mister Bob,' she said shoving the stinky ashtray away.

'You know the OTMs? Those clip-ons? Well, the young ones have been making their own jewellery using OTMs with footy and other sporting colours. Like bracelets where they thread them on to cheap wire, and earrings where they glue them onto cheap fittings. Even rings.'

Pushing the ashtray even further away, Rose chuckled. 'Clever kids.' She put her bare feet up on the chair next to her.

'I love hearing you laugh, Rose. You don't do it often

enough.' He had only heard her happy a few times, and all since she'd returned to Manila. 'Anyway, we thought about what the kids were up to and decided, let's go with it – encourage it. We're going to open a jewellery line. And my daughter, Charmaine is going to head up the new company. The pieces, like charms, won't need to be so lightweight and will be cheaper to produce.'

'Oh, Mister Bob. I am happy for you. Your daughter must be very clever.'

'It took Denise to remind me of her skills, and now Lola and Sarah are older, she needs a new challenge.' Bob sniffed the air. Something spicy was happening in the kitchen. 'But you know what that reminded me of? Maybe we can set you up with a display stand where the jewellery is available there.'

'Shhh … oh, not you, Mister Bob.' Rose laughed again. Aaron was making train noises. 'But that would be amazing – to sell some of your jewellery. When do you think you'll have them?'

'It'll mean another big launch, but that will be up to Charmaine, with my help. We'll have to open another office … find outlets. Mine is overflowing now we've expanded.'

'Will the bracelets be like charm bracelets?'

'Ah, not quite, Rose. A whole new concept. Affordable for everyone.'

'One day I'll see them in your shops, won't I, Mister Bob? And one day you'll come and see my shop.'

Rose knew she was being cheeky, but their relationship had turned a corner, and, although she respected him and saw him as her mentor, she now also saw him as a loyal friend. She heard Mister Bob's wife call.

'Dinner's ready, Bob.'

'Gotta go, Rose. Wish you could smell my dinner over the phone. Almost worth leaving our conversation for. Never mind. Till next time.'

Rose scooped up Aaron and toted him up the steps. 'You're

too big and heavy for this now,' she said, dumping him onto the floor in the kitchen, laughing again.

Rose sat at the kitchen table, where all four girls were doing their homework, and updated her shop records. She'd photograph them and send them off to Mister Bob. She relied on his feedback. No one else ever commented.

Chapter 19

Rose, when not in Bob's immediate thoughts, sat at the back, ever-present. Not so far back either, as he had seared her image into his head and it burnt brightly, often. As often as he could in the evenings, he called her.

'What hours is your shop open, Rose?' he asked.

'We keep it going up to sixteen hours a day, and only shut on Sundays. Mum and Annlyn still help.'

'What about holidays?'

'Still open. Not as busy, so I take the children to work. Jazz and Iris help. They learn what to do. Aaron's nearly four, so he's sensible now and doesn't wander. I have to get Mum or Annlyn to pick them up early from the store, so they can go to bed on time when I'm doing the late night,' Rose explained.

'Is it safe to walk home?' Bob said.

'It is now. Since Duterte is President, we have no bother with drug dealers or other hoodlums. They just shoot them. Streets are all clean now, and safe.'

'Oh, shit! I never thought of the dangers. And they just shoot them? No arrest? No trial?'

Rose laughed. 'Problem finished, Mister Bob.'

'What if you had a motor scooter or something?'

'Scooter would be good and quick and dangerous too. I might kill myself on it. But you do enough, Mister Bob. The fridge was a great gift. Thank you.' Rose was proud of her English. It was improving in leaps and bounds. She picked up some of it from Mister Bob, but also paid more attention to the words on the television.

Rose's shop had its quiet times and its busy times. During one of the lulls, she had a visit from a sleazy-looking man with long oily hair, but he wasn't planning to buy anything. His jeans were grubby, as were his sneakers, and he hadn't shaved any time recently. He stank of stale cigarettes – his very presence sucked the air out of the store.

'I come to collect the debt,' he demanded, thumbs in pockets, standing tall above Rose.

Rose had built up her confidence with the business and with dealing with business people, under Mister Bob's guidance, and refused to be intimidated. She had no idea what he was talking about, and told him so.

He whipped out a multiple-page document from his back pocket. 'These your father's signatures?' He shoved the papers towards her face, pointing.

Quizzically, she said, 'Yes?'

'See, he took out loans in your name. Three separate ones. Last year and year before. You pay. Now. They overdue. Now!' He shook the papers in her face.

Rose's legs almost gave way. *No, surely not. This has to be a con.* It was a long time since she'd felt so threatened.

'How much are they for?'

'Total 204,000 pesos and climbing.'

Rose flopped into her chair. *This can't be. It amounts to almost half the value of my shop. Impossible.* Tears gathered. She had to be strong. Maybe there'd been some mistake. She needed to speak to her father. And to Mister Bob. But how embarrassing that would be. She stood up again, legs trembling.

He leaned into her face. 'I'll be back Friday to collect.' And with a rude finger gesture, the debt collector with no name marched off.

Rose rang Annlyn to come and relieve her, so she could go home and speak with her father. Could he really borrow money in her name?

'Did you know about this?' she asked Annlyn when she arrived to take over.

'You think we managed on the morsels you sent home to us? What did you expect us to do? We always thought one day you'd send enough money to pay it off, but you just didn't live up to your promises.'

Rose's mouth gaped. But what did they think would happen when they ignored it? Did they think the debt would disappear – whomever it was who borrowed it?

Walking home, Rose called Mister Bob on her app hoping for some words of comfort. He was always her ally.

'Not your problem, Rose. If your father signed, it's his.'

'No, Mister Bob. Not like that here. He did it in my name.'

'Makes no sense. Let me talk to the Sisters of Good Grace. They'll know what to do.'

Rose found her father at the downstairs table, playing cards with Annlyn's husband. She loved and respected her father. How was she going to confront this? 'Dad, can I have a word in private please?'

Her father grimaced and raised his eyebrows before turning and nodding to Annlyn's husband. He harrumphed and walked aimlessly out into the street.

I'll bet he was behind this, Rose thought. 'Dad, I've just had a visit from a really nasty debt collector. Please tell me you didn't do this.'

'Oh, Rose, baby. We had to. You don't understand.'

'I understand I have to find the money, Dad, and I don't know how.' She sat down and put her head in her hands, trying desperately to hold back tears.

'What about your Mister Bob?'

Rose's phone rang. It was Sister Hailee. Rose turned her back on her father and moved away for privacy. 'Your friend Mr Marks from Sydney called me, Rose. He explained what happened. I am so sorry. You've certainly been through enough. I explained to Mr Marks we shouldn't hold out much hope as it is the law. But I said I'd arrange for us to go and see if we can appeal. Would you like to do that? I explained to him the official we would appeal to is like a hybrid magistrate or ombudsman in the Australian system.'

Standing in the afternoon sun, and feeling the perspiration running down between her breasts, Rose felt a tiny glimmer of hope with the kind, but, in her mind, somewhat useless gesture. She accepted the offer and walked back into the garage. Her father had fled upstairs.

She emailed Mister Bob to tell him what was happening, and thanked him for bringing Sister Hailee in to help. She received a quick reply asking to let him know the outcome.

After the depressing meeting, both Sister Hailee and Rose contacted Bob with the negative result.

'What a ridiculous decision,' Bob said to Rose. 'Let me see what I can do about it.' Bob knew Rose had no chance of paying off the debt. She'd never asked him for a cent. Not ever. He'd voluntarily paid for things all this time, and she still wasn't asking, but he could volunteer this, provided a stop was put to any future occurrence.

After a further discussion with Sister Hailee, Bob called Rose. 'I'm coming to see you, Rose, to sort this.'

'What! Oh, Mister Bob! But I am embarrassed. I have got in a mess. So sorry. I so want to see you, but not this way.'

'Not your fault, Rose. And don't tell anyone I'm coming. We'll see what can be done. I'm meeting with Sister Hailee first. And I'll have Charmaine with me. She's agreed to take a few days on her way to our supplier in Bangkok. You know she's now heading up the Marks Jewellery division?'

Georgina had booked a newish hotel for Bob and Charmaine to stay in a few kilometres away from Rose's current address and work. It wasn't as up-market as Bob would have preferred, but the location was convenient.

He and Charmaine met with Sister Hailee in a small business room in the hotel shortly after arrival. She was as warm and cheerful as she was short and wide. She seemed to know her stuff.

'So you recommend I just pay this loan shark,' he said, somewhat miffed, after listening to her explain Filipino law again.

'It's attracting twenty-two per cent interest,' she responded.

'Unreal.' He swore under his breath, then sighed. 'Okay. But if I pay now, how do we stop it from happening again. *Can* we do something?' He'd given in. There was no fighting it, and he didn't want to go head-to-head with a Filipino loan shark.

'Let me talk alone to Rose,' Sister Hailee said. 'What she must do is cut herself off from her family. They all rely on her too much. She's got to declare officially she's not responsible for their debts. She has her three children and her business. It is more than enough responsibility for a single mother.'

'Well, good luck with getting her to follow your advice,' he said to her. 'But I do appreciate all your assistance.'

Sister Hailee replied, 'And I also recommend I take the funds to the lender. Not you. They will think the Church is paying it if I do it. They might even be embarrassed and reduce the interest, but I doubt it.' She sat silently for a moment, her hands folded in her lap. 'And it will protect Rose so they won't think she has access to those amounts of pesos again.'

When Sister Hailee left, and Bob had arranged for Georgina

back in Sydney to transfer the funds to the Order, he said to his daughter, 'Let's take a look around the neighbourhood. We'll hire an air-conditioned taxi.'

Neither of them had been to the Philippines before.

After an hour, they'd not travelled very far, since dodging the cars, trikes, bikes and multi-coloured buses took a lot of nerve and a lot of patience for their driver.

'They're like huge squatters' towns dotted here and there, among the more established houses,' Bob remarked. 'The lower sections of the high rises are usually taken up with small shops, often in arcades.

'People buy fresh food daily on their way home,' he explained to Charmaine. 'Fruit and vegies, meat, or whole meals.' He'd learnt some of the cultural routines from Rose. 'Let me take you past her shop. That's sort of where she's located and it's what she does.'

He passed a piece of paper with the address on to the driver, knowing his speech, especially from the back seat, would be difficult to understand. They drove on.

'There it is,' he pointed, recognising it from a photo Rose had sent him. They didn't stop. The traffic pushed them along, although there were bikes parked on the footpath.

'How the heck does she make a living from that tiny little thing?' Charmaine said. 'But, look, there are customers.' She sighed. 'The air. This noise. Traffic. Everything ...' She waved her hands widely. 'It's all too much. It's like I'm suffering from claustrophobia. Let's get back to the hotel, Dad. I feel helpless witnessing so much hardship. Life seems such a struggle for them.'

They freshened up in their respective rooms where Bob slipped off his shoes and napped before meeting up again late in the afternoon in the bar. He wore shoes with Velcro fasteners – laces were beyond him.

After Charmaine ordered a cocktail, and Bob a scotch, he launched into his latest idea. 'I'm going to have to set Rose up in a higher-earning business, aren't I? After what you said, I think it's necessary. I've been thinking of a laundromat. I'm guessing all the high-rise offices and apartments around where Rose has her store would make it work. Has to be the right location.'

He nodded, agreeing with himself as his thoughts fell like unchecked dribble from his mouth. 'You could drop your laundry off on your way to work, and pick it up dry, folded, and ironed if necessary, on your way home. She could employ help. What do you reckon?'

'Dad, slow down. *Slow down.* I can sort-of relate to having an absentee husband and working and looking after kids, you know, and it can be overwhelming – even with my income and the help I get.'

'It's why I'm asking your opinion. But you see the hours she works now.'

Charmaine held up her finger. 'Hush. Think of this. When something happened to me, look at the support and backup I had. What if something happened to Rose? From what you say, she doesn't get much support. I gather her family takes advantage of her, and she certainly gets no financial support apart from you.'

'Not a bigger business then? Well, what?'

'No. She needs security, not more responsibility.'

'What do you mean?'

'I'm thinking,' Charmaine paused, looking for the best way to put her suggestion. 'Set her up in her own home. No rent. No hangers-on. Security for her children if something were to happen to her.'

Bob watched Charmaine lift her laptop from her briefcase, boot it up and google real estate near where they were located.

'Shit, look at this, Dad.' She turned the screen towards him. 'You can get a three-bedroom apartment near where Rose lives for 40 to 60,000 thousand dollars Australian.'

'Really? Well, they are basic. Hmm. Let me think about it.' The planted seed began germinating, the rubbing of the head facilitating it.

'You've taken on quite a responsibility here. I wonder what she's like in the flesh?'

Bob had arranged for Rose and her three children to be picked up and to come and join Charmaine and him for an early dinner. They waited in the foyer.

Rose entered, head held high, dressed in her sister's colourful top with her simple skirt. She held tightly to a little boy on her right, with two tiny attractive girls accompanying her on the left. Seeing her Mister Bob, she left Aaron with his sisters and flew across the foyer into his arms, which wrapped around her. Realising what she was doing, she suddenly stood back.

'So sorry, Mister Bob. Just so good to see you.' But she couldn't stop smiling. She turned to Charmaine. 'So rude of me. I'm Rose.' She held out her hand and shook it before introducing her children, who moved up beside their mother and stood touching her, speechless.

The girls' long black hair, tied back in ponytails, shone. They were cleanly and neatly dressed in skirts and tee-shirts, and wore sandals on their feet. Aaron, too, appeared well-groomed.

Once introductions were over, they made their way to the family-friendly restaurant on the eighth floor. Rose lingered on the way to the table, pointing out a large window facing south to her children. A major housing project was under construction and well-advanced. 'Over there is where we used to live, and that's where you were born, Aaron,' she said in Tagalog, before explaining her comments to Bob and Charmaine in her rough English.

'Wow, those must have been difficult times,' Charmaine said as they made their way to the reserved table for six. 'Sorry, that was probably a bit insensitive of me,' she added, thinking about those even more difficult times Rose had been through.

'Hmm, I did not know anything much else then,' Rose responded. 'I grew up over near the coast, and went to school there till I turned fourteen.' Rose helped her children choose from the kids' menu before resuming. 'It is not till I travel,' Rose blushed as she looked up at Charmaine, 'that I see things, you know, like I only would see on TV.'

'Like?' Charmaine prompted.

The children had been given orders to sit quietly and say nothing. The two girls were paying close attention to the conversation and appeared to have a good understanding of English, even though, when asked a question by Charmaine they spoke in monosyllables and giggles.

'Oh, things like dining in a proper dining room. A special celebration for us today would be McDonalds. Mister Bob taught me how to use cutlery and how to be confident. I do not like alcohol, though.'

Rose contentedly watched the evening progress till her three children finished with ice cream.

'School and work tomorrow. Now, what do you say to Mister Bob?'

This time Aaron spoke for the first time, and in an ever-so-clipped British accent said, 'Thank you, Mister Bob.'

Charmaine smothered a laugh at the rounded vowel sounds coming from this dear little Filipino boy. 'You speak very nice English, Aaron. How did you learn it?'

He looked to his mother for help. 'He always watches Peppa Pig. It's a British TV show for kids,' she explained, seeing Mister Bob's bewildered look.

'We need to meet up again tomorrow to talk business, Rose,'

Bob said as he escorted them to their waiting taxi. 'Charmaine and I are flying out tomorrow night.'

'I see Sister Hailee in the morning, Mister Bob.'

'She will explain everything. Let's meet after that. I'll come to the shop.'

After they'd departed, Charmaine said, 'Let's go get a drink, and you can tell me more about this woman of yours.'

Bob looked at her sharply, but held his reply till they were seated. 'She's so brave, and so strong you know. And she's so keen to learn. Like a sponge, absorbing everything I tell her. She'd never heard of a business plan. Now she can write one. Aren't you impressed by her?'

'Hmm. I meant less about her abilities and more about your relationship with her.'

Again Bob looked sharply at his daughter. 'Platonic. Mentor/mentee. Really, Charmaine?'

Chapter 20

Next morning, with no one available to relieve her, Rose closed the shutter on the shop, leaving a notice to say she'd re-open at twelve. She walked to a nearby coffee shop to meet Sister Hailee.

Being a dedicated Catholic, Rose, like the rest of her family, held all religious folk in awe and esteem. Sister Hailee was no different. Whatever she advised would be almost infallible.

After light chit-chat in Tagalog over coffee, Sister Hailee said seriously, 'How are you managing, Rose? Do you have someone to share your past experiences with?'

'You know what happened to me?' Embarrassed, Rose put her hands over her face. 'I cannot ever talk about it.'

'I'm here if you ever want to talk about it, Rose. You know you have done nothing, absolutely nothing wrong. You did what you needed to survive. You should be proud to be a survivor of such a horrendous ordeal.'

Rose had never heard such positive words about her life in Bangkok. She felt tears building. *No,* she told herself. *No, not now.* In a soft voice, she said, 'Thank you, but I will never tell anyone on the planet about those unspeakable times.'

With a conciliatory nod, the religious woman went on. 'Let's talk about this debt your father has incurred in your name. It was unfair of him to borrow the money that way. You have big responsibilities, but those responsibilities are to your three children.' She paused. 'No one else, Rose.'

She sat back and folded her hands in her lap, letting the words sink in. After a few moments, she added, 'You must ask your parents to return home. They are both still capable people. Then, you must move out of the house, since it is in your sister's name. You must move into your own place. Your sister and her family will cope without you, even though they may not like it.'

Rose's brain scrambled with the thoughts of being on her own with Jasmin, Iris and Aaron. The only time it had happened was when Aaron was born and her husband, Ramil, deserted her and his children. They were unbearable memories, as were the events that followed. *No, no. I can't be alone.* 'But I need my sister.'

Even though Annlyn complained, whinged, and even abused and bullied Rose, some family, she thought, was better than no family, surely.

'As family, and as family support, yes, you can need them. But as dependents, no. I am happy to come with you to explain it all to them.'

Rose hesitated. Her family would listen to a nun. She doubted she'd have the courage to say these things to them. She nodded slowly to Sister Hailee, who moved the conversation to Rose's children in order to leave her in a more positive state.

'I can't help noticing you and the girls all have the names of flowers. Sweet. How did it come about? And tell me, how are they getting on at school?'

Rose leaned forward enthusiastically to talk about her favourite subject. 'My mother always loved flowers, and frangipani is our favourite, but it's a bit awkward as a name.'

They laughed together for a brief moment. Rose was proud of the girls' achievements in the classroom. It wouldn't be long before Aaron started school, she told Sister Hailee.

Before parting, Sister Hailee arranged to meet Rose's family and handed Rose her business card for the second time. 'And your wonderful Mister Bob is arranging for us to pay the debt, so you never have to see these debt collector people again.'

This time, the tears trickled – tears of relief. She had gathered something had been planned, but now it was confirmed, she knew she'd have to muster the courage to follow through on Sister Hailee's advice.

Rose departed the meeting and re-opened her sari sari shop. She met the lunchtime trade with a genuine smile, and waited for Mister Bob. When he arrived, she went to help him as he slowly struggled from the illegally parked taxi. She insisted he sat in a plastic chair, and not on the stools with no back support. She then stood in front of him and thanked him profusely for releasing her from the debt, bowing as she did.

'But I'm really scared to face my family with Sister Hailee tonight,' she admitted.

Seeing customers, Rose took a moment away to serve the two men wanting to buy cold drinks.

'I see you get great use out of the fridge,' Bob said, once the customers left.

'Thanks to you again. I can never repay you.' Rose shook her head wildly.

'Rose, the more you succeed the more you repay me with that success. Now, tell me about your parents. They have their own place to go to?'

'It's a bus ride then train ride and then a ferry ride. But they have no money.'

'We can fix that one easily. You know that.'

Rose shook her head. 'Even after what my father did?' She felt uncomfortable. Why did life revolve around money? 'And the rental house is in Annlyn and her husband's name, not mine.'

'So you move out.'

'No, no. I cannot afford to move.' *Money again.* Her hands flew up to cover her face so Mister Bob couldn't see her shame. *And,* she thought, *my sister and her husband and their children can't afford to stay there without me.*

'I wish I didn't have to fly back home tonight. But we've

sorted the debt, and that's why I came. Now I want you to be free from the burden of supporting so many people, Rose. Listen to me …' He clasped both her hands and held them cosily in his. 'I have a new range of spectacles. They're going gangbusters. We've expanded into jewellery. You know that'll be fabulous too. Let me share the successes with you by getting you started in your own rented apartment?'

Buying a house for Rose and her family was complicated, Bob realised, but first, she needed to adjust to living alone. It was too early to bring it up. Go slowly and rent first, Charmaine had advised.

Rose squirmed. But, for her children's sake, she must accept Mister Bob's help once again.

As though reading her mind, Mister Bob said, 'Do it for your children, Rose.' He squeezed her hands then let go.

She nodded and smiled a brief embarrassed smile.

'And we'll put furniture in it too. When you've found somewhere, you call me and let me know the details. I'll transfer enough to cover security deposit and a bit of rent. We can act quickly.'

Peak hour was almost upon them, and Rose needed to attend to the customers arriving after work, while Bob needed to get to the airport. He had achieved more than expected this trip, although the parting of so much money for so little to see for it still rankled.

Arriving home for a late dinner, after the children had eaten, Rose said, 'Sister Hailee will be dropping in to talk to us soon.'

'What about? – no – don't worry we can guess,' Annlyn said. 'Working out how to pay the money.'

Soon enough, Sister Hailee hauled her bulky self up the stairs. 'Glad there aren't too many steps,' she said breathlessly at the top.

The kitchen was a tight squeeze. There was no lounge, nor separate dining room, and with reverence, the adults in the family stood to be introduced.

With little preamble, the nun, sitting close to Rose, launched in. 'We will take care of the monies owed this time, but never again,' she said firmly. This was how she'd pre-arranged with Mr Marks to speak about it, to protect him. 'And we will organise for Rose and her children to move into her own place. I'm sure you all understand why that is necessary.' A stunned silence hung heavily. Hostility filled the already heated room.

Rose felt a reprieve when Sister Hailee made it sound as though it was her decision and not Rose's. But she could feel herself heating up from the red-hot anger being sent to her telepathically by her family. Out of respect, they would not comment as long as the nun sat at their table.

As soon as she departed, the verbal attacks began. 'You're just Mister Bob's ugly whore. You do his bidding for money. You give him whatever he wants, and then you're so gutless you get a nun to ... '

Rose's mother cut across Annlyn's tirade. 'No more, Annlyn. The nun spoke a lot of truths. Her words hurt us. We need to consider them.' Her eyes flashed back and forth to her two daughters. 'Now click your bracelets together, look each other in the eyes and apologise.'

Rose almost choked over complying with this useless, stupid, lifelong family ritual, but not obeying her mother was not an option. Annlyn acted as disingenuous with her apology as Rose did with hers.

If it were not for the deep respect she held for her mother, Rose might have thrown her silver bracelet at her sister. But then again, it represented more than healing rifts with Annlyn. It was the only tangible object she had that linked her to her grandfather who had worked for a silversmith. She felt conflicted as the two thoughts sat in juxtaposition.

Bob and Charmaine parted ways at Ninoy Aquino airport. 'Sure you'll be okay back to Sydney?' Charmaine checked.

'I'm not an invalid,' Bob told her sharply. 'Now go get creative with Arthit.'

She gave him a hug and a kiss before he hauled himself onto an arranged electric cart that would take him to his gate.

'And talk over the house idea for Rose with Mum, too, won't you?' she lobbed at him as a parting gesture as he was whizzed away.

Rose spent a restless night, partly caused by the usual kicks and nudges from the children, but more by this new and unfolding situation. She untangled herself from the little limbs and crawled to the wall where she propped herself up. Staring blindly at the unlit single light globe dangling from the centre of the ceiling, she quickly identified, with relief, that her mother was her only genuine support. While she couldn't survive without Mister Bob, he would never understand her life here in Manila. But then, she thought, her mother would never understand her life back in Bangkok – not that she would ever try to explain it. She wrapped her arms around herself, holding tight.

Annlyn and her husband left early in the morning, saying nothing. Rose helped the children prepare for school while her father sat sullenly at the table. Rose was at a loss as to what she should say or do. Thankfully, her mother helped get the older ones off to school and kept Aaron at her side. Rose left to catch the early trade. After lunch, her mother came to relieve her.

'Go and find a place to live, Rose. This situation cannot continue at home.'

They hugged.

Rose found a small non-descript apartment in a large block

not too far from her store. *Just imagine*, Rose dreamed, *of having the shop on the ground floor and living above it. Ah, but it's just a dream.* The apartment, though, had two bedrooms. That was a bonus. And she thought she could afford it, given she wouldn't be feeding so many mouths, or clothing so many children, not to mention meeting a lower rent.

So, with Mister Bob's financial help and her mother's support, she was ready to move in a week later. The teasing, abuse and bullying she'd received from Annlyn and her husband turned into begging when they realised Rose's moving out had become reality.

'How do you expect us to survive?' Annlyn whined, while Rose packed her children's meagre belongings into plastic bags. 'We rented this place for you and your children and we took care of them. You can't just walk out.'

Rose could be silent no longer. Her voice raised, she said, 'You can't stop reminding me of what you did. What about *me*! I worked my backside off for you and your lazy bum husband and kids. You put me into …'

Annlyn screamed back, over the top of her sister, veins sticking out on her neck, 'How dare you! At least I have a husband. No wonder Ramil took off.'

Their father sat at the table, looking down at his fingernails. Their mother scuttled around, gathered up the plastic bags of clothes, and, walking out, said sternly to Rose, 'Follow me.' The situation had escalated beyond bracelet clicking.

Rose's face flushed bright red and her hands shook. On the way to the new accommodation, she said, more calmly, 'What will they do, Ma? How will they manage?'

'As the nun said, Rose, it is no longer your responsibility. I'll stay till you're settled and then go back to our own home with your father.'

'I'll cut back on my hours at the shop, and create a space there for Aaron.'

The first night in her sparsely furnished apartment, Rose put the two girls on a new mattress in one room, and slept on another new mattress on the floor in the other room with Aaron. Not only had the furniture arrived, but so had a few treats for her children. New tee-shirts for all three of them, and a basketball. She even bought a lipstick for her mother, who'd promised to be back early in the morning. When morning came, Rose smiled gently when she saw Jasmin and Iris had snuck in during the night and curled up on her mattress as well. After a whole five children, sharing with just three was a treat.

As if sensing the new era and the new needs, the two girls assumed more responsibility, organising themselves for school, under the direction of their grandmother. Aaron, now four, would go to work with his mother.

'It's lonely, Ma,' Rose admitted.

'You'll manage, like you always have, my girl.' Her mother rewarded her with a heartfelt smile.

Once at work, Rose opened her email. The message had come. From Mister Bob:

Keep Smiling.

On Sunday, Rose had the children dress in their best clothes before heading out the door to church. One of her neighbours walked with two girls in the same direction. The two women fell into step beside each other as the children ran back and forth.

Rose discovered Hazel was also a single mum. She was attractive, and so young to be a mum. Before the Mass began, they arranged to go to the local park with basketball courts once they'd been home and changed into casual clothes.

Rose sat in a pew, Jasmin on one side of her, and Iris on the other. She pulled them close, then lifted Aaron, who'd been standing in front of her, onto her lap. Aaron groaned when she hugged him tightly. She smiled a rare smile, closed her eyes and gave thanks for her current circumstances. Despite her moment of pleasure, her mind took her on a quick flashback where she saw herself tumbling out a window, half-dressed, to escape. She hated those uncontrolled thoughts, and instantly opened her eyes and drank in her humble but safe surroundings. Ignoring the priest and his words and gestures, she promised herself that she'd make an effort not to let memories dominate and disturb her anymore.

Later, at the park, Hazel and Rose sat on a bench in the shade of a Poinciana tree, both clasping cold bottles of water. Trying to cool off, they pressed them against their foreheads and on the back of their necks before they drank. They could see their children, and hear their whoops and laughter and yelling while they interacted with other kids as well. The basketball Rose had splurged on proved a big hit.

'But it's so hard being alone with so little money, Rose. How do you do it?'

Rose gave a simple explanation, disclosing nothing of her benefactor, then she asked Hazel the same question.

'I work in a kitchen at the local hotel. At least I get to bring home leftovers. But after paying the rent and other bills, there's nothing left. You know what I'm thinking?'

'What?'

'I'm thinking of working overseas. Ever thought of it?' She swung around and looked brightly at Rose.

Seeing the look on Rose's face, Hazel said, 'What's wrong? I reckon it's a great idea. A few of my cousins are doing it. I think my aunty would look after my two. Have you got someone to ask?'

Just then Aaron came running up, crying, blood running down from his knee. Rose welcomed the distraction. She cuddled him and opened her bag, extracting a plaster. In an instant, all fixed up, he slid down off her lap and ran off.

'Well?' Hazel pursued.

'Let me tell you what happened to a friend of mine,' Rose said. With a much-abbreviated version, trying not to sound emotional, Rose poured out her own experience. 'So,' she finished up, 'you can see it's fraught.'

Hazel sat wide-eyed. 'No! But we could be so careful, being warned what to watch for.'

'No. Count me out. I'm going to make the shop work now I'm on my own.'

'That was you, not a friend, wasn't it?' Hazel turned and stared into Rose's eyes.

'Hazel, listen to me, whoever it was, just don't take the risk.' Rose stood up, shrugged, and swung her head towards the basketball courts. 'Come on, let's join them and have some fun.'

Chapter 21

Bob's expanded optometry business and Charmaine's jewellery business challenged them both, but with their diligence and constant attention, the ventures were lucrative. Their patents were challenged by competitors in the industry but they defended well. Two Annual General Meetings came and went. They refused lucrative take-over offers.

It was a warm but cloudy Sunday afternoon out by the pool when Charmaine enquired after Rose's wellbeing.

'I think it's time for us to start looking at a house for Rose and her family,' Bob remarked. 'She's run the shop a couple of years now. It's not quite doing the job it should. She can't afford staff, and she needs time to tend the children. She still needs our financial support.'

'Okay, you get the ball rolling on that one,' Denise agreed. 'You and Charmaine.'

Denise disappeared inside, reappearing a few minutes later with a tray of watermelon and rockmelon topped with cherries – a treat for the grandchildren. She called to the girls who were splashing around in the pool.

'Beat ya to it,' Sarah yelled to Lola. As they clambered out, Sarah turned and pushed her sister back in, intending to reach the food first. Startled by a scream, followed by an almighty crack, the adults looked up to see Lola disappearing into the pool right on the edge. She had lost her footing and smacked her head on the side as she fell back in.

Sarah stood in shock as her sister rolled over, face down in the water, not moving. Charmaine was the first adult to reach Lola, quickly followed by Denise. They acted silently in tandem, with Charmaine jumping in and holding a floppy Lola up to her mother who dragged her out by the armpits.

Bob attempted to jump up and rush over. That resulted in his landing on all fours when his mind went ahead but the lack of dopamine being transmitted by his brain forgot to tell his feet to move with his intention.

'Is she breathing … is she breathing?' Charmaine demanded of her mother as she clambered from the pool.

'Bob, call an ambulance,' Denise yelled, still looking for a pulse. She saw Bob had fallen. 'Get up!' Looking Charmaine in the eyes, she grimaced, fingers on Lola's neck. 'Yes, there it is.' She moved back on her haunches, and they rolled Lola into the recovery position.

Sarah chewed her fist and sobbed. Charmaine looked up, rubbed her leg. 'It's alright, my love, it was an accident.' She turned to her father. He was still down on the pavers, but had crawled to the table, reached the phone and was talking.

In a matter of minutes, Bob watched the paramedics, one bloke and one woman, both in dark green garb, carrying weighty bags, sweep through the open house.

'She's stirring, Bob. They'll take her to the Children's Hospital now,' Denise reported to a shaken Bob several minutes later. 'She'll be fine.'

On that same Sunday, in Manila, Rose and Hazel were at the usual park with their children.

'Thanks again for looking after my girls in the evenings, Rose. The extra shift has made such a difference financially.' They'd upgraded from drinking water to drinking Coca-Cola. 'Are you doing enough hours in the shop?'

'Well, since you can look after my three in the afternoons it helps. But Jazz and Iris are such sensible girls. I can trust them now to look after Aaron if you're not around anyway.' She put the can to her mouth. 'My Mister Bob picks up the cost of anything important, like doctor visits.'

'What a gift he is. Pity he's not younger and available.' They laughed. 'Do you get much of a chance to meet anyone while you're in the shop?'

'A few blokes hang about. I'm not interested. Besides, I've got some useless husband somewhere on the planet, so I'm not available.'

'Yeah, same sort of thing for me. Sometimes I wish we weren't bound by the Church and could just divorce simply.' Hazel stared whimsically. 'They do it in other countries.'

'Hmm.' Rose daydreamed. But that dreaming was shattered by a piercing scream. Aaron raced at Olympic speed towards his Mum.

Rose, in turn, rose and sprinted towards him. 'What? What?' She grabbed him by the shoulders, but he continued to scream. She slapped his face. Not hard, but noisily. Abruptly silence happened.

He pointed to his bicep. 'A wasp …' He gasped hysterically. 'A wasp …'

Rose saw the stings. More than one. The area was already red and swollen. Hazel and the children formed a circle around them.

Down on her knees, she turned to Hazel. 'What will I do?' Aaron was wheezing and coughing and crying.

'Get him to the hospital.'

It took a couple of moments for Hazel's words to register. Rose disengaged one arm from around Aaron and pulled her phone from her shorts' pocket. With a shaking hand, she rang her favourite trike man, Simon. It rang a few times. She looked up at Hazel, pleading. 'It's Sunday.' She was afraid he wouldn't answer, but he did.

Hearing her distress and explanation, he said he'd come immediately. She scooped Aaron up and marched to the side of the road where Simon had asked her to wait.

Aaron continued to strain to breathe and was so sweaty he was slippery to hold. In a flash, Simon arrived, showing his concern. His tricycle opened on one side, but had a windshield in front and a roof over. It fitted Rose and the two girls easily. Aaron clung to his mother, and she clung to him. 'Hang on, everyone.' He revved the small motor and took off, arriving at the hospital in record time.

Rose ordered her two girls to sit in the waiting area while staff ushered Rose and Aaron through. They treated the stings with ice, and injected antihistamines into his arm. He lay there lethargically with an oxygen mask on his face. Rose noted nursing staff showed no great concern once Aaron's breathing became more regular. They'd wandered off to attend to others. Clerical staff took details from Rose. This visit was not free, and Rose hoped she could afford to pay, but when presented with the account, she was caught short.

'Please let me go and ask my friend outside?' she asked them.

'Simon, I am embarrassed. I have never done this, but can you please help me. I can promise repayment quickly.' She realised she couldn't afford his ride service either.

'For you, Rose, of course. How much?' He pulled a roll of notes from his shorts' pocket.

Another hour passed before she left with Aaron. Out at the trike she said to them all, once again holding Aaron, 'He's suffering from anaphylaxis. It's an allergic reaction to the stings. They said I should go to a pharmacy and buy an Epi-Pen. But it's okay for now.' She guided the girls onto the trike again, and climbed on herself. She touched Simon on his arm.

'I don't know how to thank you, Simon. Things could have been more serious without you.' Rose didn't want to tell anyone, but they'd said that if Aaron suffered another sting he might not survive without the quick injection from the Pen.

'Rose, instead of paying me back, why not just give me a credit at the shop?' Simon suggested. For the first time since Aaron was stung, Rose smiled.

Later that evening, Rose sought a bit more adult comfort after such a dramatic day, so rang her Mister Bob. He answered with his usual greeting of 'How are you, Rose?'

She replied, 'Bad thing happened today, Mister Bob.'

'You too, Rose?'

'What happened to you, Mister Bob?'

'Oh, no, all good now. Little Lola got knocked out. She's in hospital recovering. What about you?'

It dawned on Rose their relationship had transitioned from a mentor one to a friendship one. *Almost,* she thought, *a father-type one but where I can share so much more than I ever could with my father.* And she needed that since she'd been isolated from her family.

'Aaron got a bad sting. Had a shock and had to go to hospital. He is okay now. But could die if happens again, Mister Bob.'

'What sting?'

'Like a bee this time, but any sting they say is really bad. They say I need – let me look at word – Epi-Pen?'

'Can you get one then?'

'Oh, I will save for it.'

After all this time, Bob had not breached the subject of a house for Rose, in spite of both his wife and daughter being supportive. Rose never asked for money, nor anything else, but he knew she struggled in a constant battle to keep her finances above board. Having to save for an Epi-pen? Of course, he'd transfer more funds. He'd made her show him her cash flow chart from the shop from time to time. Its size and location were limitations, together with a single operator, who was also a single mum.

It is time. 'Rose, we've been thinking, rather than, perhaps, expanding your business, what do you think of owning your own home?'

He heard a gasp. 'What do you mean?'

He went through the logic espoused originally by Charmaine.

'I often dream of shop with apartment above, but I pay rent for shop and rent for apartment and never two together. I have never owned anything.'

'I'm going to leave you to think about it, Rose. Perhaps a budget of some sixty thousand Australian dollars?'

'Oh, Mister Bob.'

'Go think about it, Rose. And keep smiling.'

Apart from Mister Bob, Rose trusted no one. But he didn't understand what life was like in the Philippines, especially for a single mother trying to run a small business. She was a magnet to men, even though she deliberately wore a wedding ring. She now understood why she had been successfully recruited into sex trafficking. Many of her male customers hung around longer than they needed to, and plied her with compliments. They'd tell her she looked like a teenager even though they knew she had three children. Word was out that she was on her own, and they'd often ask how her business was going. Naturally, she always talked it up, even when it wasn't quite true. She longed for a companion, but none of her would-be suitors made her heart flutter. She made lots of friends, mainly through her shop, but relationships never went beyond chatting with them. And she would die from shame and humiliation if anyone discovered her past.

When a past memory of life in Thailand arose, Rose would

throw herself into her work, or prattle on aimlessly with a customer till those images disappeared. She kept her children close, worked hard long hours and hoped for more, now she believed one day soon she'd own her own home. But were all her losses worth it? She missed her parents and her sister the most. How would they react to this news?

Converted to Philippine pesos, Mister Bob had given her a sizeable amount for a house or apartment. She spent all her spare time searching online. If only she could find a place where she could open a shop underneath. Imagine as the children got older not needing to close and go home. The girls could do more to relieve in the shop. The idea took root, but she realised, after much research that she would need to move to a different area to find the combination within the budget.

'What you think?' she said to Mister Bob during their next conversation.

'Where are you considering?' Bob opened Google Maps, trying to follow Rose's suggestions. 'It means nothing to me, but a few things to look for would be to check that it doesn't flood, and check there's not too much competition business-wise. See if you can find an agent you can trust to start looking for you, Rose.'

Rose knew Mister Bob liked to use the face-to-face app. It chewed up a lot more of her data, but she also enjoyed watching him as he leaned back in his home office chair, and rubbed his head. 'That's a funny habit,' she said, laughing.

'More ideas get released, he said. 'Well, that's what Denise thinks.'

She and Bob discussed the properties she had inspected, month after month, till she finally saw a place in a developing area a considerable distance from her shop and home.

'It was built by a proper builder,' she explained. 'Some are not. Ground and two levels above, but you can build more levels on top if wanted.'

'Oh, they do that in Egypt too,' Bob said, recalling his days as a tourist. 'When a child marries, they simply build on to the family home.'

'One day, maybe Jazz or Iris.' Rose shook her head. That far ahead she could not imagine.

'You must send me photos and the link, Rose.'

'Mister Bob,' she said hesitantly, 'it is over budget. But it already has shop in front. No flooding. Three schools near. Trike hub.'

'What's that mean?' Bob interrupted.

'The riders gather there to pick up fares and the customers change trikes. Go to other territories. Riders have their own territories.'

'There's so much I don't know. What businesses are around?'

'Shopping centre streets away. Not like big ones. Like just stalls both sides of the street. Car repair. Honey factory. Stuff like that.'

'Send me everything you can, Rose.'

Each time Rose visited the property with the agent, she had to travel over an hour each way. She decided to be thorough this time and take a heap of photos as well as videos. She also took the children. The property was vacant, so they ran around claiming rooms for themselves. This amused Rose, since, in spite of having two bedrooms at their rental, the girls often chose, still, to sleep with their mother.

When the photos appeared online, Bob saw a solid concrete block structure with a basic interior. The floors were a mixture of tiles and timber. The concrete-floored bathroom consisted of the hole-in-the-floor toilet and the shower head on the pipe on the un-enclosed wall. There was another hole in the floor for drainage. He reminded himself that this was normal for Rose and her family, as was using a bucket and dipper. The kitchen displayed open, pine shelving in the kitchen – another norm.

The detached shop in the front was constructed of concrete blocks, unpainted, and the front lined up with the street.

Bob turned to Google Maps, and found the location, went exploring, then switched to satellite view.

He saw it was ten thousand dollars over budget.

This way, no shop rental, Mister Bob, Rose optimistically pointed out.

That evening after dinner, Bob emailed Rose.

> *So Rose, we have all looked at the photos. It's quite colourful, isn't it. We all conferred. If you think it's suitable, then so do we. It's all systems go. But don't sign anything. Send me a copy of the contract. And make sure it's in English.*
>
> *Do you have a conveyancer or settlement agent, or someone who represents your interests to make sure it's all legal and above board?*

Rose quickly responded, even though it was late on Friday night.

> *The agent introduced me to a man who will do all for me and get title, and only cost about 3,000 pesos.*

Warning bells rang for Bob when he read that. His quick currency conversion in his head said this worked out less than one hundred Australian dollars. *Ridiculous.* So he quickly sent back:

> *Just wait, Rose. I might get the Sisters of Good Grace to help again.*

Rose sighed with relief. So much cheating and fraud, and how would she tell? This was such a huge decision.

When Bob read this he wondered what the hell he was doing communicating through email. He instantly called Rose on the app.

'Of course, I'll come, Rose. I'll make arrangements and let you know.'

The next morning he rang Charmaine in her office. She had located to another building entirely to run the jewellery business. There was no room for expansion in Bob's offices, and he didn't want to move. But they'd thought it important that the OTM jewellery be located not too far from the BM spectacle and optometry store, so they were in walking distance of each other.

Charmaine came to him, arriving on the first floor via the personal lift he'd installed a few years earlier.

'So, what's up?' she asked, striding into his office, heels clicking.

'Rose. Property. Will you come up to Manila with me? As soon as we can.' He reiterated what Rose had said about settlement.

'I can work it in with a trip to see Arthit again if you like.'

'Okay, get Georgina to book us tickets. Can you stay there three days?'

'Really? Sure.'

Bob wouldn't admit to anyone his growing concern about travelling alone. His brain, he deduced, was fine, but his balance was not.

Relief flooded through Rose's blood like a shot of meth when Mister Bob told her he was coming and Charmaine would accompany him. She couldn't take the day off to meet them, but they would go straight away to meet her agent at the property. It was a long drive, she knew, from their hotel. Roads were always crowded. As the crows fly, it was only half an hour. She chastised herself for not warning them.

Sister Hailee, Bob told her, had recommended an English-speaking solicitor.

Rose waited impatiently for a message from Mister Bob to say everything had gone smoothly, but the more time that passed, the more concerned she became; she wondered if she'd have to start the house search all over again. She tried to keep her mind distracted, chatting with her regulars longer than normal.

In the late afternoon, her phone app made its unique sound.

With a slow and soft voice, Bob began, 'It's all done, Rose. It took time to understand all the different rules and regulations, but I think we've covered all bases. The contract is ready for you to see.'

'Oh, Mister Bob.' She heaved a sigh of relief. 'You don't know how happy you've made me. You are so kind.'

'I'm just organising the deposit. I'll see you at the hotel for dinner tonight and fill you in then. I'm in the car heading back to the hotel to rest this poor old body and let my brain have a rest after that lot.'

After the meal, Charmaine excused herself, leaving her father alone with Rose.

'We've come a long way from those days in Bangkok, haven't we, Rose?' he reminisced. Rose appeared younger than ever, dressed in a black and white polka dot dress with a wide belt clinching her tiny waist, and a touch of lipstick on her mouth. She rewarded Bob with her warm smile and a gentle 'Mmm,' and stroked the back of his hand that rested on the table.

'Do you have nightmares about any of it?'

'Sometimes I do. The drugs, the escape. Especially the escape. Out that window. But I wake and touch one of my children. They are always there. They still sleep with me.' She laughed. 'They do not want me out of sight.'

'What was growing up at home like?'

Rose's eyes wandered around the walls while she collected her words. 'When I was little, I slept with Mum and Dad and Annlyn. It was normal.' She stared up over Bob's head. 'I miss them all,' she confessed, fiddling with her bracelet.

'Well, can't you make contact with your sister?'

'She is not talking to me.'

'How long since you tried to talk to her?'

Rose looked thoughtful. 'Mmm. I will try again soon. Maybe she got jealous about the house.'

'So she knows?'

'She knows I was looking.'

'You should be able to move in a couple of weeks. Have you got someone to help?'

'My cousin, Joshua. He will carry everything to the shop for me. Maybe if Annlyn will talk, maybe I ask her and her husband too.'

'Is he working?'

The waiter came by, but Bob signalled to leave them alone for now.

Rose sipped her club soda. 'He gets work sometimes. He is clever with his hands. I need to fix up the shop so it is secure. He could do it. Place to cook food and sell. Oh, Mister Bob, I am so excited. You are so good to me. I will make enough money. You will be proud of me.'

'I already am, Rose. I'll come up and visit once you've settled in and got the shop up and running to see it all.'

'And now you must tell me what is happening with your Parkinson's. You listen to all my problems, but I see it is difficult for you.'

'So noticeable, huh? I had to wear a monitor, it was just a kind of watch, called a PKG. No, don't ask, I can't remember what it stands for, but what it told the neurologist is that I sort of fade out in the afternoons. Not that I needed to wear something to know that.'

'You get tired?'

'And a bit unstable. Or more unstable. So I'm supposed to rest.'

'And here I am keeping you up.'

'No, I only need to rest for an hour or two max mid-afternoon.' He slowly sipped his wine. 'Georgina protects me if I fall asleep at my desk, which I do sometimes.'

'I'll make sure we look after you better when you come next time. Do you still play your golf?'

Bob signalled the waiter for a refill for himself and Rose. 'None of that. But I exercise at the gym twice a week with my physio. Even a bit of shadow boxing.'

Rose chuckled. 'I'd like to see that.'

Bob smiled back. 'No, you mustn't laugh – although I must look a sight. I'm losing a bit of weight, you know. Well, two kilos gone.' He patted his still-firm paunch.

'Are you worried, Mister Bob?'

'What about?'

'You know. Getting worse?'

'I worry I might break a bone when I fall over. And I fall over a bit, Rose. But the more you succeed up here, the less worried I'll become. Your success is my success.'

'Are you happy?'

'You make me happy, Rose. If I don't smile much it's because my muscles don't work in my face. It's all a bit of a shit really. But what can you do?'

Chapter 22

Rose missed her sister. She relished her memories of their childhood together, which she found herself revisiting regularly during quiet times at work. They had experienced a simple and relatively carefree life in a basic house, much like all their neighbours. They had responsibilities, like feeding the hens, sweeping, disposing of rubbish, learning to help in the house. They attended school together right up till they were fourteen. They wore only thongs on their feet, as did most of the others. The walk to and from school took them more than thirty minutes, and they sometimes explored the streets around their school after it had finished in spite of their mother insisting they must always come straight home.

Rose, in her loneliness, and searching those memories of happier times for solace found one particular disturbing episode she and Annlyn had shared all those years ago. It kept raising itself like a screaming baby, demanding to be attended to. What had really happened? What did it mean? The time had come to call Annlyn and make peace. The time had also come to try to understand just what they'd been through together all those years ago.

She asked Annlyn to visit. They smiled tentatively at each other and Rose made coffee, but avoided mentioning the split in the relationship for the last couple of years. Instead, she launched in with, 'Do you remember as kids when we'd wag school and go to that man's house and clean it for money?'

Annlyn's mouth gaped. 'What? Oh, you mean that man with

the puckered lips. Mr Poo-face. What about him?' Rose was grateful Annlyn's voice held strength and acceptance.

'Do you realise now what a dangerous situation we'd put ourselves in?' It was a huge relief to Rose they were talking normally again. 'I didn't know at the time but I do now. I remember how he promised to pay us double if we worked wearing just our nickers after the first visit. Came up with some nonsense about the heat. I can't believe our behaviour, Annlyn. How we didn't end up as his prisoners, or worse, I don't know. We were just kids. So young. So innocent. No one would have found us.'

Annlyn, stirred up by Rose's recall of Mr Poo-face, became animated. 'When he chased us, that was some escape, Rose, me shoving you out the window then jumping myself. I remember we laughed, but it wasn't funny. I was scared.'

'In hindsight, we should have told someone.'

'Well, Mum and Dad would have killed us if they knew.'

'Or killed Mr Poo-face.'

Now they'd broken through the years of impasse, Rose said, 'Oh, Annlyn, I've so missed you.'

'Me too.'

'Let's meet up on Sunday. Bring the kids. We've got a lovely local park.'

The following Sunday after Mass, Rose explained to Hazel she planned to meet her sister and needed some private time with her, but all the children could play together.

Recognising her sister walking across the park with her two girls following, Rose leapt up and ran to her. They threw their arms around each other, cheeks touching, tears combining. When they detached, each hugged the other's children. Aaron stiffened to Annlyn's touch.

'You used to love my cuddles,' she teased.

When the children ran off with the basketball, the sisters silently wandered, slowly, arm in arm, towards a vacant bench.

After catching up on family news, Annlyn said, 'What made you think of Mr Poo-face?'

Rose swung her body so she faced her sister. Their knees touched. She clasped both Annlyn's hands in hers, squeezed them, and, looking into her eyes, said, 'A couple of Mr Poo-faces got me, Annlyn.'

Annlyn frowned. 'I don't understand? Not your Mister Bob?'

'No, no. He saved me.'

Rose shared, for the first time, just a brief sample of some of her shocking early experiences, beginning with her captors, Mr Wang, Mr Wong and Mr Lee, and her co-prisoners, Angel and Princess, Maria and Marisol. The horror and then the distress Rose saw on her sister's face made her hesitate and pull back. She silently used her thumb to swipe away the tears on Annlyn's cheeks. Realising her disclosure was too much for her sister to absorb any further, she decided to leave the episodes of the enforced drugs and her captors' selling of her to another monster, and the ensuing violence for another day.

Thoughts about her extraordinary escape through a window from such extreme violence had brought back the memories of Mr Poo-face. But she'd explore more with Annlyn another day. Nothing but relief flowed through her body now she had her sister back.

One month later Rose relinquished her month-to-month tenancy of her shop and packed up the merchandise. As Rose had never driven a vehicle, her cousin Joshua, equipped with a driver's licence, stepped in to help load up the truck she'd rented before driving it to her apartment where they loaded on the pieces of furniture, along with her other meagre belongings stuffed into garbage bags. The children had left their school, ready to start anew. They all piled into the rental truck and headed off.

Jasmin and Iris helped with the unpacking while Aaron went out through the gate to explore the neighbourhood.

Kids played in the street. Next door a boy Aaron's age dribbled a basketball.

'He'll be right,' Rose said to the girls, returning through the gates after checking on him.

Once the truck was unloaded, Rose's cousin inspected the shop at the front. The empty shell measured about five metres by five metres with power and water connected and a door onto raised concrete outside before the step down to the street.

'Have you thought about what you want?' he asked, pad, pencil and tape measure in hand.

'I think I'll let those who want to eat here come into the yard if the weather's okay. I'll put out some tables and chairs. But one bench and a few stools in the store. In fine weather, I'll cook outside. Just the rice cooker and slow cooker.' Rose had a clear vision. I need the fridge and freezer inside for drinks and ice blocks. I'll need shelves and maybe more display cabinets.'

'What about security? I see there are already bars on the windows. Want to sprinkle broken glass along the top of the concrete layer on the fence?'

'That's a bit grim.'

'Easy to do. And keep your family safe.'

They were busy times. They were happy times. Aaron walked to the local school with other children. The two girls took a trike to a bus stop to attend a secondary school. They did their homework in the bus on the way home so they could do their chores once home.

A steady flow of customers on their way to work or school arrived at *Rose's Place* from 5 am to 9 am. A mid-morning lull followed, before the lunch crowd arrived, mostly workers from local factories and businesses.

Annlyn popped in occasionally to visit. On one visit mid-morning, as she and Rose stood in the shop drinking coffee, a skinny, stooped woman with a limp came in. 'How much for a bowl of rice?' she asked, holding out a handful of coins.

'Twenty-five pesos.' Rose saw the customer count all her coins which amounted to eighteen pesos.

'Here, sit down.' Rose pointed to the stool and doled out rice into a bowl from the huge rice cooker. 'No, keep your money,' she said gently, closing the customer's hand over her paltry coins.

'I remember hunger,' Rose whispered to her sister.

Annlyn nodded before collecting a couple of tubs of instant noodles from the shelf and throwing them in a bag. 'I'm off.'

'What's that husband of yours up to now? Picked up more work?'

'He hangs out at the docks. Piecemeal stuff.'

The sisters gave each other a peck on the cheek as Annlyn departed. Rose watched her climb into a trike out on the concrete roadway. *That useless husband of hers*, Rose thought, *gets between Annlyn and me. Stirs things up. Nasty man. Well, he had been friends with Ramil, my own cowardly husband, so what else could I expect!*

Rose's frail customer beckoned her over. 'Do you get busy? Do you need help? I'm very good at cooking and cleaning.'

Rose parked herself on the bench and introduced herself. 'I do get busy. But I'm new here and can't afford to hire anyone. I'm sorry.'

'I'm Mirikit. I used to work in a restaurant, but I had an accident. I'm fixed now.' Rose saw the scars from burns on Mirikit's weak leg. 'I just need a chance. What if I worked for no money, but you feed me?'

Rose hesitated. What harm could this woman do? She

wouldn't be a threat to her or her children, and Rose could
certainly do with help early in the morning when the children
were getting ready for school and the shop ran full-steam ahead.
Rose always started preparations at 4 am so the food, which the
children also ate for breakfast, was ready for the first customers.

'Tell you what,' Rose suggested, 'if you can be here by 4 am
tomorrow, I'll show you the ropes and you can eat here all day
tomorrow in return for your help.'

And so Mirikit, who became known as Merry, elbowed her
way into Rose's life and Rose's family, so much so, she also
moved in to the house. Rose had no regrets. Board and food in
return for work from 4 am to 2 pm five days a week. And the
food selection improved into the bargain.

More trike riders now chose to eat at *Rose's Place* — partly
because of Merry's contribution. Another reason was to enjoy
each other's company in a shady and friendly environment. But
the greatest reason for these highly fit men was their attraction
to Rose. She enjoyed the attention they gave her but never let
the flirting go too far. She was alert to their belief that, by their
standards, she was a wealthy single woman.

Willie was her favourite customer and she'd occasionally sit
and have a cup of coffee with him, as she did now, under the
huge mango tree behind the store.

'Would you like to come and see a movie with me?' he asked.
'*Three Billboards Outside Ebbing* looks great.'

Rose grimaced. She was tempted. A bit of her yearned for
male companionship, but her brain took her to past experiences
and told her to steer away. The only decent male she could think
of was her Mister Bob. *Besides*, she thought, *I am married, and
nothing good can come of a new relationship.*

'Well?' he prompted her for a reply. 'What are you thinking
about?'

'Oh Willie, that's so nice of you. But I have responsibilities.'

He reached across the table and took her hand. She reacted as though she'd received an electric shock, and Willie withdrew his touch instantly.

'I'm sorry, Rose. I didn't mean to offend.'

'You're a good friend, Willie, but can we leave it at that?'

Just as life tootled along kindly for Rose, with happy children and the business doing well, Annlyn arrived with news.

'Ramil is back. He knows where you are, Rose. And you know what that means. He has claim to this house.' Annlyn spread her arms in a wide-sweeping semi-circle. 'And his children.'

'He'll have to kill me first. And Mister Bob after me,' Rose's chilled voice declared. *Ramil won't want his children. He ran from them. But the property?* She clenched her fists and her jaw. 'I going to ring Mister Bob.'

'He can't save you or your house this time, Rose. It's the law you know. Husbands own all the property.'

'You told him our address, didn't you?'

'He came to us. It wasn't me though.'

Rose turned her back on her sister and called Mister Bob on her app.

'Rose,' he said, 'lovely to hear your voice. What's happening?'

After Rose explained, he said, 'Well, you know what to say to him if he shows up. Are you frightened? Do you want me to fly up?'

'That's too much.'

'Be strong. Firm. Assertive, Rose. Call Sister Hailee if you need urgent help. Let me know the outcome?'

As if summonsed by this emergency phone call, Rose turned towards the road to see Ramil step off a trike driven by one of her friends. Annlyn stood beside Rose and watched as Ramil approached, arms outstretched, looking to give Rose a hug and a kiss. She stretched both arms out in front of her, her palms facing out, preventing him from closing in on her.

'Aren't you going to greet me and ask what I've been doing?' he said boldly. 'I can already see what you've been doing. And with someone rich. You *slut*!'

Rose felt her neck and face flush with anger. With her hand gripping her neck, she took a few deep breaths telling herself to be calm. 'You cannot claim any of this,' she hissed. 'And you can leave now.'

He sneered. 'You think? Not likely. By law, you know this is all mine now, you bitch.' He stood square on, close to her, his arms folded.

'Let me show you who owns this property,' Rose said angrily, adding, 'and it's not me.'

'What are you talking about?'

'I'll get the papers.' She turned about-face and strode off. She acted a lot stronger than she felt as she tried to control her weak knees. But Mister Bob said it would work.

She ran back down the steps of the house with the documents in her hand, and thrust them at Ramil. 'Here, read that, you derelict monster.' She folded her arms and waited for a response.

He read the first page. 'What's this shit? My kids own this?'

'No, they don't. It's being held in trust for them till Aaron turns twenty-two, and then all three of them own it. Under the law, you have no rights to their property. You cannot touch the trust in the meantime. I own nothing.'

Sarcastically, she added, 'Just like I did when I lived with you.' She wished she'd had her phone recorder on to catch the startled look on his face. She never dreamt this moment would happen, but it gave her enormous satisfaction, and she felt chuffed that Annlyn had witnessed it. Annlyn would report back to her husband, who, no doubt, was the one who disclosed Rose's whereabouts and circumstances.

'You've not heard the end of this,' Ramil said, shoving the

documents back at her before walking out, a scowl decorating his weather-beaten face. 'Want a ride back, Annlyn?' he shouted over his shoulder.

'No thanks.'

Merry had been handling customers in the shop – mostly regulars – but there was a general sense among them that all was not well outside under the mango tree. When Ramil disappeared, one of the trike riders came around the side of the shop to check on Rose.

'I'm fine thanks, Willie.' She continued to be careful not to encourage him romantically but appreciated his concern.

The children would be returning from school soon. They brought normality and purpose to her life. She shook her head to clear the shock of seeing Ramil again.

After checking Merry could handle the shop for a while, Rose took Annlyn into the kitchen on the ground floor while she prepared the children's lunch from the food taken from the shop. The children had been gone since 5.30 am.

'Are you going to tell the kids their father just visited?'

'Do you see him even bothering to ask after them? Showing any interest? Bet he'll be back though, once he's taken in the fact that, one day, they'll own all this.' She waved the spoon in her hand widely.

'You and your Mister Bob really do have it all tied up. He must have found out about our laws to have set it up so safely. Tell me, Rose, be honest, what is it with you two?'

'Not now, Annlyn. Let's have this conversation another time.' The children burst into the house, ate quickly, then, with no encouragement, went straight to do their homework.

Walking back out to the shop with Rose, Annlyn said, 'How do you get them to do that without asking?'

'Ah, Mister Bob says education is the answer. He gets all their report cards. And we try to practise speaking English at home.

He says it's really important for them to speak it properly, not just learn it at school.'

Annlyn sat on a vacant stool and watched Rose with the customers. Some of the local schoolchildren who'd finished the early shift were eating before they walked or triked home. Rose lifted down a small packet of crisps, turned and, with a smile, raised her eyebrows at one of the young children. The returned smile confirmed she had remembered the child's favourite food. 'There you go, Jessa.' She knew all their names too.

When the lull came, Merry left to take a break, lying on the mattress in her room, with the fan beside her set on high.

After Rose and Annlyn cleaned up, Annlyn again persisted in finding out more about Mister Bob.

'I've told you what happened to me,' Rose began.

'Not very much of it. Tell me about meeting Mister Bob.'

'I used to tell almost every man who hired me I'd been kidnapped. There were hundreds of them, Annlyn.' Seeing Annlyn's jaw drop, Rose added, 'You cannot begin to imagine. I don't really want to talk about it, but most didn't care. They bought my body to play with. They thought I was a teenager or something.' Again she saw her sister's shocked look. 'Well, my youthful looks apparently appealed to them. Gross, I know. I'm tiny and look young. But I couldn't make much money because I refused to do certain things …,' Rose's voice held an iron strength, '… even though some were violent and forced me.'

Annlyn wiped her eyes with the back of her hand. 'Oh, Rose.'

'No more tears, my love.' Rose reached over and put both her arms around her sister. "No pity. My life has turned a corner and that is thanks to Mister Bob.'

Chapter 23

The end of semester arrived – the end of the school year – which meant a long holiday break too. Rose had heard no more from Ramil. He showed no interest in his children during these holidays, much to Rose's relief. She didn't know what he was doing, and hushed Annlyn when she tried to tell her.

She read each of the children's report cards before scanning them and emailing them for Mister Bob's perusal and comments. *He should be impressed. I am.* Jazz had come second overall in her classes and Iris topped many of her subjects. Even Aaron excelled, especially in the English language.

Compliments of Mister Bob, the family now shared a computer, scanner and printer. Rose was grateful for the large desktop monitor as her phone had been her only online source and her eyesight troubled her. She secretly hoped for a call from Mister Bob once he'd read the reports so she could discuss Jasmin's future education now the results were in. Any further schooling had to be paid for, as it was only free to year ten. And Jazz had told her she wanted to go to university.

Twenty-four hours passed with no word. Rose worried, but decided not to appear super keen or expectant, so she waited.

The call finally came. 'Sorry, Rose. I had a bit of a fall. Denise called an ambulance, and I was out of it for a while. Back on deck now.'

'Are you on a boat?' Rose asked, even more troubled.

His soft chuckle gave comfort. 'Just a saying – means I'm all better. Rose, these report cards are excellent. I've shown them to Denise. She says a reward is in order for all of you. What do you think everyone would like?'

'No, Mister Bob. First, tell me how you fell. It makes me sad to hear.' Her mind went into overdrive. What if something happened to him? How would she manage? How bad was this disease he had? How awful was she to think about herself?

'I certainly don't want to make you sad. In retrospect, I was an inelegant sight, to say the least. One you don't want to imagine. On the bathroom floor after my shower. Banged my head. But let's get back to talking rewards.'

'And you're all better? What can you do so it doesn't happen again?'

'Since you ask, I'm thinking about brain surgery. What happens is that my feet actually freeze, but I keep going. I'm like this big tree falling in the bush. Crrrash!'

'And will that surgery fix it? It sounds scary.'

'Not entirely. It'll just help produce more dopamine. That's …' But Bob realised explaining the neurotransmitter and what it does, together with stimulating parts of the subthalamic nucleus to stimulate the dopamine was almost beyond his comprehension, little less someone without a broad knowledge of English. 'Let's talk about some kind of treat for you and the children. I'll let you know if I decide to have an operation.'

Bob reached for his scotch, but realised he didn't have one. No drinking for a bit. Instead, he opened his desk drawer and broke off a bit of dark chocolate to pop in his mouth.

'What kind of treat you have in mind?'

'Oh, I don't know – what about a weekend at the beach?'

'I can't shut the shop, Mister Bob. But nice idea. Maybe – can I talk to you about something else – another type of reward?' Rose pondered if this was the right time, given Mister Bob was recovering from a bang in the head. But she forged ahead, explaining again about the education system, and about Jasmin's ambitions.

'I'm sure we can help Jasmin, but what about Iris and Aaron?'

'Maybe we all go for a special dinner?'

'It's a while since I've seen you all. Maybe I'll come too. I can see your shop in operation and your house being lived in.'

'We would love that, Mister Bob.'

'I'll let you know. And how much for another year of school for Jasmin?' When Rose told him in pesos, he worked out that was only about one thousand dollars. 'I think she'll need her own laptop too.'

'Should you check with Ma'am Denise?'

'Ah, she's powerfully behind educating girls. You know that.'

They terminated the call with Rose floating in a world of plus signs and positivity. She couldn't wait to tell the children.

Bob snuck another square of dark chocolate from his desk drawer, savouring its richness. His world was being taken over by women, and he relished the experience. He had acquiesced to Denise's suggestion to begin training Charmaine in the management of his optometry business. But he had no intention of letting go of the reins any time soon. Charmaine had well and truly proven herself with her contemporary ideas for the jewellery business and he had no doubt, given the opportunity, she'd be introducing them to optometry soon.

He worked shorter days, sure, but he was still on top of it even if his energy ran low at times. He was determined, in spite of it all, to pay a visit to Rose.

'C'mon, Dad. I'll call in there with you when I next see Arthit.'

Bob hated to admit the amount of help he was compelled to accept to travel, but his inexplicable desire to see Rose made him swallow his pride.

True to her word, Charmaine escorted her father from home

to their hotel in Manila where he rested till the following day when the hotel limo drove him to *Rose's Place*.

Rose had lined up her children, as well as Annlyn and her two girls, along with the trikers who were not busy, to welcome her Mister Bob. Refusing Willie's helping hand, he stepped slowly from the vehicle and stood amid the balloons and streamers that hung everywhere.

In an act of spontaneity, Bob said, 'Let's all celebrate by having lunch together.'

Everyone looked at each other in amazement.

'Oh, but we can't. We all work, Mister Bob.'

'Well, let's have caterers in here now for those who can stay. Rose, ring and order heaps for all of us. No limits. Go!'

Charmaine, having been introduced to everyone, along with her father, smiled benevolently and nodded her approval. Within an hour a service vehicle with trestles and cloths and chairs set up under the trees. Then along came the food.

The neighbours had come out to see what all the fuss was about.

'Invite them in too, Rose. Plenty to share.'

Rose watched with delight as all the neighbourhood children on holidays revelled in the deep-fried chicken and fizzy drinks. *That's my Mister Bob*, she thought.

While they feasted, Bob said to Rose, 'Can you give me a quick tour of your house?'

She led him across the yard to the front door, quietly nodding to Willie and his mate to follow. They walked around the ground floor which housed the kitchen and living areas. Bob insisted on going up the stairs to the next level, where some bedrooms and the bathroom was. Rose stood back to let Willie walk beside Bob, and Willie's friend followed close behind. When Bob saw the basic bathroom hadn't changed, he decided he'd get it upgraded in the future.

Coming down the stairs was more complex. Willie caught on quickly and walked in front of Bob, so if he fell forward Willie could brace him while his mate walked beside so Bob could put his hand on his shoulder. Bob threw one leg out in front, then allowed himself to drop. It was an exhausting venture, but one Rose acknowledged he was determined to achieve.

Bob expressed his gratitude to his helpers. Rose silently expressed relief.

The tour of the shop was, by comparison, quick and simple, till Bob ventured off, shuffling down the rickety roadway on his own. Seeing this, Charmaine called quietly to Rose. Again, Rose signalled Willie and his mate, who both escorted him. She watched from the shop as passers-by turned to look at the tubby, bald westerner staggering about with two local escorts; she turned to Charmaine. 'He doesn't mind the attention, does he?'

'That's my father.'

Rose had never felt happier. She was surrounded by all those who cared about her. Grinning, she said, 'Mister Bob deserves the attention.'

Charmaine laughed. 'Nothing will stop him. But I should get him back to the hotel for a rest. Will you join us for dinner at the hotel?'

Over dinner, they discussed business. 'Rose, the next step in building up business for you is to borrow against your house and branch out into something new. You use the house as collateral to start a new business.'

Shocked at the suggestion, Rose said, 'The bank would laugh at me.'

'Not at all. You'd be surprised.'

Rose stared at him. 'And you say another business? As well as the shop?'

'How about buying a vehicle and becoming an Uber driver, or a taxi, or maybe dedicate yourself to a hotel?'

'But I don't even drive.' She put her knife and fork down and shook her head in amazement. *Surely, he is joking?*

'Well, not yet. But you could find a driver, couldn't you? Come to some sort of financial arrangement – maybe with one of your trike riders?'

Rose looked across at Charmaine to see if she thought Mister Bob was serious. The reply consisted of a smile and a nod in return.

'Let the idea sit for a while, Rose, and if the idea grabs you, start investigating. Begin a new business plan. Cost of loan repayments, cost of running the vehicle, cost of a driver. All of that. We can talk more on the phone later. But the girls are getting older and can help Merry more in the shop too, can't they?'

Bob returned to Sydney, utterly exhausted. The next time he wanted to see Rose, he decided she'd have to come to Australia. Overseas travel was a step too far. As well as working part-time, he kept up his weekly Lions' meetings. He went to monthly lunches at the golf club with his buddies. He attended the gym with his specialist instructor twice a week. He communicated regularly with Rose, either by email or by Facetime.

'Mister Bob,' she said, beaming at him from his computer monitor one evening, 'I visited the bank. They were not all that helpful or nice to me, so I went to another bank. They were different, and explained things. You would be so proud of me. I have all the documents to read and fill in. Can I send them to you to go over?'

This was no chore for Bob. No one was going to take advantage of Rose again if he could help it.

A couple of months later, in early 2019, after many discussions over the previous months, Rose called Bob from outside her store. 'Look, look at me, Mister Bob,' she said, laughing loudly, as she sat on the bonnet of a fire engine red Toyota Vios, one arm thrown in the air.

Bob roared with laughter seeing her posing like a movie star on the screen in front of him. 'Well, they'll certainly see you coming, Rose, with that colour car.'

'I will find customers. Willie will drive. I trust him. I will get my driver's licence and then we share the driving.'

'I know you will do this well, Rose. These are exciting times for you.' He paused and looked serious. 'How serious is it with Willie?'

Rose blushed. 'Oh, no, Mister Bob. You have it all wrong. Nothing going on.'

'Didn't look like it to me.' He grinned.

Rose was well supported in her little community when the neighbours left her fresh fruit from their trees in return for her tiny favours such as delivering when they were unwell. But finding enough business for her *Red Rocket,* as she'd named her car, was harder than she thought. Willie's connections were not in the same league as those customers who would hire a car and driver for a day or part thereof. And learning to drive in Manila to Rose was akin to balancing on the edge of a cliff top in a high wind. She was sure she left nail prints in the steering wheel each time.

She finally passed the test, but her anxiety level stayed balanced on that cliff edge.

One regular job she picked up was a three-times-a-week delivery of an esky of fresh seafood from a wholesaler to a restaurant. All they asked was reliability, so if Rose had another commitment such as taking one of the children to the dentist, Willie stepped in. Any jobs he found were his.

Rose preferred transporting people rather than goods. From her Bangkok experiences she had gained confidence and become adept at dealing with and connecting with passengers, not to mention contracting prices. She made her passengers feel at ease by fussing over them and chatting with ease.

Through a contact she'd made at a nearby hotel, she picked up one of their clients at the hotel front door under the porte cochere. As usual, leaving the air conditioning on high, she ran around from behind the wheel to the passenger side to introduce herself and help him into the back, while pointing out the complimentary bottle of water and sealed hand refresher.

He slowly eased himself into the seat. Not as slowly as Mister Bob, she noted, and this guy was much bigger and just as bald. He wore suit pants, pink business shirt with the top button undone and pink striped silk tie hanging. She'd learnt long ago to notice such things. A quick assessment told her he should tip generously. She took his jacket from him and hung it on the hook. He ignored all Rose's words and actions and didn't divulge his name.

Fair enough, Rose thought. But, in spite of his ignorance, she decided she'd still try to converse with him while they travelled the long distance to his destination. She used her GPS navigation to guide the way.

Because he hadn't said a word, Rose had no idea what language he spoke. He appeared western, and not Asian. *Here we go,* she thought, and said in English, which she'd been using prior, 'May I guess where you're from?' She paused to give him time to respond.

Nothing.

'American?'

'Ah, Rose Petal, you guessed it in one.'

In shock, with thoughts of her past life in Bangkok scrambling through her head, Rose hit the accelerator instead of the brake. *Who is he? What does it mean?* As though she'd been attacked by a thousand knives, she flew through a tee intersection, and smashed head-on into a concrete block fence. The screaming, crunching metal noise terrified her. Her airbag activated. Her head jerked forward into it, hurting her face. Smoke rose from the engine. *Oh, no! Oh, no! What have I done?* she thought. Then she suddenly remembered she had a passenger. And not just any passenger.

Having crumpled the airbag, she turned her head. *Ouch*, she thought as she touched her face, tenderly checking it. She turned to the back seat. 'Are you alright?'

'Crazy whore! Call me another vehicle now!'

A sense of relief overcame her as she watched him open the door, grab his jacket, and step out, uninjured. *Hopefully he's not just out of my car but out of my life, whoever the hell he is,* she thought. Those who understood her passenger's English, moved away from him, as a crowd gathered trying to help her out.

But her door was jammed.

Through the open back door, she could hear the American ranting. 'Someone just call me a fuckin' taxi and get me the fuck away from this crazy slut.'

Ignoring him, a woman climbed into the back seat and touched Rose's shoulder. In Tagalog she asked Rose if she was hurt. Rose tried to move her legs. Relief. They both seemed okay. A man from outside yelled to her, 'Turn the ignition off, quickly.' That action would never have occurred to Rose.

Her new backseat passenger encouraged Rose to try to manoeuvre herself out and over the front seats. Slowly she drew herself up and, contorting her body, she slithered over into the back seat and out of the car with the help of bystanders. Thankfully she wore long shorts for modesty. Someone guided her to sit down on some of the concrete blocks she'd knocked out of the wall.

She watched, still stunned, but somewhat relieved, as the American climbed into another vehicle. She then turned her attention to her *Red Rocket*. Her next thought was, *what will Mister Bob say?* She was almost devoid of emotion, feeling numb, not just from the accident, but also from having been exposed. Or had she?

Police appeared and asked for her licence. Her lovely rescuer lady clambered back into the vehicle where she retrieved Rose's papers from the glove box and her phone from a stand where the GPS was still screening.

The owners of the smashed fence demanded details from her. Still numb, Rose complied with the requests made of her without speaking. When the crowd dispersed and everything calmed down, she gathered her thoughts, and with prompting from her original helper, she rang Willie, who organised a tow truck and a ride home for her.

That evening, with some trepidation, Rose called Mister Bob on her app to report the accident. But his only concern was her and her welfare.

'Oh, I'm a bit battered and sore, but okay.'

'And the car?'

'They say a write-off. But it's insured.'

'Follow through on that, won't you, Rose?'

Months passed. Rose continued to pay the bank for the loan on the *Red Rocket,* which was drawing zero income but the insurance had not paid her out.

'What do I do, Mister Bob?'

'Look up the insurer and visit them personally, Rose. Don't leave until you have some answers you're happy with. Think you can do that?'

Rose, standing in her front yard, one hand on her hip, took a deep breath. She hated conflict and was sure this meeting would be confronting. But she'd made no advancements via phone calls. And she wasn't managing financially with the extra burden.

But how could she tell that to Mister Bob.

As though her thoughts fed telepathically through the app, Mister Bob added, 'And Rose, I'll meet those repayments, as long as you get an answer from the insurance company.'

'Thank you. We would never manage without you. Always you ask about us and look after us, but how about you, Mister Bob? And Denise, and Charmaine? Tell me how everyone is?'

'Hmm. Charmaine has grown into an effective chief executive. I watch her. She knows everyone's name and what they do and what their strengths and weaknesses are. You know me. I rely more on reports and figures and outcomes,' he said, 'but her approach gets results too.'

And Denise?'

'She's always strong.'

'And you? How are you?'

'Me, I'm the same.'

'How your Parkinson's treating you?'

'Ah, I'm falling over more now, but all that blubber on me helps me bounce back.'

Rose didn't laugh. She wished she could do something for him.

Another month passed. The rep from the insurance company had assured her the money would be in her account soon. She realised she should have had him define the word *soon*. The time it took to visit the company was daunting, but at least she had a name.

Yet another month went by. Rose decided she'd default on the loan repayment for that month to see if that might prompt action. She went to the bank and explained why and asked them to follow up so they could get their money. To her utter amazement, they called the insurance company while she was there. Sure enough, the money appeared in her account within three days. But it wasn't enough to replace the *Red Rocket*. She decided she'd purchase a good secondhand vehicle, and had Willie help her choose it.

But her repayments remained the same yet her insurance costs went up. When she complained about it to Mister Bob, he told her that was normal.

'How is your health, Rose? You never tell me.'

'The children go to the dentist, and Jazz now has braces. But I cannot stand these headaches I get every night. I cannot sleep when it is dark. The pain, it is bad. I go to the hospital. They say dry eyes. They give me drops. It did not help.'

'I think you might need an optometrist, Rose.'

'An eye doctor, like you?'

Rose took Bob's advice and after testing, was prescribed glasses. They made no difference. She admitted she could see a little better, but the headaches persisted.

'We'll see if we can get you to Sydney and check it out. I think it might be more than eyesight.' Bob was pretty sure Rose would need laser treatment, which fell beyond his expertise. 'First, you'll need to investigate getting a visa, Rose. Can you go online and start making enquiries?'

One part of Rose got excited. Her dream was coming true. *Me visit Australia.* But real-world problems collided with her dream. 'Not sure I can get away, Mister Bob. Ramil might come back. Who will look after the girls and Aaron?'

'The girls are surely almost old enough. Can you call on your sister or your mother? Will your sister help Merry to run the shop? Is there enough room for Annlyn to bring her children to stay? Someone strong enough to handle Ramil?'

There was quite a bit of planning and organising, but not more than Rose had needed to undertake in the past. When she looked online to begin the exercise of acquiring a visa, she found the agency wanted ten thousand pesos. This converted to almost three hundred Australian dollars. How could that be?

Rose glanced up from the laptop and saw, out of the window, white ash falling gently from the sky like snowflakes. She abandoned her task and walked out to check, instantly screwing up her nose at the acrid gassy smell.

'Yuk,' she exclaimed, pinching her nose. She'd heard the warnings about the Taal Volcano earlier. It wasn't very far south of where she lived, and there had also been warnings of possible earthquakes. She stood stock still, but thankfully felt nothing.

She returned indoors and turned on the radio. They'd raised the level of alert to a four. Level five was the highest. An explosive eruption could occur any time they announced. Looking up into the sky, she saw the great plumes of white. Thankfully they were some distance away.

'Close the store, Merry,' she said, this time wearing a mask. 'I'll go and get a box of masks. Probably need them for a least the next couple of days.'

With the radio constantly updating the situation, Rose next heard there was a chance of a tsunami.

'Thank goodness,' she told the girls who'd arrived home from school, 'that your grandparents are on the other side of the island.' The following bulletin declared the ash clouds stretched sixty-two miles north of the volcano. It extended way past where they lived. It had become so serious over the islands the International Airport had been forced to close.

The following day she called Mister Bob. 'And President Duterte has ordered all the schools to close, and all government work to stop,' she told him.

'Yes, we're hearing all about it here too. Are you all okay?'

'Sure. Smelly and dusty. But Mister Bob, the agency wants lots of money for the visa,' she said, changing the subject.

'No, Rose, you don't need to use an agency. You can do this

for free yourself. Go to the official Australian Government site. I'll send you a link. It's a Visitor visa you want.'

'She called him back once she'd begun the application. 'It wants to know date and flight details.'

'Sounds a bit back-to-front. Give me some dates that work for you and I'll get Georgina to book something.'

The erupting volcano and the emergencies surrounding it lessened over time. The waiting-for-a-visa time began. During the wait, without warning, Ramil appeared again at the house one morning. He had three burly mates with him. The children were at school. Three trike riders sat at a table under the massive mango tree having a cold drink.

'You can't stop me moving in,' Ramil challenged, shaking off a large, heavy backpack and moving towards the house, backed up by his entourage.

Willie, the biggest and loudest of the riders, stood and moved towards Rose. She smiled at him. 'I've got this, Willie,' she said firmly, although her legs were shaking as she pulled out her phone and, on speaker, pressed 911 and loudly asked for Police. Her ears pulsed in sync with her racing heart. She'd never done anything like this before, but Mister Bob and Sister Hailee had instilled in her to take this action should she feel threatened.

Ramil, seeing the look of determination and confidence on her face, snarled, 'You still haven't heard the last of this.' He turned to his mates and, using his head, beckoned them to leave.

Rose cancelled the emergency call before rushing over to a seat by the trike riders and collapsing.

Willie said, 'Rose, it's time to get a Barangay Protection Order. What a monster. And while it's in place, because it's only good for a couple of weeks, why don't you file for a Temporary Protection Order? It can last for as long as you want. It will give you peace of mind.'

'But doesn't that mean going to court?'

'Yes, but don't worry. We'll be witnesses.' He turned to his fellow trike riders. 'Won't we?'

They nodded. Rose hated to appear vulnerable, so smiled and nodded back. With a sense of discomfort, she set those wheels in motion.

The shop performed reasonably well. Merry often disappeared in the afternoons, and always disappeared on weekends. Rose didn't mind and didn't ask why. The busy times were early mornings and lunch times during the week as well as late afternoons, and Jasmin and Iris now pulled their weight in the late afternoons.

Christmas 2019 came and went, and still no visa had been approved. The shockingly painful nightly headaches continued. On the positive side, Rose felt comforted to hear from her brother-in-law that Ramil had returned to work on the cruise ship.

Months went by. Mister Bob told her he was frustrated with the time it was taking to get a visa. For the third time, he instructed Georgina to change the flight booking, always with a return flight, this time in March.

'I tried to move it along this end, Rose,' he said. 'But it has to be your end.'

Rose was doing all she could. Not only did she feel that same frustration, but also the nighty pain behind her eyes.

Finally, with great excitement, she received her approval to travel. She called Mister Bob on Whatsapp. 'It's here. I have it! I have it!'

Bob didn't need to ask her what she had. 'So you can get on the March flight?'

'Must organise now, Mister Bob. Will I see kangaroo? Can I hold koala? Will I see Harbour Bridge?' she gabbled excitedly.

Bob laughed. 'We'll make sure you do all those things, Rose.'

'But they said I should carry US dollars.'

'Good idea. I'll send some extra funds for emergencies. US dollars speak everywhere.'

'Will I need warm clothes?'

'Rose, anything you need here we'll find for you, but, no, it won't be cold.'

Chapter 24

Rose's mother moved in to look after the children. Merry asked if her son could move in during Rose's absence to give her a hand.

'I didn't even know you had a son, Merry.'

'Ulan's a nice boy, a kind boy. He's twenty-five. He likes to go out at night.'

Rose noticed she said it almost as a question. 'As long as he helps you at busy times.'

Merry smiled weakly.

The household grew in preparation for her trip. Rose felt blessed by what she had and was unperturbed by the crowding. She soon discovered what Merry's vague comments about Ulan meant. He did indeed go out evenings – to some kind of club – where he sang on stage. And, much to Rose and her children's surprise on the first night, he went dressed as a woman. Rose was almost envious of his makeup, and his wigs were monumental masterpieces. Provided it was not beyond their bedtime, Jasmin and Iris gathered at night to watch him prepare and apply his makeup.

Before she left, Rose arranged all kinds of rosters, including one for the bathroom, now there was an older male in the house.

Rose's flight in early March, arranged by Georgina with cost in mind, had a brief stop-over in Singapore. Rose's level of anxiety had escalated at Changi airport, even though she was nowhere near Thailand. She managed to find her way to the departure gate, and once on board, she relaxed again, having faith Mister Bob would be at the other end to meet her.

Going through Immigration frightened her. Mister Bob had warned her they may ask a lot of questions, even though she had her Visitor visa. He'd sent her a letter to print out and carry, but it wasn't needed. She cleared Immigration easily and walked into the Arrivals Hall, her eyes scanning the people for her Mister Bob.

Her tiny face-masked figure, which didn't appear much taller than the trolley she pushed, walked along slowly.

Then there he was! Mister Bob, wearing no mask, raised his arm and waved enthusiastically before moving towards her. Denise stood back waiting.

'Hello, my beautiful little Rose,' he exclaimed, taking her in his arms. 'Come and meet Denise.' His 180-degree turn took some shuffling on his part.

She handed control of her cart off to him when he reached for it.

Denise greeted her. 'Hello, Rose. And you can take the mask off now. Not needed here.'

Rose felt the warmth in the motherly hug, noting she only reached Ma'am Denise's chin.

'I brought a box of masks for you,' Rose said, producing them from her carry-on.

'I'm sure it won't be long before we need them, and there's a massive shortage. So thoughtful of you.'

'I brought hand sanitiser also,' Rose added.

'Oh, my goodness. You were thinking. Can't be had for love nor money.'

Rose looked at her oddly.

'Sorry. I'm going to have to be careful with the sayings I use. Now, come. Bob, you can push the cart again. The car's in a special disabled bay because of Bob, so we're fortunate we don't have far to walk.'

They set off slowly. Rose watched Bob walk competently with the cart in front of him.

'How's your head?' Bob asked Rose.

'Same. Only comes at night.'

Denise said, 'Well, Charmaine's mother-in-law is a doctor, and we have an appointment for you tomorrow to get the ball rolling. Complete check over.'

'You're very kind, Ma'am Denise.' Rose felt like crying, being swamped by all the concern.

'Oh, you must call me Denise.'

Once home, Denise parked the car and ushered Rose inside. Rose stopped dead, her eyes trying to take in all she saw – the space – the luxury – the colours. Through the door to her right, she could see a sparkling pool with underwater lights glowing. Her hand flew to her chest trying to hold in her overloaded emotions. Turning to Denise, she said, with a lopsided smile, 'My whole house fits in this one room.'

'It must be overwhelming to see all this. Come. I'll take you to your room, and then we'll have a cup of tea?'

As Rose climbed the staircase after Ma'am Denise, she feared her manners were not fine enough for these fine people. She'd only ever seen Mister Bob overseas in hotels or in meetings.

She glanced back at Mister Bob at the bottom of the stairs. He nodded and called, 'Keep smiling, Rose. It's all happening.'

The guest bedroom and ensuite had the same effect on Rose as the open-style living room downstairs. *My whole extended family could sleep in here and there'd still be heaps of room*, she thought. Then Ma'am Denise showed her how to use the controls for the air-conditioning on the remote and passed it to her. Rose was overcome with uncontrolled and unrecognisable feelings. She sat on the edge of the huge bed with tears in her eyes, and shortness of breath.

'Oh, Rose, it must be so different, and so difficult. You know what … let me leave you for a few minutes. I'm sure you must want to call your family and freshen up. You just come down when you're ready.' She kissed the top of Rose's head. 'And I've left the Wi-Fi password on the bedside table.'

Rose had never known such a beautiful gesture from someone who was almost a stranger to her. More tears flowed. She knew Ma'am Denise was aware of her past, but Ma'am Denise always seemed so business-like when Rose saw her on the face-time chats with Mister Bob. Now, here she was, as kind as a mother cat with her newborn kittens.

Finding herself alone, Rose called home on her app. 'Oh, Jazz,' she said to her older daughter, 'how are things there?'

'Mum, you haven't been gone very long. It's late. We're all good. You okay?'

'I'm in Paradise. I feel like a pop star on tour. They treat me so well. One day, maybe you'll get to visit Australia too.'

After Rose sorted out how to get warm water from the mixer tap, she washed her face and brushed her teeth, and went back downstairs to find Ma'am Denise and Mister Bob with drinks in their hand.

'Would you like a drink, Rose?'

'Do you have coffee?'

'Come with me and I'll show you so you can help yourself any time.'

Another new thing to learn. A coffee machine. Pods. It seemed easy enough. With her small china cup, Rose joined them for a further chat before they all headed to bed.

On the way to the doctor's the next morning, Ma'am Denise offered to come into the consulting room with Rose, in case language became a barrier. Charmaine's mother-in-law had been briefed. 'You're in charge, Rose, so you can choose what you want checked.'

It was a delicate topic but Rose caught on. There was no way she would let anyone invade her privacy. There'd been more than enough intrusion. As they drove along, Rose noticed the orderliness of the traffic. It wasn't a mad scramble like at home, and the drivers seemed to obey the rules.

When she heard her name called to go in to see the doctor, her legs trembled as she stood, but she indicated to Ma'am Denise she wanted to go in alone.

The doctor behaved kindly and respectfully as she progressed slowly through a range of tests and measures, explaining as she went. 'I'll get the nurse to take some blood for testing, too, now we've finished,' she told Rose.

When they left, Denise said, 'Let's have a bite to eat before we go to Bob's place to get the eyes tested.'

They were tucked into a booth at a little café after Denise had parked in the visitor park at the back of Bob's store in Chatswood. 'Now, here's the menu. Pick whatever you like.'

Rose sat with a booklet menu in her hand, trying to make sense of a *salmon and avocado sammich*.

'Naughty of them,' Denise replied when Rose asked. 'It's just a cheeky name for sandwich.'

Rose had found Ma'am Denise intimidating from the brief conversations she'd had in the past. But here they were sharing jokes about languages.

'I still have to ask the waiter when I see a foreign word I don't understand in a menu. I remember when *jus* first popped up,' Denise added.

'*Jus?* Well, it Spanish for *juice,* no?'

Denise smiled. 'And French, as I found out. But hey, so you speak three languages. Spanish too.'

'I am not sure I speak English. What do you think?'

'I think your English is 100 per cent better than my Spanish, Rose. I rate mine a zero.'

They both ordered a Caesar salad. 'There are so many variations of this. Got a favourite?' Denise said.

'No, I have never tried it.'

'I love to see you are so brave, Rose … out there trying new things, moving forward and fronting the unknown. How did you go with the doctor today?'

'She wanted to talk, but I did not. Put everything all behind me. Just go forward, like you say.'

The salads arrived. A mouthful fell off Denise's fork straight onto her red, black and white top. 'Damn,' she said, realising if she scrubbed it with the thick red serviette, the colour would run onto the clothing. She opened her bag and used tissues, but the mark stayed. 'Hmm. I guess I'll have to put up with that mark.'

Rose thought Ma'am Denise represented a walking ad for fashion for her age. Even at breakfast time, she wore a gown matching her pyjamas. Rose's wardrobe, in comparison, consisted of skirts, shorts and tee-shirts and not much else. Easy to change tee-shirts halfway through the stinking humid days at home.

As if reading Rose's mind about clothes, Denise said, 'Maybe, if there's time, we'll go shopping for some clothes for you and your children after your eye test? And we must pick up some OTMs for your children too.'

'OTMs? I know Mister Bob told me, but what does it stand for again?'

'Oh, it's On The Marks, Marks being the spectacles. They were originally just clip-ons for the Marks spectacles, but now they're also a jewellery line. The popular ones are in the colour of your favourite team. You follow footy? Got team colours?'

'Oh, you mean football? We are mostly basketball now. Football okay. Our national teams' colours are blue, white and red.'

Bob greeted them in his shop, and introduced Rose to his store manager, Barbie. 'She will take you through all the processes, and call me when you're finished, Rose. Then you can join Denise and me for afternoon tea with Charmaine.'

Sometime later, Barbie escorted Rose upstairs, with a frown on her face and a file in her hand. Handing Bob the file, she shook her head.

'Sit down and explain to all of us, Barbie.' He looked over at Rose. 'You don't mind, do you?'

After a smile and a nod, he turned to Barbie. 'Simple to understand language, not technical.' Bob avoided speaking when someone else could.

'The Tonometry test – it's where the little puff of air in each eye was done – showed intraocular pressure inside your eye,' Barbie said, directing her comments to Rose. 'The condition is called broadly, glaucoma. In brief, you'll need to get the pressure down. If you leave it untreated you could go blind.'

'Whoa,' Denise threw in. 'That's a lot of information at once, and pretty dramatic. How are you feeling, Rose?'

Rose found herself short of breath with anxiety. 'Can you fix it?' she whispered.

'We have caught it early.' Bob calmed the environment and Rose's nerves, even though he hadn't read the formal diagnosis. But he would have bet on the result, just from hearing the symptoms from Rose from the Philippines. He was alarmed, though. It wasn't good. That was why she was in Sydney.

'It's nothing you've done, Rose. It is sadly found more frequently in the Asian population. But we can arrange treatment with the ophthalmologist. Barbie, can you call in a favour from Max and get an early appointment? Tell him I'll call him soon.'

Rose underwent the first laser treatment the following day, and Denise brought her home with watery eyes, blurred vision and drops. 'I gather you should be okay tomorrow, so we'll go visit a place down on Darling Harbour where you can nurse a koala. But, Rose, I'm not sure Bob can walk the distance. Are you okay with just me?'

'If you have time, Ma'am Denise.'

'One – you can just call me Denise, and two – I am happy to take you. Afterwards, we can do a bit of souvenir shopping if you like.'

Rose felt awkward. She wasn't sure how to say she had no money to spend.

As if seeing her discomfort, Denise added, 'They'll be gifts from us. Why don't you budget one hundred dollars per child, and the same for yourself?'

In the evening Bob, Denise and Rose gathered out by the pool. The sun had set, and to Rose, the pool lights and spot-lit trees created an atmosphere of holidaying at a luxurious destination.

The main topic of conversation was Covid-19. Everywhere. Not just in the backyard. Denise, who'd heard snippets on the radio said, 'So we've had a case that's not from overseas. It's got them stirred up. The *Diamond Princess* episode off Japan was diabolical. I don't think people fully understood what was going on. They've now called it a floating petri dish. Those poor souls. We were a bit late getting our Ozzies back, but they're home.'

She reached for her white wine. 'But they got on the cruise ship, you know, after all the warnings.' She shuddered. 'I heard there were six positive cases, but they're all okay after quarantining in Darwin.' She looked at Rose. 'I worry about you getting back home safely.'

'One more treatment. Then I go home. My mum worries too.'

'I'll bet she does.'

Anxiety hung in the air like a storm cloud about to burst as they listened to news broadcasts and updates. Official predictions of tens of thousands of deaths of the vulnerable sent strong messages of hand-washing, social distancing, quarantining, lock-downs and masks.

'Well,' Denise went on, 'we can't buy hand sanitiser anywhere. We've only got what you gave us, Rose. I'm thinking we're going to need lots more. But next door have aloe vera growing in a pot and I've got a recipe for it based on aloe vera.'

'I will help you.'

'Maybe tomorrow? Could be messy.' Denise laughed. 'And have you ever heard of PPE before? No, I hadn't either. They say we have a shortage in the hospitals as well as face masks.' Denise explained Personal Protective Equipment to Rose. 'At least we have masks. Again thanks to you.'

Next morning, Rose surfaced elated. 'No pain. All night I sleep. So happy.'

After breakfast, Denise rang the neighbour, who brought over six long stems of aloe vera in a plastic bag. 'I'll give you a bottle of it if it works,' Denise said as thanks.

Rose and Denise, up on bar stools, tried with a potato peeler to skin the plant. It was akin to cutting thin slices of jelly. They tried with sharp knives and finally had a transparent slimy substance on their board with no sign of green matter. First, they attempted to chop it finely. Rose got a swift nudge from Denise, who was rocking with laughter. 'This isn't going to work. Imagine those lumps on your hands. I'm going to put it in the blender with the alcohol and scented oil.'

Rose watched the process, fascinated by this complicated lady, the wife of her benefactor. She seemed so sophisticated, yet she behaved so normally. Rose knew and understood Mister Bob. Not Ma'am Denise though. She was hard to read. She wondered how two people could be so different yet be together.

As if Denise had read Rose's mind again, she said, 'I had no idea what you would be like, Rose. Sure, I'd seen photos, and Charmaine said you were lovely. I knew you'd been through a shocking experience, so my main thoughts were those of sympathy.' Denise had turned the blender off, and leaned back against the bench. 'But now, I see you're just a mum trying to do her best. I'm so glad Bob is helping you, and you have my full support.'

With trepidation, Rose said, 'You not angry with Mister Bob?'

'Oh, I'm angry all right. But …' she was about to say *that's got nothing to do with you,* then realised it had everything to do with Rose. '… it has everything to do with Bob's behaviour, and not yours. His initial secretiveness, his deceptiveness.'

Seeing the puzzled look on Rose's face, Denise simplified her comments. 'Bob's been naughty not looking for help from us earlier.' Lining up some small jars, she added, 'But you have done nothing wrong, Rose. Nothing.'

Rose picked up one of the empty jars, with a partial label stuck to it saying *Vegemite.* 'This?' she asked.

'Ha. Must get you a tube of it to take home. It's our national food. I'll let you try it.'

Rose watched Denise mix a teaspoon of the black paste with cream cheese, then coat a stick of celery.

'Go on, give it a go.'

Rose tried to keep a neutral face, but a few twitches gave away her opinion. She couldn't say it, but she thought it was disgusting.

'Not for everyone, hey,' Denise smiled.

After a light lunch, they headed off to the Wild Life Zoo at Darling Harbour. Rose wanted to cling to Ma'am Denise's arm, wondering what would become of her if she became separated. *But then,* she thought, *I could always call Mister Bob.*

Friendly kangaroos allowed themselves to be touched. Rose

stood cuddling a koala while her photo was taken. She was almost living the dream, but she longed for her children to be beside her. Everything she did, everything she saw, made her think of their joy if they had been there. When she signalled she'd seen enough Australian wildlife, Denise took her to purchase some stuffed toys for the children before taking her on a ferry ride, where she felt awed by seeing the Harbour Bridge and the Opera House from the water.

The days flew by for Rose as she was escorted all over Sydney. But an air of urgency, fuelled by her need to receive her next eye treatment then return home to her children, stripped her of full enjoyment. On the TV news, she watched visuals of women fighting over toilet paper.

'I don't understand?' she asked Denise.

'Me neither. But just look at them.' The comical ad showed a twenty-pack of toilet paper for $7,999 and a free pool table thrown in.

The day of the final laser treatment dawned.

They were gathered in the kitchen when Bob said, 'I just got a text. Your flight's been cancelled, Rose. They haven't offered another.'

Rose felt sick. 'What can we do?'

'The airlines have stopped running to timetables. It's just chaos. I'll get on to Georgina. Don't worry. We'll get you home one way or another.'

Rose managed to get on a flight to Kuala Lumpur with a tight connection to the Philippines the same night. Airports were shutting down, Georgina advised them. Covid-19 had turned international travel into a nightmare.

Max, the ophthalmologist, told Bob when he collected Rose after her second treatment, he was not at all happy she was flying out of the country straight away. 'I really do need to check on her in another few days.'

'No, I must go now,' Rose insisted.

Bob was adamant too. Rose had to hurry back to the Philippines.

Bob and Denise told Rose their friends were in quarantine in their own homes. They'd been doing business in South East Asia when they heard the news the Government told all Australians to return home immediately. They rang Qantas who told them which flight to get on the next morning, and they could sort out payment later.

While Rose underwent her treatment, Denise, wearing a mask, did her friends' shopping to leave at their front door. 'It's all so surreal,' she told Rose later. 'There's not much on the supermarket shelves.'

In the late afternoon, Bob and Charmaine escorted Rose to the airport. When they fronted up to the Malaysian Airlines counter for check-in, Rose was refused boarding. Rose stood, helpless. She wasn't sure how many more barriers she could jump over. Bob demanded an explanation from the ground crew.

A supervisor explained, 'The connecting flight to the Philippines in KL departs from another terminal, not easily accessed from Arrivals, and there is not enough time if there is any delay. We are closing KL International Airport at midnight tonight.'

'What do we do?'

'Try Air Asia.'

Rose followed Charmaine over to Air Asia's counter, only to find they could not purchase a ticket at the airport. Rose watched Charmaine ring her mother at home.

Denise hopped online, and found a flight with Air Asia the next day to Singapore, connecting to the Philippines. But it would land, not at Ninoy Aquino, the main Manila Airport, but

Clark International Airport. To her surprise, she saw the Ninoy Aquino was also closing that same day to international flights. She quickly rang Charmaine to check if Clark would work for Rose.

'It is long way from home, but it gets me there.'

Denise booked the ticket then checked on her granddaughters who were staying with her.

Rose, tired, disappointed and watery-eyed, returned to the Mark's home with Bob and Charmaine.

Her heart ached for her Mister Bob as she watched him stagger to the compact glassed-in lift tucked into the curve of the staircase. She wondered if he'd even find the energy to undress himself. She realised he really was becoming frail, in spite of his size.

Downstairs, Denise said, 'Well, the WHO has called it a pandemic. We're all in unchartered waters. Some States are closing borders. See they are suggesting hotel quarantine instead of home quarantine for returning overseas travellers. So many restrictions, so many unknowns. Rose, we must get you home.' She put her arm around Rose's shoulders and gave her a comforting squeeze. The kettle had boiled and Charmaine, pouring hot drinks, glanced at Rose and saw, in those bloodshot and watery eyes caused by the laser treatment earlier in the day, a deep sadness.

'Of course, this must be so frightening. What word from home, Rose?'

'They wipe all the shop all the time with alcohol. Wear masks.' The effort to try to explain the worries she had in English, and the worries her mother had was too great. She took a few sips of her hot chocolate, and bowed, 'Please, can I go to bed now?'

Again Denise squeezed Rose's shoulders, then, arm still around her, escorted her to the lift with her bag. 'Sleep well. We'll get you home tomorrow.'

She left her at the door of her room, feeling her concern.

The following afternoon Rose departed. The calmness she felt sitting in her allocated seat swept over her like a refreshing shower after a hot day. A sense of achievement overtook her when she found her way to the correct departure gate at Changi Airport. Mister Bob had warned her it wouldn't be easy. She felt double the relief when she boarded the plane to Clark Airport in the Philippines, even though it was running late. She knew no one would be there to meet her, even if they were willing, because the whole country was now in lockdown.

They landed in the middle of the night. Rose passed through Immigration and Customs with ease. Hearing and speaking Tagalog filled her with a comfort she'd been longing for. But she was startled to see so few people about, and no taxis waiting outside. Although it was late, Rose called Mister Bob on the app from inside the terminal with anxiety levels rising yet again.

'I do not know how to get home. No transport. What do I do, Mister Bob?' Her vision was still a little blurry, but the watery eyes were not from the laser procedure.

Without hesitation, Bob replied, 'Listen, Rose, you are carrying the answer. Those US dollars. Use them. Bribe your way. You've been in worse situations. You play it strong. You can do this.'

A surge of electric current coursed through her veins. *Yes, I can do this. I faced more daring challenges than this one.* She marched out onto the road and hailed a delivery truck. She waved two fifty-dollar notes at him. 'You take me home?'

He went to reach for the notes, but she pulled back. 'I'll give them to you when we get there.' She walked around to the passenger side, hefted her bag up, and climbed in. Her family were waiting up for her.

When she arrived home, from deep within she pulled up energy, trying to sparkle for the excited mob through her exhaustion. She pulled gifts out for everyone, the biggest hit for all being the OTM jewellery.

Chapter 25

The Philippines certainly was in lockdown. 'They only let one person in house out for shopping,' Rose reported to Mister Bob. 'We must show pass. That person is my cousin mostly. He came to help and is stuck. My Mum sad; she cannot go home. She is also stuck here now and not happy. No school for kids. They must learn at home.'

'For what it's worth, things are not good here either, Rose. How's the shop doing?' He wanted her to feel as though she wasn't alone in these highly uncertain times.

'Oh, everyone stocked up big before. But from supermarket, not from me. And no one is at work, so no breakfast or lunch here at the shop. Not on way home from work either. No money.' Rose explained all non-essential business had shut.

'So you have no income?'

'I trade mangoes for other foods. We are okay for now. Eat our own stocks.'

Typical Rose, he thought. She still supported a houseful and didn't complain.

Because the Prime Minister had shouted out to all Australians to get home, Charmaine's husband abandoned his overseas work, jumped on the next available flight, and quarantined for two weeks at home, after being tested. Charmaine and the twins moved in with Bob and Denise again to allow that to happen.

The New South Wales Premier, Gladys Berejiklian, also announced non-essential businesses and activities would cease to function, although, for now, schools would remain open. But parents were encouraged to keep their children home.

Curious to compare, the next time Bob called Rose, he said, 'Tell me about what a usual day looks like for you?'

Rose laughed. 'Jazz is now part-time teacher as well as online student. This is her final year high school. She teaches Iris and Aaron, and Charlie.' She hesitated.

'What? Who is Charlie?'

'You remember Joshua, my cousin? He moved in. He is very good, but has no work. Where he used to live, his next-door people got killed in car accident, and their little boy was on his own, so he is here now.'

'So let me get this right. You, your three children, your Mum, your cousin and his kid neighbour. If I've counted right, there are seven.'

'Don't forget Merry. She does all the cooking and helps with cleaning for shop and house. But her son moved out to stay with friends.'

'Eight. Oh, Rose, I'll need to start sending you money again. You take on such responsibility.'

'They had nowhere else to go.'

After the call, Rose felt a pang of guilt. She'd been trying to help her sister Annlyn and Annlyn's family as well. But stock and funds no longer stretched to helping the extended family to any extent. There were no reserve funds and almost no income. She didn't know how to tell Mister Bob so she'd just have to stretch what he sent as widely as she could.

The following week, Willie, her favourite trike rider, came to ask if she was able to help any of them. These were her neighbours, her friends, who supported her shop, and here she was, getting extra money from Mister Bob, but how far could she stretch it beyond family? She knew they could see she was able to afford to feed her extended family, and by their standards, was judged as wealthy by those in her own neighbourhood.

The next time she talked to Mister Bob, she told him, 'Big problem, now starvation is setting in. People actually die. Not just from Covid. No food.'

He heard the distress in her clipped words. 'Tell me the truth, Rose, how many are you trying to feed?'

Rose avoided the question. 'You are very kind Mister Bob. We try to manage.' Her voice quavered, tinged with anxiety. 'But so sad for my friends.'

Bob was deeply troubled by what he was hearing, not just in the words spoken, but in Rose's tone.

'I'll call you back later, Rose. In the meantime, please take care and stay well.'

Bob found Denise at her desk. It was becoming more and more difficult to manoeuvre himself around the house. He stood with his hand on the wall for balance. Denise rose and cleared off a chair for him to sit on.

Bob related Rose's concerns and fears over the suffering of her friends and neighbours who couldn't access food. 'Starvation, Denise.'

'What are you proposing? We're sending thousands already. We can't feed the whole of the Philippine population, Bob.' Denise leaned forward. 'So much need. It's overwhelming.'

They were both silent for a while.

Denise smiled sneakily at him. 'I've got it. We'll do a fundraising campaign.'

Bob caught on. 'Yeah, yeah. Just think. We have a little neighbourhood in a third-world country and we know the heart of that neighbourhood. We know Rose could operate the charity as a business. Fully trustworthy. We could make it personal.'

'This will certainly keep you busy, Bob. It will need a name, some photos, a brochure with a simple explanation. But mostly it will need personal contact from all of us to our networks.'

'Any ideas for a name?'

They bandied ideas back and forth. 'Sometimes the simplest is the best. Why not just the basic *Project Hand to Mouth*?' she said.

'So, let's do a trial run, and see what happens. Send $5,000 to Rose.'

Bob couldn't believe the degree to which Denise committed to helping out. 'I'll call her to suss it out.'

Rose was initially speechless when she listened to Mister Bob. 'Really, you are serious? Oh wow! I will get plenty of help.' They discussed the types of essential supplies.

It had been Rose's habit to forward photos to Mister Bob of her life and her children in action, not just their report cards, but also her shop, her neighbours, her trike riders and even her mangoes, to keep him up to date and informed. From the photos sent, Bob enjoyed building the story of Rose's life in his imagination. Now he might learn more about the neighbourhood.

'You'd need to keep records for the donors. Do you think there'd be any costs?'

'I will get Willie to pick up rice at the warehouse on his trike. Maybe fuel? And maybe he needs a permit.'

'Can you sort permits and the like while I start to bring in funds? I'll send 5,000 Aussie dollars in pesos to start. And can you send me some photos to use?'

Bob sat down with his computer feeling a sense of accomplishment, even though he hadn't yet achieved anything, and tapped out a draft to send to his network of friends. It read:

> *Hello..........,*
>
> *Some of you would be aware of the circumstances*

around Denise, Charmaine and my involvement with a family in Manila over the last several years. For others of you, it will be the first time you have been made aware of it and I would be happy to explain in a little more detail by separate correspondence if you wish.

Having been fortunate enough over the years to travel extensively, I have no doubt in my mind that we live in the best country on the planet. While we sit at home in splendid isolation during the Covid-19 virus crisis there are millions of people in other countries who are doing it infinitely tougher. One of those countries happens to be the Philippines where people are experiencing total lockdowns, which means no income from any source and a government that has insufficient funds to feed the population. As I understand it, the government there will be faced with a very difficult decision in the next few weeks to either lift the restrictions and risk a serious outbreak of the virus or keep the restrictions and face the possibility of famine amongst the population.

When speaking with Rose (the matriarch of the family) the other day, it became apparent to me that many of her friends, neighbours and other associates were literally starting to starve to death for the want of some food. Having finished the call and speaking with Denise, we decided we could no longer sit back and ignore the plight of the families and children associated with Rose.

Being new, and a little naïve, I guess, when it comes to being in the front line of the philanthropic business, I have been overwhelmed by their response to our early support. However, there comes a time when you reach the bottom of your own pockets, so to speak, and have to admit we are now close to that point.

Feeling dejected about the financial limitations we now face, it occurred to me that I have many friends and acquaintances out there in the wider world who might like to join me on this journey. I've called it PROJECT HAND TO MOUTH.

The organisation I admit does not look as professional as some of the larger charities you are no doubt familiar with, but believe me it is functional and working very well. Rose, her three children and extended family are carrying out a wonderful job of purchasing, repackaging and distributing the food parcels to families in need in their neighbourhood (see attached photos).

In simple terms it is costing about $23 per food parcel (or bag) which consists of 10 kgs of rice, 10 satchels of coffee and other miscellaneous goodies which I am informed would keep a family of 2 adults and 2 children in food for 5 to 7 days.

Rounding up the numbers means the following,

1. A donation of $100 would see 4 families eat for a week.

2. A donation of $500 would see 20 families eat for a week.

3. A donation of $1000 would see 20 families eat for 2 weeks.

I know you must be inundated with requests for money from charities and, like myself, have a plethora of other needs to satisfy, but if you can spare a few dollars for a worthy cause it would be very much appreciated.

All funds can be forwarded to the following account. Trust me when I say there are no indirect costs involved.

Denise had forwarded their initial formal donation via internet banking to Rose to kick off Project Hand to Mouth.

Bob sent off a letter for Rose to give to Willie or whoever would transport the rice purchased from the first $5,000.

Later in the evening, he again called Rose.

'I got your letter and printed it and gave to Willie, Mister Bob. He will be a big help. And my cousin Joshua too. But how are you, Mister Bob?'

'Denise is a great support, Rose. This damn Parkinson's is getting worse. And I can't go to my doctor or physio yet. But why am I complaining? We have enough to eat, even if it's not always what we'd normally have.'

'What do you miss doing? Things you did before this Parkinson's.'

'You sound like the neurological psychiatrist. He asked me the same question.'

'What is that? Never heard of that.'

'He did testing to see if I'm okay for the brain surgery – the deep brain stimulation one.'

Rose put her hand over her mouth in surprise. They were not using Facetime. *Thank goodness he can't see me,* she thought. 'When are you having surgery?' She tried to sound casual, but everyone knew how dangerous and risky any brain surgery was. What would happen to her if something happened to her Mister Bob? Her hand went from her mouth to her heart.

'Oh, haven't finished all the testing, and now with Covid, no surgery.'

'So what is testing like with this man?'

'Oh, you know, answering stuff like "Who is the Prime Minister" and "What day is it" and then there's maths and English.' Bob gave his head a quick stroke at the memory of some of the testing. After the silence, he added, 'I'm really good with numbers. I can count backwards in sevens from one hundred quickly, but ask me to name words starting with the letter b in a time frame of one minute, and I'm a disaster, a failure.'

'I think you're great with words, Mister Bob. But you didn't answer me earlier. What would you like to do now that you can't?'

'Travel alone. Not need help.'

'Where would you go?'

'Where do you think? I worry about my little Filipino family all the time – even more so now Covid is raging and people are dying of starvation. Of course, they wouldn't let me travel now, even if I was physically capable. I would love to see you again, Rose. You know that?'

'You are very important to all of us, Mister Bob. I don't know how to show you how much.'

'Just keeping everyone going is enough for now. And Denise and I have sent out a letter to all our friends and colleagues to see if they'll help with our Project Hand to Mouth.' Bob paused.

'Hmm. That was days ago. Let me call Denise and see if she can check the account. I'll call you right back.'

Bob found Denise in the kitchen with her laptop open on the kitchen bench. She tapped in the password after opening the bank icon before clicking on the account. 'Oh, my goodness, Bob.'

'What?'

'There are three amounts of ten thousand dollars!'

'Who?'

'Well, there's my lovely old Aunt Risby. I'm stunned she can even use internet banking. Good for her. I'll give her a call in the morning. What an amazing woman she is. Eighty something and still secretary of her local Probus too.'

'And the others?' Bob hauled himself up onto a bar stool, more interested in Project Hand to Mouth than old Aunt Risby. Not that he didn't appreciate the donation, but he was frightened of calling her because she'd talk the legs off him.

Denise turned the laptop around. 'Your mates?' She pointed to deposits from names she didn't recognise.

There were several other donations for varying amounts from one hundred dollars to one thousand dollars.

'Wow, Den. Will you look at that! I'm just going to call Rose back and tell her.'

Rose wept silent tears when she heard the news. That total strangers were prepared to help her feed her friends and neighbours was like winning a major prize in a competition you'd not even entered.

Chapter 26

When the first donation arrived from Mister Bob, Rose called a meeting of her mixed household to tell them everyone would be working to help feed the neighbours. She called Willie, the trike rider, who grabbed hold of Rose and twirled her around, yelling, 'Celebration time everyone! Here comes the food.'

His job was to collect food from the warehouse and help Rose identify those who needed food the most.

Rose wrote out the first order. After rice in 30-kilogram bags, powdered milk for babies was next on the list, then, finally, coffee. 'And we need big quantities of plastic bags to put the rice into once we've weighed it up,' Rose added.

It took several trips for Willie to complete the order. On one trip, he was pulled over by the police who asked for his permit.

Arriving back at Rose's store, he said, 'I thought they might just take some of the rice. There's so much corruption and then there's the black market, but they were decent human beings and let me go when they saw your Mister Bob's letter.'

The front room of Rose's home was converted, as plastic bags were filled with rice by a conveyor belt line of people from her household, including the children. Bags were topped off with packets of coffee.

Word was out. Rose locked her shop. There was nothing left to sell, and there were no neighbours with money to buy anything anyway. Her gates were also locked, with her new little car sitting uselessly inside like a sailing boat without sails. Neither was going anywhere. Her car was too expensive to run, even if there had been somewhere to go.

Once the parcels were ready, she opened the shop to control the crowd outside. They'd serve from there. Willie stood outside trying to manage the mob. At least they were wearing masks, but there was no social distancing in their excited state.

'But Willie, we need a system, so the same people aren't back tomorrow,' Rose suggested after they'd shut shop.

'I'll do up a roster. And there's the Castillo family down that road,' he said, pointing. 'The grandmother is overseas working. But she can't earn a living or support the family because the Saudis are in lockdown too. Her daughter has terminal cancer. The husband looks after the three little children. We need to deliver to them.'

'They are exactly the ones to help. Twice a week to them. Who else?' Rose said.

Willie identified a family with a two-year-old with encephalitis.

'Yep, powdered milk, twice weekly for them.'

And so it went on. Name after name, list after list.

Rose took the time to snap some photos of the work and some of the recipients. When Willie showed up on his trike laden with bags, holding a cardboard sign reading: *Thank you, Mister Bob,* Rose couldn't resist another photo.

She was pleasantly surprised to find gifts placed outside her shop the day after the first food relief went out. A small bag of guavas, a pawpaw, a few cobs of corn, a bottle of sanitiser and a pair of socks. It lifted everyone's spirits to have something fresh to eat, not to mention their job of giving others around them food and hope. 'But I'm not sure we're desperate enough to eat socks yet,' Rose announced. 'And with no school, there's no need for wearing any.'

As for homeschooling, Jasmin was in her element, supervising and sharing her knowledge. Her only problem, she explained to her mother, was she needed time for her own work. She wanted to study at university to be a pharmacist, so her workload was greater and harder, demanding outstanding results for entry acceptance.

'We must work something out for you,' Rose declared, knowing what a gifted child she had. There was no doubt in Rose's mind Jazz would achieve her goal. Rose sent all the children's report cards to Mister Bob, letting him know his support was not just achieving good financial outcomes – well – not so much right now with the pandemic, but overall. But Rose was not sure how to give Jazz the support she needed.

'Oh, Mister Bob,' she said when he rang, 'I do not know how best to help her. I know nothing of what she does.'

'Well, first we need to see she has a laptop of her own. No use trying to share one among the whole family.'

Rose gasped. That was not expected, but it made sense.

'And Rose, as I've said before, it's critical they all speak good English. I know it's a compulsory subject for them, but I don't mean just writing it. Although that's important too. Why not get them to email me once a week in English with a report on what they are doing? And then we could even move up to talking to me once a week.'

Rose looked over at the children affectionately. 'You sure about that? Good practice for them, but what about your time?'

'Never a better time, Rose. And another suggestion. For, say, one hour each day while you're all together, just speak English? There'd be no better practice.'

'My English is awful. They do not learn from me.'

'Aha – maybe they teach you, Rose.'

What a smart man to suggest these things. But, oh, the energy some of the ideas take, she thought. As it was, she still rose at five in the mornings, and didn't hit the bed till very late, working all day. The burden of being responsible for so many weighed her down.

How could she explain it to him?

She rounded up her three around the dining table and said, 'We are all going to work together. Not just managing the Project Hand to Mouth for our community, but to let Mister Bob know you are keeping up with your work. Every Friday, I want you to send him an email with what you've been doing for the week. You can check each other's English. Okay?'

'That's scary, Mum. Can't you do it?'

'Been doing it for years and years. Now it's your turn. Jazz, he's buying you your own laptop so you no longer have to share.' She looked each of them in the eye. 'And,' she went on, 'we are going to talk to each other in English over breakfast every morning. And that doesn't mean not talking. It means just the opposite, so you can correct each other.'

This suggestion met with laughter, till Jasmin said in accented English, 'Dear Mister Bob, Thank you most sincerely for the extra lessons.' Again they laughed.

Tens of thousands of dollars poured into Project Hand to Mouth as photos of bags of rice with signs on top acknowledging and thanking specific donors were sent to Bob, who, in turn, forwarded them on to an original donor.

Bob's Lions' meetings resumed, but via Zoom, since indoor crowds were not permitted. Bob nominated Charmaine as a guest speaker in order to explain the plight of Rose's community whilst maintaining her privacy. And so more funds poured in.

The Fridays with his golfing buddies had ceased due to Covid-19 restrictions, but Bob contacted them all by email to harness their support too, so the donations kept rolling in.

Restrictions continued for Rose in the Philippines but relaxed somewhat for Bob in Sydney.

'I go to the office most mornings, Rose. We've got

government assistance for our workers via a program called JobKeeper and there's lots of paperwork to handle. They've been doing it tough too.' Bob realised that was a bit insensitive. 'Nothing like how tough you've been doing it though,' he corrected, realising how lucky Australians were by comparison.

'Some emergency relief is getting out here,' Rose replied. 'But we are in an area they don't consider needs help. Lots of homelessness now. More than before.'

'What we are doing, Mister Bob, is growing more food on the bits of vacant land around, even at the school. We are drying seeds and sharing.'

'A few donations still trickle in. Some donors had set up monthly transfers of a couple of hundred dollars each time, Rose.'

'We are all grateful for anything, Mister Bob. But enough about that. How is your Parkinson's?'

'Oh, Rose, that! You'd laugh if you watched me try to roll over in bed. I'm like a beached whale. Just stuck.'

Rose giggled at the analogy.

'It's not funny. You're laughing,' he accused good-humouredly.

'You just told me I'd laugh,' she said mischievously.

'Worse still, Rose,' he said, still in good humour, 'Denise has kicked me out of the bedroom. Apparently, I thrash about in bed all night now. But, and no laughing again, Rose, Denise is going to get me satin sheets and I'll have to wear satin boxers to bed so I can roll better. Roll! Can you imagine? I'll probably slide right off the bed.'

Rose chuckled again. 'Waste of satin sheets,' she added.

He laughed at the thought. 'But my bonus is that I get to watch TV through the night when I can't sleep. Couldn't do that before.'

Over the years their conversations had become much more

relaxed. As his disability claimed more of him, and Rose's capabilities grew, the relationship seemed to Rose to be on a more even keel.

'How is Ma'am Denise? What is she doing?'

'Oh, she's back teaching. It's all a bit foreign to me, but she's highly competent at what she does. Like you. Competent. Like Charmaine. All these talented women I'm surrounded by.'

'I didn't ask after Charmaine.'

'She pretty much runs all the business now. I oversee decisions, but I must have taught her well.'

'Taught me well too, Mister Bob.'

Chapter 27

Rose and her extended family, like all families in the Philippines, were still in lockdown, with just one nominated person per household allowed out unless it was an emergency.

Warnings sounded everywhere around the Philippines. As if Covid-19 wasn't enough to cope with throughout 2020, Rose thought, these warnings are about an enormously destructive typhoon on its way.

She quickly emailed Mister Bob.

> *We may lose contact, Mister Bob. Big typhoon on the way. Really bad. Do not worry if you do not hear from me. Maybe no connections to anything soon. Joshua nail everything down for me.*

Bob emailed back:

> *Please keep safe. I'm sure you know what to do. It seems like just yesterday you were dealing with a volcano erupting. We have bushfires delivered straight from hell, Rose, but honestly, you seem to win regularly in the lottery of disasters delivered on your doorstep. Keep Smiling.*

Rose had turned everything electrical off, and with Merry's help filled every container she could find with water. They moved everything outside inside, and they all gathered together on the ground floor and waited calmly. This was not the first time, but ones this big were rare.

On their battery-powered radio, Rose heard it called

Typhoon Ulysses. Then they heard the wind. Rose and Joshua pushed the kitchen table into a solid corner; she gathered the four children and pushed them together in that corner, instructing Merry and Joshua to form a barrier around them with her. The wind picked up in intensity till it sounded like a train was about to hurtle through the house.

No one spoke. They couldn't have been heard above the smashing and crashing anyway. And then came the water. Under the doors, under the gaps around the boarded-up windows. Their bottoms were wet. The children clung to each other as Rose, Merry and Joshua tried to comfort them. Petrified, Rose wished someone was there to give her solace.

Then a calmness fell on them all, as heavy in its silence as the deafening roar of the wind earlier. Rose stretched her cramped limbs, as did the others. 'Come, we'll close that side of the house and open the other to relieve the pressure, so the windows don't blow out.' Joshua and Merry followed. This was always what occurred in the eye of the typhoon. It was only half over and so far their home had held together, even if it was leaking a bit.

The radio broadcast a litany of static.

'Everyone back into position,' she ordered, realising once again her enormous and lonely responsibility and the burden it carried. If she got it wrong, someone could die.

And so, surrounded again by a noise like a continuous line of freight trains hurtling by, they sat in personal silence, each of them alone with their thoughts as they rode out the rest of the typhoon.

A second silence came, broken only by the creaking of broken branches and the dripping of water onto the outside pavers. They crawled from their wet shelter. Rose opened the door and peered outside. The others gathered behind her, and with a bit of pushing, they all soon tumbled outside. What they saw left them speechless.

There was barely a leaf left on any tree. Branches were down, leaving no clear ground to walk on. But there were no broken windows, or structural damage. The power was out. And there was no water. From past experience, Rose doubted they'd see either of those services restored any time soon.

The freezer had been turned off long ago, and the tiny amount of food in the fridge would need to be consumed soon, but the green vegies growing in pots, which had been move into the store, would serve them well.

Rose went back inside and upstairs with a straw broom while the children explored in wonderment. She began swishing out the water from the top floor down. Joshua took down the boards from the windows before going back inside to throw them open.

'We don't want to deal with mould or mildew,' Rose said as she thanked him. Already in the moist heat, steam rose from the wet baked tiles in the yard.

Merry, meanwhile, true to her skills, threw together a cold meal for everyone. 'I'll get a fire going outside so we can heat water and cook food before we lose it,' she said. 'We'll preserve the gas bottle.'

Rose left the radio on, hoping a voice would break through the static.

Jasmin opened the gates.

Rose heard her gasp and went to look, the sight too much to take in. Wreckage from homes that had been destroyed littered the narrow roadway, and was even stuck up in trees. Power lines were tangled on the ground. She immediately forbade the children to exit their property.

The water, Rose realised, would need to be rationed. So much water had come down, but there had not been enough utensils to gather it in. Communications were down.

Bob's attempts to make contact with Rose constantly failed. The longer it went on, the more concerned he became. Typhoon Ulysses with its Category Four strength featured in all the major news bulletins. The typhoon had caused the worst flooding in the Philippines since the 2009 typhoon. These reports left him feeling helpless. Powerless.

The scenes on TV showed floodwaters up over rooftops, the homeless wading through water up to their neck with a bag of possessions held high over their heads. Others struggled through almost knee-deep mud.

'Unreal,' Bob muttered to himself. He bowed his head and stroked it with both hands. Were his little family even still alive?

More images showed boat rescues, but also reported many dead or missing. He attempted again to call Rose on their shared app. Still no response.

Eventually Rose called her Mister Bob. Relief washed over her like a cool welcome breeze when she heard his voice. It was such a difficult time to navigate through without his support. 'Oh, Mister Bob, Mister Bob. Awful here. I will send pictures.'

'But are you all safe?'

'All safe. Yard a mess. No running water. No power.'

'And the house?'

'Strong. Water came in, but we sweep it out.'

'It must have been very scary for you all.'

'We closed all on the side of the direction it came in. We hid together when it hit. So loud.' Rose breathed heavily, reliving the fear. 'You never been in a typhoon?'

'I've heard about them from friends in Queensland. We call them cyclones, but the same,' he explained. 'So you have no electricity or water?'

'All food in fridge is gone. Nothing in shop fridge or freezer. We are not selling anything anyway. No one has got money. We have still got rice. We cook over open fire.'

Bob heard the tension in Rose's voice but struggled to grasp the enormity of the problems she faced. After all, if a disaster such as this occurred in Sydney, the authorities would pull out all stops to get everything restored urgently. But no such priority in the ravaged country existed when people were dying from causes other than lack of fresh water or electricity.

Puzzled, Bob said, 'So what are you drinking? How do you wash?'

'We go to my sister's house. She has got water. Shower, wash clothes there. We are okay. Can't do Covid lockdown now.'

Bob's phone beeped. He saw on his desktop the photos Rose sent via Messenger. Sure enough, huge branches covered the ground in Rose's yard. Corrugated iron from other premises had blown in. Bob was overtaken by frustration and helplessness. Money wasn't going to make life easier for his little family so far away. Being overpopulated and under-financed, the country was fraught with disasters.

A few days later, Rose emailed a number of photos to Bob. He looked at them before reading the email. In the photos Rose and Merry worked with the children, parcelling up donated clothing and domestic bits and pieces such as kitchen items and towels and bed linen. Other photos showed them ploughing through deep thick mud and passing over the parcels to rough temporary homes surrounded by filthy mud-coated rubbish that had once been prized possessions from within their home.

The pictures raised mixed emotions in Bob. He felt both sad and proud – sad for the people's losses, and sad his little family had been exposed to so much drama and trauma over the years, yet proud they had come so far that they were able now to help others.

The email read:

We are okay this time. Others are not okay. Our house is the centre for 'Reach Out'. You help to teach our kids well, Mister Bob.

Keep Smiling.

Rose.

Appendix:

Courtesy of Dr Marinella Marmo,
A/Professor, College of Business, Government and Law,
Flinders University, Adelaide.

This story is based on facts. The woman protagonist has experienced the brutality of sex trafficking. She was rescued by an Australian man. A religious group stepped in to help in the rescue and repatriation stages. It is a story that can be read in one day: in one day we are exposed to a life trajectory made of dreams for a better life, shock, fear, sufferance, abuse, humiliation and lots and lots of hope for a different ending. The story indeed ends well for the protagonist in her real life and she devotes herself to help many others, supported once more by the same Australian family.

And yet, one cannot stop thinking about this story as a drop in the ocean. This book sheds light into the immense problem of severe exploitation of human beings for personal or commercial gain that occurs everywhere. Indeed, while reading this book, my mind went to the millions of faceless children, women and men subjected to slavery and slavery-like practices in the so-called modern slavery industry. We will never hear about these stories, about their hope and sufferance, and yet we are geared to produce empathies only if we can connect to a story. And there are lot of these unheard stories.

While the hidden nature of this type of serious crime makes producing an accurate prevalence measure difficult, an estimate of 40.3 million people subjected to any form of slavery has been suggested by the United Nations' International Labour Organization (ILO) and the Walk Free Foundation. This is more than three times the figure during the transatlantic slave trade between the 15th and 19th centuries. This means that, nowadays, one every 200 people worldwide is in a condition of slavery or slavery-like practice. Women and girls comprise 71% of all victims and children are calculated as making up 25% of the total numbers. People subjected to this heinous crime are often hidden away, difficult to reach, very likely unable to leave their situation, and/or may not come forward because of fear of retaliation to self or family, or other reasons such as shame.

Modern slavery takes many forms, from sex to labour exploitation, from organ trafficking to child soldiers, from forced marriage to servitude. The book makes a brief reference also to the plea of domestic servitude, where it recounts the experience of a woman treated very badly and her freedom removed altogether working as a domestic aid. The protagonist does not want to end up in a similar situation, and yet.

In all cases of human trafficking there is deception. Deception and consent are inherently linked. In this book we see deception, but we need to be aware that deception can take many forms.

Typecasting deception in only one typology can cause stereotyping slavery and slavery-like practices through a tunnel vision, because it can produce the expectation of an ideal victim and an ideal perpetrator. The blur between the lines can be present and so is the victim-perpetrator cycle, where the victim may become the perpetrator of a similar form of crime. Law enforcement and social services are fully aware of these nuances, proving we are at a point in time where we are actually making massive progress in addressing the issue. Nevertheless, the biggest jump in progress would come from a concerted effort. In the case of this story, we see that many people are involved in making this crime a reality, not just organised crime: from the 'clients' to the hotel concierge, from the police to border officers, the problem is bigger that what may seem because lots of people are earning their share. The anecdotal evidence portrayed in the book demonstrates that this form of crime generates an incredible profit with many beneficiaries that permits its endurance despite the many laws in place. ILO estimates that this sector generates as much as $150bn (AU$207bn) in profits every year. They estimate that, on average, sex traffickers can earn around $36,000 (AU$49,000) per victim.

And, as the book indicates, the Covid-19 global pandemic pushed a further strain in already vulnerable populations. In 2020 the United Nations warned us that more cases of severe exploitation will occur as a direct result of the pandemic, and now that the pandemic has being prolonged we can only expect a bleak future unless we all stand up against it.

Therefore, if this book touches you and you are determined to take action, there are many options:

- discuss this issue with at least three people around you within a week from reading the book to help raise awareness;

- be more conscious and shop ethically: support the businesses trying to do the right thing;

- donate your time or money to this cause;

- organise an awareness-raising event or attend one.

By writing this book, Shirley will help many people to develop an understating of the complexities of modern slavery and an empathetic gaze that we can apply to the faceless victims. As the book's profit is donated to a service working in this sector, by purchasing the book you are already helping with addressing the issue.

A/Prof Marmo holds a PhD in Applied Social Science (University of Lancaster, UK) and an LLB (Honours) (Università di Salerno, Italy). She joined the Flinders Law Schook in 2005, after having held positions in the UK (University of Leicester and the Liverpool John Moores University).

A/Prof Marmo is a leading expert on human mobility, human rights and cross-border migration. Her research has been cited by academics and senior policymakers worldwide, profiled by several prominent international and national media outlets, formed the base for a British Parliamentary Q&A sessions and used to inform a documentary in Britain. She is an active contributor to national and state inquiries.

At present, she is leading a research project on contemporary forms of modern slavery in South Australia which is contributing to shape local policies (@stopslaverysa).

About the Author

Shirley worked in the welfare sector for over 35 years including seven years with Lifeline WA, where, with her background in psychology, she trained counsellors, and volunteered as one herself. She travelled the State, disseminating suicide intervention strategies, after which she wrote *Twenty-Four Seven* and its sequel, *Georgie-Girl*, fictionalising her experiences.

Prior to this, she wrote *The Rocky Girl*, which chronicled life during the 1950s and '60s in Central Queensland. This was the forerunner to the true crime story, *Mima – A case of abduction, rape and murder*, which was published in 2016. Mima was a work colleague of Shirley's in Rockhampton in the 1960s and was murdered while working for the electricity authority. Her last work was *Edwin – Flamboyant Australian Pioneer*, a work of historical fiction.

Woman for Sale is, like its predecessors, based on real events. It is yet another story that deserves to be told.